THE LAST GUNFIGHTER: MONTANA GUNDOWN

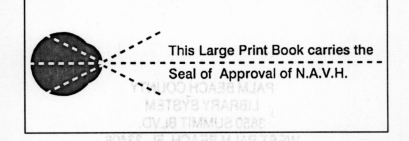

This Large Print Book carries the
Seal of Approval of N.A.V.H.

THE LAST GUNFIGHTER: MONTANA GUNDOWN

WILLIAM W. JOHNSTONE
WITH J.A. JOHNSTONE

WHEELER PUBLISHING
A part of Gale, Cengage Learning

GALE
CENGAGE Learning·

Detroit • New York • San Francisco • New Haven, Conn • Waterville, Maine • London

GALE
CENGAGE Learning®

LIBRARY OF CONGRESS CATALOGING-IN-PUBLICATION DATA

Johnstone, William W.
    The last gunfighter. Montana gundown / by William W. Johnstone with J.A. Johnstone. — Large Print edition.
        pages cm. — (Wheeler Publishing Large Print Western)
    ISBN 978-1-4104-6595-5 (softcover) — ISBN 1-4104-6595-0 (softcover)
    1. Large type books. I. Johnstone, J. A. II. Title.
PS3560.O415L35528 2014
813'.54—dc23   2013041267

Published in 2014 by arrangement with Pinnacle Books, an imprint of Kensington Publishing Corp.

THE LAST GUNFIGHTER: MONTANA GUNDOWN

CHAPTER 1

It was nice to be home.

Of course, a man like him didn't have a home in the strictest sense of the word like most folks did, Frank Morgan reflected as he and his friend, the old-timer named Salty Stevens, rode through a valley with majestic mountains looming over it.

There was a good reason Frank was known as the Drifter. Every time he had tried to put down roots in the past thirty years or so, something had happened to prevent it.

Often something tragic.

Despite that, he had grown to regard the entire American West as his home. Recently he had spent time in Alaska and Canada, and while he had to admit that those places were spectacularly beautiful, it was nice to be back in the sort of frontier country where he felt most comfortable.

Cattle country, like the places where he

had grown up in Texas, even though this particular valley was located in Montana. Frank saw stock grazing here and there on lush grass. This was his kind of territory, and his kind of people lived here.

"Pretty, ain't it?" Salty asked, as if reading Frank's mind.

Frank nodded and said, "Yep."

"Well, don't get all carried away and start waxin' poetical about it."

Frank grinned. The expression softened the rugged lines of his face . . . a little.

He was a broad-shouldered, powerfully built man who had been wandering the West for more than thirty years since coming home to Texas as a youngster after the Civil War. It was not long after that he discovered, through no fault of his own, how fast and deadly accurate with a gun he was.

Other people became aware of that natural talent of his. Some tried to use him to their advantage. Others just wanted to test their own skills against his in contests where the stakes were life and death.

And with each man that fell to his gun, Frank Morgan's reputation grew. He left his home in search of peace, but gun trouble followed him, and as years passed and men died, the reputation became more than that.

It became a legend.

He was tagged with the nickname Drifter because of his habit of never staying in one place for very long, but some folks had started calling him the Last Gunfighter. In these days when the dawn of a new century was closing in fast, most people considered the Old West to be finished.

Hell, it had been more than twenty years since Jack McCall put a bullet in the back of Wild Bill Hickok's head in the Number 10 Saloon in Deadwood. Wes Hardin was dead, too, also shot in the back of the head by a coward; Ben Thompson had gone under; Smoke Jensen was living the peaceful life of a rancher in Colorado; and nobody quite knew what had happened to Matt Bodine.

So it was understandable that people considered Frank Morgan to be the last of a dying breed, that of the shootist and pistolero. In truth, he wasn't. There were still quite a number of men in the West who were quick on the draw and deadly with their guns. They just didn't attain the notoriety such men once had. The newspaper and magazine writers liked to write about how modern and civilized everything was.

Only the dime novelists still cared about the frontier. They never got all the details right, but there was some truth in the feelings they conveyed. Even Frank, who had been cast as the hero of a number of those lurid, yellow-backed, totally fictional tales, had come to this realization.

Clad in worn range clothes, including a faded blue bib-front shirt and a high-crowned gray Stetson, Frank rode easy in the saddle of a leggy golden sorrel stallion he had dubbed Goldy. He was leading the rangy gray known as Stormy, and a big, wolflike cur called Dog trotted alongside the horses. Frank, Stormy, and Dog had been trail partners for a long time, and although Goldy was younger, he had fit in with them, too.

Salty wore a fringed buckskin vest over his flannel shirt with a battered old hat pushed down on his thatch of white hair, which matched his bristling beard. He rode a pinto pony and led a sturdy packhorse. The packs were full of supplies given to them by Bob Coburn, an old friend of Frank's and the owner of the Circle C ranch where they had spent the past few weeks.

Dog, Stormy, and Goldy had been watched over by a livery owner in Seattle for months while Frank was off adventuring in the Great White North. But on receiving a telegram from Frank, the man had put the animals in a livestock car and a train had delivered them to a siding near the Circle C. Frank and Salty had ridden down from Canada to pick them up at the ranch, and the reunion between Frank and his old friends had been a happy one.

For a while, Frank had been content to stay there and visit with Bob. He got a kick out of demonstrating gun and rope tricks for the rancher's ten-year-old son. Salty spent hours telling wild, hair-raising stories to the youngster, who seemed to have a knack of his own for yarn-spinning. It was a pleasant time.

Eventually, Frank got up one morning and knew it was time to move on. That was why he and Salty were now ambling along this valley in a generally eastward direction. Where it would take them, Frank had no idea.

He didn't figure it really mattered all that much.

"Are we still goin' to Mexico?" Salty asked. "We been talkin' about it for a good long time."

"We said we were going to spend the winter there," Frank pointed out. "It's not winter anymore. It's the middle of summer, and a beautiful one at that."

"Yeah, but Mexico's a long ways off. Take

us a pretty good spell to get there, especially since you don't believe in gettin' in no hurry. I figure we should start thinkin' about headin' in that direction."

Frank nodded slowly and said, "We can do that. Start thinking about it, I mean."

"You're a dadgummed deliberate cuss, you know that?"

"A man gets that way when the years start piling up on him."

Salty snorted and said, "There's been a heap more of 'em pile up on me than on you."

They could have bantered like this for hours, rocking along peacefully in the saddle in the midst of this spectacularly beautiful scenery.

Unfortunately, trouble reared its ugly head in the form of an outbreak of gunshots somewhere not far away.

Both men reined their mounts to a halt. Salty looked over at Frank and said, "Oh, Lord. You're thinkin' about gettin' in the big middle of that ruckus, whatever it is, ain't you?"

"I'm curious," Frank allowed.

The shots continued to bang and roar. They were closer now. Frank's keen eyes suddenly spotted movement in a line of pine trees about two hundred yards ahead.

A second later, four men on horseback burst out of the trees. They lashed at their mounts with the reins, urging every bit of speed they could out of the animals.

"They're headed for them rocks!" Salty exclaimed.

Frank saw the clump of boulders off to the left and knew the old-timer was right. The rocks offered the nearest cover for those fugitives.

They might not make it, because an even larger group of riders emerged from the pines about a hundred yards behind them. More than a dozen men were all throwing lead after the four fugitives.

Most of them were using handguns, and Frank knew the range was too far for such weapons. A few of the pursuers had Winchesters. The sharper crack of the repeaters mixed with the boom of the revolvers. A lucky shot might bring down one of the men fleeing toward the boulders.

"What're you doin'?" Salty yelped as Frank reached for his own Winchester.

"Figured I'd even the odds a little."

"We don't know who those hombres are," Salty argued. "Might be owlhoots, and that could be a posse after 'em."

"That's why I intend to aim high," Frank said as he levered a round into the Winchester's chamber and lifted the rifle to his shoulder.

He knew Salty was right. It wasn't very smart to get in the middle of a fight when you didn't know who the sides were or what stakes were involved.

But when Frank saw four men being chased by fifteen or twenty, the sense of fairness that was a deeply ingrained part of him kicked up a fuss. He just didn't like the odds.

"Aw, shoot!" Salty muttered. "Well, it's been more'n a month since anybody tried to kill us, so I reckon we're overdue."

He reached for his own Winchester and pulled it out of its sheath.

Frank aimed over the heads of the pursuers, who appeared not to have noticed him or Salty, and pressed the trigger. The Winchester cracked and spat flame.

Now that the ball was open, Frank didn't hesitate. He cranked off five shots as fast as he could work the Winchester's lever. Beside him, Salty's rifle barked several times as he joined in.

The pursuers must have heard the shots, or at least heard the bullets whistling over their heads, because they slowed suddenly and started milling around in confusion. The delay was enough to give the four fugitives a chance to reach the safety of the rocks. As they disappeared behind the boulders, the men who had been chasing them swung around to face the new threat.

They charged toward Frank and Salty.

"Uh-oh," Salty said as he lowered his rifle. "I don't think they're firin' warnin' shots, Frank!"

Salty was right about that. He and Frank were the prey now.

CHAPTER 2

"Come on, Dog!" Frank called as he jammed the Winchester back in its sheath and hauled Goldy around. From the corner of his eye he had spotted a small knoll about fifty yards to their right. That was the closest cover he and Salty could find.

Leading Stormy and the packhorse, the two men pounded toward the little hill. It was barely big enough for all of them to crowd behind it. As they reached the knoll, Frank sensed as much as heard the passage of a bullet close beside his left ear.

The varmints were getting the range.

He swung behind the hill and instantly dropped out of the saddle, pulling the rifle from its sheath as he did so. His feet had barely hit the ground when he charged ten feet or so up the slope and threw himself down on his belly. He yanked his hat off so the crown wouldn't stick up over the top of the knoll and get ventilated by a bullet.

It was a good hat, and he didn't see any point in letting it be damaged.

Also, the grass growing on the knoll would make it harder for the gunmen to see where he and Salty hid. The old-timer bellied down beside Frank and thrust the barrel of his Winchester over the top of the hill.

"We still aimin' high?" Salty asked in a scornful tone that made it clear he didn't think that was a very good idea.

"Reckon we'd better," Frank said. "Those fellas could still be lawmen."

"Mighty trigger-happy badge-toters, if they are," Salty muttered. He squinted over the barrel of his Winchester and squeezed off a shot.

Frank did likewise. He had lowered his aim a little, hoping that some bullets whizzing around their heads would make the men think twice about continuing this fight.

One of the riders suddenly threw up his arms and half-fell out of the saddle, catching himself at the last instant. The man slumped on the back of his horse, obviously badly wounded.

Frank was about to say something to Salty about not following the plan, when he saw puffs of powder-smoke coming from the rocks where the four riders they'd seen earlier had taken shelter. Those fugitives were taking a hand in this game, and considering that they had been the object of the chase to start with, Frank supposed he couldn't blame them.

With the four men in the rocks and Frank and Salty behind the knoll, the gunmen were caught in a cross fire. First one, then another and then the whole group yanked their horses around as they must have realized the bad position they were in. They spurred their mounts and galloped back toward the trees.

Salty lowered his rifle and crowed, "They're lightin' a shuck!"

"For now," Frank agreed as the men disappeared into the pines, including the one who had been wounded. "We'd better be careful, though. They might double back and try again. I think we'll stay right here for a while."

"Really? I figured we'd go talk to those other fellas and find out what this is all about."

"If they want to palaver, they know where to find us. They're probably pretty curious who it was that pulled their bacon out of the fire."

Curious maybe, but definitely cautious. Long minutes crawled by with no sign of the four men emerging from their cover in the boulders.

But then one rider appeared, guiding his horse with his knees and holding his rifle ready in both hands, and the others trailed slowly out of the rocks behind him. They were on the alert for trouble as much as the first man was.

Nothing happened, though, as the four men rode across the grassy flat toward the knoll. Frank and Salty watched them come. When they were about twenty yards away, the men reined in, and the one in the lead called, "You still up there?"

"We're here," Frank said.

"Who are you?"

"Could ask the same thing of you, mister."

The man sheathed his Winchester. He took off a flat-crowned brown hat and sleeved sweat from his forehead. He appeared to be in his midtwenties, a well-set-up young man with brown hair and the sort of permanent tan that indicated he spent his days working outdoors.

Without putting the hat back on, he looked up at the top of the knoll and said, "My name is Hal Embry. My father is Jubal Embry. This is his range we're on, the Boxed E." Hal turned in the saddle and waved his hat at the other three men. "These are three of our hands, Bill Kitson, Ike Morales, and

Gage Carlin." The young man put his hat back on. "Now you know who we are. Reckon it's only fair you return the favor."

"I'm Frank. My pard here is called Salty. Just a couple of rannies riding through these parts."

"Well, we're surely obliged to the two of you for taking a hand in that fight, Frank. If you hadn't, Morgan and his gunnies might've done for us."

At the mention of that name, Frank stiffened and glanced over at Salty with a frown. The old-timer shrugged. It wasn't like Morgan was such an uncommon name. There were plenty of hombres carrying it around, all over the West.

Hal Embry went on. "Why don't you come back to the Boxed E headquarters with us? I know my pa would like to thank you, too, and we can offer you a mighty fine dinner in partial payment of the debt. Our cook's the best you'll find in Montana." A sudden grin split the young man's face. "She's my ma."

Salty scratched his beard and said quietly, "I could do with a home-cooked meal. It's been a few days since we left the Circle C, and trail grub just ain't the same as woman-cooked."

Frank felt an instinctive liking for Hal Embry, and the men with him seemed to be sturdy cowhands of the type he knew well and admired.

Besides, he wanted to know more about this man called Morgan, who evidently led a crew of killers.

"All right," Frank called down to Hal. "Hang on, and we'll join you."

He and Salty went down the hill and retrieved their horses. They swung into leather and rode around the knoll, leading Stormy and the packhorse, and Dog came with them.

As they came up to the other men, Frank saw that the three punchers were keeping a watchful eye on the trees. They were being careful, too, in case the gunmen came back and started shooting again.

Hal Embry nodded and said, "I'm pleased to meet you fellas. Just passing through these parts, you said?"

"That's right," Frank told him.

"You don't happen to be acquainted with a man named Gaius Baldridge, do you?"

"Guy Us," Salty repeated with a puzzled frown. "What in tarnation sort of a name is that?"

"Latin," Frank said. "The ancient Romans used it some." He had unexpected bits of knowledge in his head because he was an

21

avid reader and always had a book or two in his saddlebags.

"Well, as far as I'm concerned, it's Latin for low-down snake," Hal said. "You don't know him, then?"

"Never even heard of him until just this minute," Frank replied with a shake of his head.

"That's what I figured, since Brady Morgan works for him and that was Morgan and his men you were shooting at. But since you just rode into this part of the country, it was possible Baldridge might have sent for you."

"To do what?" Frank asked, although he suddenly had a hunch that he might know the answer.

"To sign on as regulators for him."

That was what Frank expected to hear. It must have taken Salty by surprise, though, because the old-timer exclaimed, "Regulators! You mean we just waltzed right into the middle of a dadblasted range war?"

Hal smiled thinly and said, "I'm afraid so. Baldridge is an old open range man. He doesn't like it that my pa filed an official claim on part of this valley last year and moved out Baldridge's stock. He's been trying to run us off ever since."

"And he brought in regulators to do it,"

22

Frank mused. "Most of the time, that's just a fancy name for hired killers."

"Brady Morgan and his crew sure fit the bill," Hal agreed. "But there's no need to sit around here all day jawing. It'll be nigh on to suppertime before we get back to the house."

He lifted his reins and turned his horse. Frank and Salty fell in beside him. The three cowhands brought up the rear, spreading out some and riding with their rifles across the saddle in front of them.

"Those gunnies jumped you for no good reason?" Frank asked.

"That's right," Hal said. "The boys and I were just checking on the stock in this part of the valley when Morgan and the others showed up and started shooting. We lit out, but I don't figure we would have gotten away if you and Salty hadn't pitched in and given us a hand."

"They still outnumbered us by quite a bit."

"Yeah, but we were forted up good in those rocks, and it wouldn't have been easy to roust the two of you from that knoll. Plus we had them between two fires. Morgan may be a lot of things, but he's not a fool. Once he saw the layout, he knew he'd suffer some heavy losses, even if he managed to kill us all. I guess he figured it'd be better to wait and try to wipe us out some other day."

Frank nodded. Hired guns were nothing if not practical. A hired killer would risk his life for wages. That was part of the job. But he wouldn't do it foolishly. Frank had known plenty of them even though he had never sold his gun himself, his reputation to the contrary. He fought only for causes he believed in.

"You said this isn't open range anymore," he commented to Hal Embry. "I haven't seen any fences."

"We haven't gotten around to fencing off most of the Boxed E just yet. Barbwire costs money, and we're sort of cash poor. And to tell you the truth, my pa is enough of an old-fashioned cattleman that he doesn't like the stuff. He's a little slow to change. It took my ma and my sister quite a while to convince him to file a claim on the land legal-like, but he finally saw that that's the way things are going these days. The land's ours, all right. The claim's on file official and proper down in Helena."

"I don't doubt it," Frank said.

"Yeah, things are changin' all over," Salty put in. "Most of it sticks in my craw, too."

"You'll get along with my pa, then," Hal

said with a grin.

True to the young man's prediction, the sun was almost directly overhead when the six men rode up to the ranch headquarters. It was a nice-looking layout, Frank thought, with a two-story, sturdy-looking log ranch house, a bunkhouse and barn made of whipsawed planks, and several pole corrals. A smaller pen near the ranch house held a couple of milk cows, and someone had put in a vegetable garden, too. There was nothing fancy about the Boxed E, but it had a comfortable look about it, as if a family could make a good home here.

If they got the chance.

Several shaggy yellow dogs came bounding out from the barn to greet the newcomers. They stopped short, their legs stiffening and the hair raising on their necks as they spotted Dog and caught his scent. Growls came from deep in their throats, and the big cur answered in kind.

"Dog!" Frank said. "Easy."

The ranch dogs approached warily. Considerable sniffing and circling went on, then Dog turned his back on the other canines and strode on next to Frank and Goldy, his disdain for the ranch dogs palpable.

The ranch house had a big porch along the front of it. As the riders approached, a heavyset man with thinning gray hair and a gray goatee stepped out of the house with a double-barreled shotgun in his hands. From the man's powerful bearing, Frank guessed this was Jubal Embry, the owner of the Boxed E.

"You all right, Hal?" the man asked in a challenging tone as the riders drew rein in front of the porch. "One of the hands said he thought he heard some shots coming from the west pasture a while ago."

"He did hear shots," Hal said. "Brady Morgan and his gun-wolves jumped us while we were checking the stock over there. Might've done for us, too, Pa, if these drifters hadn't come along and helped us out."

"Drifters," Jubal Embry muttered. Then his eyes widened abruptly in recognition, and the shotgun in his hands came up. "Hal, you damned fool!" he shouted. "That's Frank Morgan, the gunfighter! He's Brady Morgan's father!"

CHAPTER 3

Frank didn't know what was more of a shock: having that scattergun pointed at him, or hearing that he was the father of a regulator, a hired killer.

Frank had one son, Conrad Browning, who had been led by tragedy to abandon the life of a successful businessman and now roamed the Southwest, using the name Kid Morgan. And there was a girl down in Texas named Victoria who *might* be his daughter. Frank wasn't sure about that, and Victoria's mother had always refused to say positively one way or the other. Victoria was confined to a wheelchair, the victim of a bullet intended for Frank himself, but she was married to Frank's old friend, Texas Ranger Tyler Beaumont, and he knew she was doing well. Every so often, one of her letters caught up to him.

Those were his only two children, as far as he knew, although to be honest he had been with other women from time to time over the years. None of them had ever said anything to him about being in the family way. But maybe they wouldn't have.

And he hadn't learned of Conrad's existence until the young man was nearly grown, he reminded himself. Was it possible that he had other offspring out there somewhere?

He had to admit that it was.

Those thoughts flashed through his head as he looked down the twin barrels of Jubal Embry's shotgun. He hadn't budged since Embry pointed the Greener at him. He didn't want to give the rancher any excuse to jerk those triggers.

"Pa, wait!" Hal said. "You must have it wrong. These hombres helped us."

Embry squinted at Frank over the shotgun's barrels and said, "Are you denyin' it, mister? Are you Frank Morgan or not?"

"I'm Morgan," Frank said. "But I never heard of anybody called Brady Morgan until today."

Hal stared over at him. "I trusted you," the young man muttered.

"Are you loco?" Salty burst out. "You trusted us for good reason! We kept those no-good varmints from gunnin' you!"

One of the ranch hands spoke up, saying,

"That's true, Mr. Embry. As soon as they saw what was goin' on, they opened fire on Baldridge's regulators."

Hal glared at Frank and asked, "Why didn't you tell me your real name?"

"I did. Frank's my real handle. But once you started talking about somebody else named Morgan, I thought it might be a good idea to wait a while and see what else I could find out about what's going on around here."

"Well, now you know," Embry said. "That bloodthirsty whelp of yours is workin' for Baldridge and tryin' to run us off land that's rightfully ours. But he can't do it. He can't get rid of us without killin' us."

"I believe you," Frank said. "But Morgan's a common name. Just because the man ramrodding Baldridge's regulators is called that, it doesn't mean he's related to me."

"Then why does he keep goin' around tellin' everybody he's the son of the famous gunfighter Frank Morgan?"

Frank couldn't answer that, so he just shrugged and shook his head.

"All I can tell you, Mr. Embry, is that Salty and I didn't know anything about any of this until today. Not about Baldridge, not about the trouble you've been having, and

29

for sure not anything about this Brady Morgan."

Doubt began to appear in Hal's eyes. He said, "I suppose he could be telling the truth, Pa —"

"You think it's a coincidence they showed up just as those gunnies were tryin' to kill you?" Embry demanded. He didn't lower the shotgun. "Don't be so blasted dumb. It's a trick, that's what it is! Baldridge is tryin' to slip these men in amongst us, so they can work against us."

"I don't see how —"

"Did they shoot any of those regulators?"

"Well . . . no," Hal admitted. "I think it was Gage's shot that plugged one of them. Looked to me like they might've been firing high."

Embry snorted. "Ain't that a surprise," he said. "I swear, boy, they've pulled the wool over your eyes! But they can't fool me." The shotgun's barrels shook slightly from the depth of the rage that possessed the man holding the weapon. "Get off my range! Get out now before I blow you both out of the saddle like I ought to!"

"You're makin' a mistake, mister," Salty said. "You got it all wrong."

"I don't think so. Now *git!*"

30

Frank lifted Goldy's reins and said, "We're going."

He was angry, too, but he could see that he wasn't going to be able to change Jubal Embry's mind. Circumstances had conspired to convince the rancher that he was right, and he wouldn't be swayed, no matter what.

"Hal, get in the house," Embry went on sharply. "You three, ride along with Morgan and whatever that old pelican's name is, and make sure they get off our range. If they give you any trouble . . . shoot 'em!"

Hal looked over at Frank and said, "I'm pretty mixed up about all this, but I appreciate what you did for us."

"You're welcome," Frank said with a faint smile.

"Hal!" Embry roared. "Now!"

Frowning in embarrassment and anger, Hal dismounted while Frank and Salty turned their horses away from the ranch house. Frank saw that several more punchers had emerged from the bunkhouse and the barn. The men watched with wary, slitted eyes as Frank and Salty rode past. They had heard enough of Embry's bull-like bellowing to believe that these two strangers were enemies of the Boxed E.

"Maybe this'll break you of the habit of

goin' around tryin' to help folks," Salty said as they rode east and the ranch headquarters fell behind them. "That's the most surefire way of gettin' in a heap of trouble I ever saw."

"Seems like when you and I met, I was trying to give you a hand," Frank drawled.

"Yeah, well, that was different."

The three cowboys trailed behind them, rifles still held at the ready. But when they were out of sight of the ranch house, one of the men nudged his horse up alongside Frank's mount.

"Gage Carlin," he reintroduced himself. He was middle-aged, with the rawboned, weather-beaten look of a veteran cowboy. "For what it's worth, Mr. Morgan, we're obliged to you, too, like Hal said."

"Thanks, Gage," Frank replied. "And also for what it's worth, I was telling the truth back there. I don't know this Brady Morgan, or Gaius Baldridge, either."

"My bones say you're tellin' the truth. Can't go against the boss, though. No offense."

Frank nodded and said, "None taken. I've ridden for the brand in my time, too."

"Not for a while, I expect, judgin' by the stories I've heard about you."

"Not for a while," Frank admitted. "But

some of those stories you mentioned were likely just big windies."

"Some, maybe. Not all, I'll bet."

"No," Frank said, "not all."

They rode on for a while, and finally Salty asked, "Is there a town somewhere the way we're goin'?"

"Yeah. Settlement called Pine Knob. Didn't start out as much, but it's growin'."

"Does the railroad pass through there?" Frank asked.

Carlin shook his head and said, "Nope. Closest train station is in Great Falls. But there are a couple of good eatin' places in Pine Knob, and a decent hotel if you're lookin' for a place to stay." The cowboy grinned. "And some nice saloons, too."

Salty licked his lips and said, "Now you're talkin'."

Frank was still curious and asked, "Where does Baldridge's range run?"

"He has the whole eastern end of the valley," Carlin said. "Pine Knob sits in between, right on Loco Creek. Folks call it that because of the way it twists around so, but it runs generally north and south and cuts the valley right smack in half."

"Baldridge used to run his stock from one end of the valley to the other?"

"Yep. But he never filed claim on any of it

except the land his headquarters sits on, at the far end of the valley. Miss Faye is the one who figured that out."

"Who's that?"

"The boss's daughter. Smart as a whip, she is. I probably shouldn't be sayin' this, but she got the head for business that Hal didn't. He's a top hand and as good a ramrod as you'd ever want to work for, but . . ."

"I understand," Frank said. Hal Embry could handle the day-to-day details of running a ranch but didn't know how to go about doing so profitably.

Like most cowboys, Gage Carlin was talkative once he got going. He continued, "Yeah, Miss Faye found out her daddy could file on the range and wouldn't have to share it with Baldridge's B Star spread anymore. We've always had trouble with Baldridge tryin' to hog the grass and water. Once it was done, we pushed all the B Star stock east of Loco Creek. Baldridge pitched a fit, but there was nothin' he could do about it. Not legally, anyway. So he filed on his half of the valley and started tryin' to crowd us out with regulators."

"Ain't there no law in these parts?" Salty asked.

"Pine Knob's got a marshal, but he don't

take no sides in what goes on outside of town. And a deputy U.S. marshal gets up this way from Helena now and then, but you can't count on him bein' around whenever there's trouble. Folks still handle most problems on their own."

Frank nodded. That was the way it had been on the frontier for a long time, and despite the inexorable advance of so-called civilization, it was likely to remain that way for a while longer.

"We've had potshots taken at us before," Carlin went on, "and there's been trouble in town between our crew and Brady Morgan and his men, but today's the first time they've tried to out-an'-out murder some of us on Boxed E land." The cowboy shook his head regretfully. "It probably won't be the last."

"No," Frank agreed, "it probably won't."

They rode over a shallow ridge, and Frank spotted some buildings on the flats about a mile away, where a line of cottonwoods marked the twisting course of a stream.

The men reined in, and Carlin pointed.

"That's it," he said. "That's Pine Knob."

"Why in blazes do they call it that?" Salty asked. "I don't even see a knob, let alone one covered with pines."

"Well, it's not much of a hill," Carlin

35

explained, "and you can't see it because it's on the other side of the creek, past the settlement. A few years ago it was covered with pines, but then folks came in and started the town, and they cut 'em all down for lumber to make the buildin's. I guess you could say the name's all that's left of the original pine knob."

"If that don't beat all," Salty muttered. "Folks are too quick to tear down and build things that ain't as good as what was there to start with."

"You could be right, sir. But I gotta admit, I do like havin' a place closer than Great Falls where a fella can get a drink."

"Well, you may have a point there," Salty admitted.

"We'll head back now. You fellas will keep goin', right? You don't aim to make any trouble for the Boxed E?"

"That's right," Frank said. "You have my word on it."

"Good enough for me," Carlin said with a nod. He turned to Morales and Kitson. "Come on, boys."

The three men turned and rode back toward the ranch headquarters.

"We didn't get that dinner the Embry boy promised us," Salty said. "And I was sure lookin' forward to it. What say we find us a hash house down yonder in the settlement, get a surroundin' in our bellies, maybe wet our whistles, and then ride on? Might be able to get out of this valley by dark."

"I thought you might want to spend the night," Frank said. "Fill up on something besides trail grub and sleep in a real bed for a change."

Salty looked over at him for a long moment, then abruptly jerked his battered old hat off and agitatedly ran his other hand through his tangled white hair.

"Dadgummit! I knowed it, I purely did. You can't just ride away, can you? You got to mix in and get to the bottom of this whole range war mess. You got to find out what the story is on this Brady Morgan varmint!"

"Wouldn't you be curious if you found out you might have a son you didn't know about?"

Salty pulled on his beard and said, "I just might. I wasn't always a scruffy ol' billy goat, you know. I used to have a way with the ladies."

"I don't doubt it. Anyway, I didn't say we were going to get mixed up in any range war."

"You didn't have to say it," Salty replied with a sigh. "I've rode with you long enough now to know how trouble follows the Morgan clan."

He heeled his paint into motion.

Frank rode after Salty. He hated to admit it, but the old-timer was right. For decades now, trouble seemed to follow Frank wherever he went, and from what he knew of Conrad's life now, the same was true of Kid Morgan.

He supposed he couldn't expect things to be any different with this Brady Morgan . . . whoever he was.

CHAPTER 4

Most of Pine Knob's buildings were on the east side of the creek. Gaius Baldridge's side, so to speak. But as Frank and Salty rode into the settlement from the west, they passed a few businesses and some residences.

Among the businesses were an adjacent black-smith shop and livery stable and a couple of saloons, one called CORRIGAN'S CASINO, and another that was, according to the sign, THE POPULAR SALOON.

Judging by the sleepy appearance of the place, that was wishful thinking.

Of course, at the moment none of the establishments in Pine Knob seemed to be doing much business, Frank noted as he and Salty rode over the bridge that spanned Loco Creek. The shoes of their horses clapped loudly against the planks.

A few horses were tied up at the hitch racks in front of the boardwalks on both sides of the main street, and a wagon was parked in front of the general store. The heads of the mules hitched to the wagon drooped, and their tails flicked lazily at flies. Frank looked along the boardwalks and didn't see any other movement.

"Ain't what you'd call a bustlin' settlement," Salty commented.

"It's siesta time," Frank said.

"Yeah . . . in Mexico. Which is where we were supposed to be headin', remember?"

"We'll get there one of these days," Frank told him. "And folks like a little nap after dinner anywhere it gets hot in the summer."

"We ain't had dinner yet. Is there somethin' wrong with your memory?"

Frank grinned as he brought Goldy to a halt. "No, and my sense of smell is just fine, too. Take a whiff of that."

Salty reined in as well and took a deep breath. An expression of awe appeared on his grizzled face.

"Oh, Lord, where's that comin' from? I smell pot roast and taters and fresh-baked bread and . . . and . . . is that apple pie? Point me to the Pearly Gates, 'cause heaven's gotta be around here somewheres close!"

"It's not exactly heaven," Frank said, "but those smells seem to be coming from that building over there."

It was a frame structure that had been painted the same shade of red that was usually used on barns, and appropriately enough, the name on the sign propped inside one of the front windows was THE FEED BARN.

Frank and Salty dismounted in front of it and tied up their horses. Frank told Dog to sit and stay, and the big cur obediently lowered his rump to the ground beside the horses. He would watch over them until Frank returned.

The two men went inside through a door that had plaid curtains over the glass in its upper half. The curtains matched the ones hanging at the sides of the windows and made for a nice homey touch.

The mouth-watering aromas were even stronger inside. A couple of men sat on stools at the counter to the right, and one of the tables covered with blue-checked tablecloths was occupied. The midday rush seemed to be over, which was fine with Frank. He had never cared much for crowds.

As domestic and appealing as the surroundings seemed, the man behind the counter wearing an apron was just the opposite. He was tall, but he carried himself hunched over with his head thrust forward so he seemed to be shorter than he was. He was mostly bald, with a fringe of white hair around his ears and several days' worth of stubble on his cheeks. His left eye was covered with a black patch, and his right glared at the newcomers with suspicion.

"Well?" he snapped as Frank and Salty came up to the counter. "What do you want?"

"Couple of meals, whatever you're serving up will be fine," Frank said.

"Damned right it will be," the man said. "You come in here, think you can push around an honest man —"

"Whoa up there, hoss," Salty broke in. "Ain't no call to get a burr under your saddle. We ain't tryin' to push anybody around."

The man pushed his head even farther forward, so that he looked more like a buzzard than ever.

"Are you callin' me a liar?" he shouted.

At that moment, the door into the café opened again with a slight tinkle of the bell that hung over it, and a woman came inside. From the corner of Frank's eye, he saw the startled look that came over her face. She hurried toward the counter, saying, "It's all right, Solomon. I can take over out here.

You just go back in the kitchen."

"Better be careful, girl." Solomon jabbed a finger at Frank and Salty. "These two gunnies came in and started givin' me trouble. Maybe you better go fetch Marshal Trask."

"I'm sure it'll be fine," the young woman said as she went behind the counter and took the man's arm. Gently, she steered him toward the open door that led into the café's kitchen. "Don't worry, I'll take care of it."

Still grumbling warnings, Solomon disappeared into the kitchen. The woman paused, took a deep breath, and turned to face Frank and Salty. She rested her palms on the counter.

"I apologize for my uncle," she said quietly. "I wasn't really expecting any strangers to come in at this time of day, so I thought it would be all right if I ran over to the store for a few minutes."

Frank had noticed that the other men in the café hadn't seemed surprised by Solomon's hostile attitude. He said, "Your uncle doesn't cotton to strangers, I reckon."

She smiled sadly and shook her head. "No, I'm afraid not. He's been this way ever since he came back from the war. He was with Grant and was wounded at the Wilderness. My father looked after him for years, but now . . . well, we're all that each other has left. He's really a very sweet man, once you get to know him."

Salty grunted and said, "If it was up to me, we wouldn't be around that long. But I just got one question, missy."

"What's that?" she asked.

"Is that cantankerous old codger the one who does the cookin' for this place?"

"That's right."

"And it tastes as good as it smells?"

"That's two questions," she said with a smile, "but yes, it does."

"Well, then, bring it on. Anything that smells that good, I don't care if ol' Santy Anny himself cooked it!"

She nodded and said, "Two pot roast specials, coming up."

A few minutes later she emerged from the kitchen and put two plates heaped high with food in front of them. Then she filled two cups with coffee from a pot that was simmering on a small stove and passed them to Frank and Salty as well.

"By the way, I'm Katie Storm," she said. "You already met my uncle Solomon."

"I'm Frank; this is Salty."

Once again Frank failed to provide their last names, but this time there was a reason for it, instead of just happenstance as it had been starting out with Hal Embry. From everything he had heard, the name "Morgan" was bound to raise most eyebrows around here.

"Are you just passing through Pine Knob?" Katie asked.

"That was the plan," Salty said. "For some of us, anyway."

Katie looked a little puzzled, but Frank didn't try to explain. He said, "We'll probably be here for a day or two."

"You're not . . ." She hesitated. "You're not gunmen like Solomon said, are you?"

"Who do I look like?" Salty asked. "Wild Bill Hickok?"

"Not exactly." Katie rested level blue eyes on Frank. "But you're different."

"We're not hired guns," he told her.

"But you've heard about the trouble here in the valley? Between Mr. Baldridge and the Embrys?"

"We have," Frank said. He wasn't going to lie to her. "But it's not what brought us here."

She smiled again, but the expression held a hint of a chill now.

"But it might be enough to make you stay a while, is that it? Now that you've seen you can hire on with Brady Morgan and the rest of Baldridge's regulators?"

"Not interested," Frank said, his voice flat.

The food wasn't going to taste as good now, he sensed. Even though this young woman didn't know who he was, she was starting to grow suspicious of him.

Maybe he ought to wear a sign on his back giving the number of men he had killed in his life, he thought. Salty could come along with a rag and a piece of chalk and change the total every time he had to shoot somebody else.

Katie looked at him intently for a long moment, then nodded slowly.

"Maybe you're telling the truth," she said. "I've got a hunch you are." She shrugged. "But it's none of my business anyway. Let me know if you need that coffee heated up."

She turned away and went along the counter to talk quietly with the two men sitting at the other end.

Salty leaned closer to Frank and said, "The folks in this town are crazy or touchy or both. You sure you don't want to just finish this meal and then leave?"

"I'm sure they'll all warm up to us once they get to know us," Frank said. "Like Solomon there."

He inclined his head toward the kitchen door, which was only open about an inch now. But Solomon Storm's good eye was visible in that narrow crack as he stood on

46

the other side of the door and peered suspiciously at them.

"Good Lord," Salty muttered. "That hombre gives me the fantods."

The little bell rang again as the café's front door opened. Frank heard the distinctive sound of booted feet on the floor, along with the jingle of spurs. He looked over his shoulder and saw that three men had come in. One was the leader of the trio. That would have been obvious from the way he carried himself even if the other two hadn't hung back slightly.

He was young, in his twenties, but his eyes seemed older than that. His Stetson was thumbed back on a shock of thick black hair. He wore a wine-red shirt, a black leather vest, and dark gray trousers tucked into high-topped black boots. Two pearl-handled revolvers rode in black holsters on his hips.

A lot of men who dressed like that were just putting on a show, Frank knew. They wanted people to think they were more dangerous than they really were.

That wasn't the case here. The eyes were the giveaway. This man's eyes were cold and reptilian.

"Those horses who are tied up out front," he snapped. "The sorrel, the gray, and the pinto. Who do they belong to?"

Frank turned on the stool and stood up, his movements easy and deliberate, nothing that would spook a man into drawing.

"Who wants to know?" he asked, although he was certain he already knew the answer.

"Brady Morgan, old man, and if those are your horses, you better get ready to die."

CHAPTER 5

Frank said to Katie Storm, "Ma'am, you'd best go back in the kitchen."

The café's customers had gotten to their feet already and were edging toward the back door.

Her face tense with worry, Katie said, "Mr. Morgan, I don't want any trouble in here —"

Frank knew she was talking to the younger man. So did Brady, because he grinned and said without looking at her, "It won't be any trouble to kill this pair of old fools, sweetheart." The grin vanished almost as soon as it appeared, to be replaced by a sneer as Brady went on. "Well, what about it? I asked you a question, mister."

"Those are our horses," Frank said.

"I thought so. I don't know if it was you or one of those worthless Boxed E hands who killed Jack Simmons, and I don't care. I'll settle with them later. I've got you here right now."

"You ambushed those cowboys on their home range," Frank pointed out. From the corner of his eye, he saw that Salty had shifted slightly on the stool so that he could get his gun out quickly if he needed to. "They were just defending themselves, and we gave them a hand."

"Home range," Brady repeated with a contemptuous snort. "That claim Jubal Embry filed is phony as all get-out! Mr. Baldridge will prove it in court, too. He owns all this valley, and the Embrys are nothin' but damn squatters!"

Hal Embry hadn't said anything about there being a legal dispute over the claim, but it didn't really change anything. Fifteen men trying to gun down four was still going to raise Frank's ire.

"Ma'am, I sure would appreciate it if you'd go out into the kitchen," he said again to Katie.

He didn't look at her as he spoke. Instead he searched the face of Brady Morgan, hunting for any sign of resemblance to the face he saw in the mirror every time he shaved.

Frank looked for other resemblances as well, to women he had known twenty-five to thirty years earlier. The problem was, he

50

wasn't sure if he could remember all of them, and even the ones he did, their faces had faded in his memory.

Brady didn't really look like him, he decided, but the young man was of a similar size and build, and although Frank's hair was graying now, in his youth it had been dark like Brady's. And there was something else, a vague familiarity . . .

"What the hell are you starin' at, old man?" Brady demanded. "Trying to memorize the face of the man who's gonna kill you?"

"That's enough," Katie said. "Nobody's going to kill anybody, at least not in my café."

Frank heard fear in her voice, but he heard resolve, too. She was stubborn and wouldn't back down.

Neither would Brady Morgan, and Frank knew he was about to kill a man who just might be his son . . . or die at the hands of that same man if Brady was fast enough. That was doubtful, but Frank couldn't rule it out.

The last customer to slip out the café's back door had left it open, so Frank didn't know anyone was there until he saw Brady's eyes flick past him in that direction. It wasn't a trick. Brady looked distinctly annoyed.

"Like the lady said, nobody's killin' anybody," a voice spoke harshly, "unless you hombres force me to use this Greener."

Brady snapped, "This is none of your business, Marshal."

"The hell you say. Blood bein' spilled anywhere in the town limits is exactly my business."

Somebody must have scurried down to the marshal's office and told him there was trouble brewing at the Feed Barn, Frank thought. Gage Carlin had told him the lawman wasn't taking sides in the feud between the Boxed E and the B Star, but obviously the man intended to maintain law and order inside his jurisdiction.

"Miss Storm, you need to either get down behind the counter or go out in the kitchen," the marshal went on. "If I touch off both barrels, it'll be a clean sweep in here."

"And it'll do a lot of damage and get blood all over the floor and everything else," Katie said.

A grim chuckle came from the lawman.

"You can always go through their pockets and collect enough to pay for your trouble," he said. "I expect the magistrate would approve that. The money might be a little bloodstained, but it'll still spend."

With the air still thick with the tension of impending gunplay, the sudden jingle of the bell over the front door made Salty jump a little and exclaim, "Jehosaphat!"

Frank kept most of his attention focused on Brady Morgan, but he glanced over Brady's shoulder at the man who stood in the open door way. The newcomer was medium height and very slender, with long, snow-white hair and a close-cropped beard of the same color. He wore a black suit and black bowler hat. When he spoke, it was with a British accent so faint as to be almost indiscernible, as if he had been in America for most of his life.

"Brady, I've been looking for you and your men. I saw your horses outside."

Brady's mouth tightened into an angry, frustrated line. "Sorry, Mr. Baldridge," he said. "The boys and I were on our way back to the store from the saloon when we spotted those horses at the hitch rail. I recognized them. They belong to the men who helped Hal Embry earlier today." Brady's lip curled again. "The men who shot Jack Simmons."

"We didn't shoot anybody," Frank said. "We were just trying to spook you and make you turn tail." He paused. "Which you did."

He probably shouldn't have added that last comment. He knew it would just fan the flames of Brady's anger. But it was the truth, and anyway, Frank was tired of this standoff.

"I'm ready to go back to the ranch," Baldridge said with an impatient tone in his voice. "It's your job to accompany me. Go outside, and I'll join you in a moment."

"Mr. Baldridge —" Brady began.

"Now, please, before Marshal Trask loses his patience and creates an incredible mess in here."

Brady dragged in a deep breath and let it out in a sigh. He turned to the other two men, jerked his head toward the door, and said, "Let's go."

The three of them trooped out as Baldridge stepped aside to let them pass. Brady Morgan was the last one out the door, and he paused long enough to glare over his shoulder at Frank.

"This isn't over, old man," he said.

"I figured as much," Frank replied.

When the three gunmen were gone, the marshal circled around Frank and stepped in front of him. The lawman was stocky and middle-aged, with a well-fed look and gray hair above a broad, florid face. Again the eyes were the most telling sign, Frank thought. This badge-toter wasn't as soft as he appeared to be at first glance.

The marshal had the double-barreled shotgun in his hands pointed at the floor now. He looked at Frank and Salty and grunted.

"I saw you fellas ride in a while ago. Didn't take you long to land in hot water, did it?"

The white-haired cattleman came forward and said, "I apologize for the part my men played in this near disaster, Marshal. Brady is a fine young man, but a bit impetuous at times."

"Like I've told you before, Mr. Baldridge," the lawman said, "you and Jubal Embry can work things out between yourselves or in court, that's none of my business. But I won't tolerate any gunplay here in town."

"Yes, and I've spoken to Brady and the other men about that," Baldridge said. "I shall do so again and attempt to reinforce their understanding of the issue."

"You do that," the marshal said with a curt nod.

The rancher turned his level, gray-eyed gaze on Frank. "My name is Gaius Baldridge," he said. "I own the B Star Ranch."

"I know who you are, Mr. Baldridge," Frank said.

"I want to extend my apologies to you as well, sir."

"Not necessary."

"Oh, I think they are." Baldridge regarded Frank for a moment with a keen, speculative look. "Do you happen to be looking for work at the moment?"

The question brought a humorless laugh from Frank.

"I don't think that young fella who just left out of here would be interested in working with me."

"Yes, but he doesn't make the decisions," Baldridge said with a hint of ice and steel in his voice. "I do."

Frank shook his head. "Sorry. We're just passing through."

"If you change your mind, the headquarters of the B Star can be found at the eastern end of the valley." Baldridge nodded politely. "Good day to you, sir."

He left the café. When the door was closed behind Baldridge, the marshal said, "Don't let the way he looks and talks fool you, mister. Gaius Baldridge was the first white man to settle in this valley. He's fought Indians, rustlers, and Montana winters for a long time, and he's plenty tough. My name's Trask, by the way. Roy Trask."

"This is Salty Stevens," Frank said with a

nod toward the old-timer. "My name's Frank . . . Browning."

He hoped Trask hadn't noticed the slight hesitation, or thought anything about it if he did. Frank had decided on the spur of the moment that it would be wise to conceal his true identity, and he'd come out with the first name that sprang to mind, that of the woman he had once loved and of the son she had given him.

Appropriate, he thought, since for the time being he didn't want that hired gunman who might also be his son to know who he really was.

"What did you do to get on Brady Morgan's bad side?" Trask asked.

"Poked our noses into somethin' that didn't concern us," Salty answered.

"Morgan and more than a dozen other men were trying to kill Hal Embry and some Boxed E hands while they were on Boxed E range," Frank elaborated. "We happened to be riding through there, saw what was going on, and pitched in to give Embry and his punchers a hand."

"Yeah, I reckon that'd do it, all right," Trask said. "Baldridge keeps Morgan on a pretty tight rein here in town, or at least tries to, but everywhere else in the valley, Morgan seems to think he's a law unto himself." The marshal grunted. "He's just about right, too." He straightened and went on, "You say you're just passing through?"

"That's right."

"Probably a good thing for you to keep moving, then, as soon as you finish that food."

"It's gone cold by now," Salty complained.

"I'll get you some food that's hot," Katie offered.

"We'd be obliged to you, Miss Storm," Frank said.

"Remember what I said about moving on," Trask advised.

"We're not likely to forget," Frank told him.

But they might not be following that advice, either, he thought.

CHAPTER 6

Katie offered Marshal Trask a cup of coffee, and the lawman accepted.

"Might be a good idea for me to stay here while you fellas finish your dinner," he said as he settled onto the stool to Salty's right. Frank had sat down again already on the stool to the old-timer's left. "Morgan and the others are probably on their way back to the B Star with Baldridge by now, but it never hurts to be careful."

Katie poured the coffee for Trask, then pushed open the kitchen door and said, "Solomon, I need a couple more plates out here."

"I heard, I heard," came the quarrelsome reply. "Just gimme a minute."

Trask nodded toward the kitchen and asked, "Did you meet Solomon?"

"We did," Frank said.

"His bark's worse'n his bite, as the old saying goes. He's really a pretty nice fella."

"That's what I told them," Katie said. She took away the plates with the cold food and replaced them with fresh meals a few minutes later.

As they dug in, Frank leaned forward to look past Salty at Marshal Trask and said, "What's behind all the trouble between these two ranches, anyway?"

Trask blew on his coffee for a few seconds before asking, "And what business of yours would that be, Mr. Browning?"

"Well, since Salty and I got shot at once today because of it and nearly did a second time, I figure that gives us a right to know what it's all about."

"You could have a point there," Trask said, nodding slowly. "Like I told you, Gaius Baldridge was the first white man in this valley. The first one who came to stay, anyway. Reckon there were probably a lot of explorers and fur trappers who passed through here, back in the Shining Times. But Baldridge came and started a ranch. The place didn't even have a name at first, because there wasn't any need for one, or for brands on his cattle. All the cows in this valley belonged to Gaius Baldridge."

"Then Jubal Embry came in and started *his* ranch," Frank guessed.

"That's right. From what I hear — be-

cause I wasn't around these parts then —
Baldridge wasn't too happy about it, but he
figured there was enough range for both of
them. They weren't what anybody would
call friends, but they got along all right.
They even closed ranks now and then and
worked together to keep out anybody who
wanted to come in and start a smaller
spread."

"But that all changed when Embry filed
on the half of the valley west of Loco
Creek."

Trask frowned at Frank and said, "How
come you asked me about this when you
seem to have all the facts already?"

"I don't know all of it," Frank said. "Brady
Morgan said that the claim Embry filed was
no good."

"That's what Baldridge's lawyer down in
Helena says. Accordin' to him, when Embry filled out the paperwork, he got some of
it wrong. Of course it was really Embry's
girl Faye who filled out the papers, more
than likely, or at least told Embry what to
put on them. That girl's got plenty of
smarts."

"So I'm guessing Baldridge filed a coun-
terclaim on the western half of the valley,
and now the whole thing is waiting for a
judge to come along and straighten it out."

"That pretty much sums it up," Trask agreed. "Except Baldridge has gotten impatient and brought in Brady Morgan and some other men who don't have any rope burns on their hands, if you know what I mean."

Frank knew exactly what the lawman meant. Brady Morgan and his men hadn't been hired because of their skills as cowboys.

They had been hired for gun work.

"I don't know who's right and who's wrong," Trask went on. "All I know about the law is how to enforce the town ordinances. I don't mind tellin' you, though, I'm not real happy about Baldridge bringing in regulators. Sooner or later there's gonna be bloodshed, and I don't want it in my town."

"Can't blame you for that," Salty said. "Why don't you send for the sheriff or the deputy U.S. marshal and let him keep the peace in the valley?"

Trask said, "The folks down in Helena know what's going on up here. You'd have to ask them why nobody's done anything about it yet."

"I never heard of this Brady Morgan," Frank said. "Has he got a reputation?"

"As a fast gun, you mean? Well, sure. He's

the son of Frank Morgan, after all. You're bound to have heard of *him*. The gunfighter they call the Drifter?"

"I've heard some about him," Frank said, nodding.

"Brady inherited Morgan's speed with a gun, I guess. He's killed several men in fair fights. I don't know exactly how many. And the men he brought in with him still have all the bark on 'em, too." Trask shook his head. "Nobody on the Boxed E can match up to that bunch when it comes to gunfighting. What I worry about is that Jubal Embry will bring in some hired killers of his own, and then it'll be outright war. Not much doubt about that."

Katie Storm had been moving around some behind the counter, doing this and that, but she stopped across from the three men and said, "Marshal, don't be so gloomy. Hal will figure out a way to keep things from getting that bad."

"I know you'd like to think so, Katie. So would I. But I'm not sure it's gonna happen that way." Trask swallowed the last of his coffee and set the empty cup on its saucer. He started to reach into his pocket, saying, "I'd be glad to pay you —"

"Not for coffee," Katie said. "It's on the house."

"In that case, I'm obliged to you." Trask grunted as he hauled his heavy carcass off the stool. He picked up the shotgun he had set down on the counter and looked at Frank and Salty. "I don't mean to be inhospitable, but I really would like for you fellas to be out of town by sundown."

"Oh, no, ain't nothin' inhospitable about that," Salty said in a tone dripping with sarcasm.

Trask grinned. He nodded to Katie, touched a finger to the brim of his hat, and left the Feed Barn the same way he had entered, by the back door.

Frank and Salty were the only customers in the place now. The ones who had fled earlier from the impending gunfight hadn't come back.

"Looks like we cost you some business," Frank said as he glanced around the place.

Katie shook her head. "Don't worry about that," she said. "When it gets closer to suppertime, they'll be back."

"After eatin' your uncle's food, I would be, too, if I had my druthers," Salty said. He used the last bite of a biscuit to mop up the remaining gravy from the pot roast and popped the succulent morsel into his mouth. Around it he said, "But we just got run out of town by the marshal."

"I thought you wanted to ride on anyway," Frank said.

"I did. I do. I ain't in the market for trouble. But this food is mighty good."

Katie smiled. "I'll be sure to tell Solomon that you liked it."

Frank was thinking about several things she had said. He commented, "From the sound of what you told the marshal, you and Hal Embry are acquainted."

A faint flush appeared on Katie's face, confirming Frank's hunch.

"No offense, Mr. Browning, but who I'm acquainted with isn't any of your affair, is it?"

Frank smiled and shook his head. "No, ma'am, it certainly isn't. But from what I've seen of him, he seems like a fine young fella."

"He is. He just doesn't need to always let his father and his sister tell him what to —" She stopped short and shook her head. "Never mind. That's —"

"None of my affair," Frank finished for her.

After a moment, she said, "I'm sorry I misjudged you earlier, when I thought you were here in Pine Knob to hire on with Baldridge. I didn't know you'd already had trouble with Brady Morgan."

Frank sipped his coffee and then said, "No way you could have known. And I'm sorry there was almost blood all over your floor and bullet holes in your walls."

She laughed. "When you put it that way, I feel guilty. I just didn't want anybody getting hurt."

"Don't blame you for that." Frank reached in his pocket. "We'd better settle up. We owe you for four meals."

"You only ate two."

"Yeah, but it wasn't your fault the first two went to waste." Frank slid a ten-dollar gold piece across the counter. "Is that enough to cover it?"

Katie's eyes widened for a second before she controlled the reaction. "More than enough," she said. "That's too generous, Mr. Browning."

"Well, I thought maybe I ought to pay for the marshal's coffee, too, since I had something to do with him being here in the first place."

"Even so . . ." Katie shook her head. "It's not going to do any good to argue with you, is it?"

Salty said, "It never does me a blasted bit of good."

She picked up the coin and said, "All right, then. Thank you, Mr. Browning."

66

"You're welcome," Frank told her as he stood up.

Money didn't mean much to him. Vivian Browning, Frank's old flame and Conrad's mother, had been a very, very rich woman, with lucrative business interests scattered all across the country. After she'd been murdered by outlaws, Frank and Conrad had inherited equal shares of her estate. That made Frank one of the richest men west of the Mississippi, even though no one would know it to look at him.

That was because most of the money went into the bank and was administered by trusted teams of lawyers in Boston, Denver, and San Francisco. As long as Frank had enough funds for trail supplies, feed for his horses, ammunition, and books, he had everything he needed.

Salty climbed off his stool, too, and doffed his battered old hat.

"We're much obliged to you for the fine meal, ma'am," he said with rough gallantry.

Katie smiled and said, "Stop by any time you're in Pine Knob, Mr. Stevens."

"After today, it ain't likely we will be, ma'am. You heard the marshal."

Katie glanced at Frank, who kept his face expressionless. "Yes, I did," she said.

Salty looked at the kitchen door, where

Solomon Storm was peeking through the narrow gap again, and called, "So long, fella!"

Solomon's head jerked back, and they heard him muttering and stomping back across the kitchen.

Frank and Salty left the Feed Barn. The horses stood at the hitch rack, with Dog sitting nearby. Frank had worried a little that Brady Morgan and his men might have tried to mess with the animals, but he didn't think that was likely.

If that had happened, they would have heard the ruckus inside the café as the big cur tore into the gunmen.

"We should've seen if we could beg the bone from that pot roast for ol' Dog," Salty said as they mounted up. "Still can, if you want."

"No, I think we'd better get on out of town," Frank said. "You heard what the marshal told us."

Salty frowned. "Yeah, I heard it, but I didn't expect you to pay no attention to it. You ain't in the habit of worryin' about what a lawman thinks."

"That's where you're wrong," Frank said. "I'm a peaceable man."

Salty just snorted as they turned their horses toward the eastern end of Pine Knob.

When they reached the edge of town, they could see the slight elevation that gave the settlement its name. As Gage Carlin had told them, it had been cleared of trees, but a number of stumps remained. It was an ugly sight, sad in its way.

They rode past the knob and followed a fairly well-defined trail that ran toward the eastern end of the valley. They would have to go past the headquarters of the B Star if they continued in that direction. After the settlement had fallen out of sight behind them, Salty said, "Those hills to the south don't look too rugged. I'll bet we can cut through that way."

"I was thinking the same thing," Frank agreed. They swung their mounts off the trail and led Stormy and the pack horse toward the hills.

Before they reached that long line, however, Frank pointed to the west and said, "Maybe we'll turn back that way."

Salty reined his paint to a halt and let loose with a blistering stream of profanity, which Frank endured stoically. Finally, Salty said, "You just can't stay out of it, can you? If there's bullets flyin' around, you got to be in the big middle of 'em!"

"I don't know who started out right and wrong in this," Frank said, "but it looks to me like Baldridge has stacked the deck against the Embrys, and that's wrong. I've got a hunch that if Baldridge really believed he could win in court, he wouldn't have brought in a bunch of hired guns."

Salty tugged at his beard and grimaced. "You're probably right about that," he admitted. "So what are we gonna do? You heard Jubal Embry. If we go back to the Boxed E to try to help him, he's liable to shoot us both on sight!"

"Well," Frank said with a smile, "we'll just have to change his mind."

CHAPTER 7

When they came to Loco Creek, they had to ride along the winding stream for a ways before they came to a place where they could ford it. The creek widened and grew shallower as it leaped and brawled over a gravel bed dotted with sandbars. With pine-covered hills and grassy meadows all around, and snow-capped mountains rising majestically in the distance, the scene's beauty was a vivid reminder of why Frank loved the West so much.

Once they were back on Boxed E range, Salty kept turning his head from side to side, peering around suspiciously.

"You reckon there are bushwhackers behind every tree or something?" Frank asked.

"There could be!" the old-timer replied. "After seein' how all Hades usually breaks loose wherever you are, I wouldn't doubt it a bit. Anyway, we've already seen some

Boxed E stock since we crossed the creek, and where there's cows, there's bound to be cowboys. Embry could'a given his punchers orders to ventilate us."

"I suppose you're right. It won't hurt to keep our eyes open."

"Durn right it won't," Salty said with a satisfied nod.

They angled back toward the center of the valley, and soon Frank began to spot some landmarks he recognized from their ride through here earlier in the day, accompanied by Gage Carlin and the other two Boxed E hands. They were retracing their path, and if they continued in this direction, it would take them straight to the ranch headquarters.

Frank reined in and said, "Maybe we'd better be a mite more discreet about this. See that little ridge off to the left? There are enough trees on it to keep us from being spotted easily."

"Good idea," Salty agreed. "Out in the open like this, I always get the feelin' somebody might be lookin' at me over the barrel of a rifle."

They headed for the ridge and climbed into the pines. When they reached the top of the slope, Frank turned to the right. That would take them in the general direction of the Boxed E headquarters.

It was past the middle of the afternoon, but the sun was still fairly high in the sky. The days were long at this time of year. Every now and then Frank and Salty saw a puncher or two on horseback in the distance, but none of the riders came close to them.

Frank reined in and motioned for Salty to do likewise when he caught a glimpse of movement through a gap in the trees to their left. At first he thought it might be one of the Boxed E ranch hands he had spotted, but as he looked closer, he made out two riders, and there was something furtive about the way they were ambling along, using the pines as cover in much the same way Frank and Salty were doing.

"Who do you reckon they are?" Frank asked in a whisper as he pointed them out.

"Danged if I know," the old-timer replied. "Some o' Embry's men, maybe?"

"Embry's men wouldn't have any reason to be sneaking around like that." Frank reached a decision. "We're going to follow them."

"That's what I figured," Salty said with a resigned nod.

For the next few minutes, Frank and Salty trailed the two riders, gradually working their way closer. While they were screened by a thick stand of brush, Frank halted long enough to dismount, take a pair of field glasses from his saddlebags, and push some branches aside to create a gap through which to study the two men.

He didn't recognize either of them. They wore range clothes, but neither man carried a rope on his saddle. That was a sure indication that they weren't cowboys. The holstered revolvers on their hips were rather low-slung, too.

"Gunmen?" Salty asked in a raspy whisper when Frank returned his horse.

Frank nodded as he put away the field glasses. "That's what they look like to me," he said.

"And I reckon you'd know. Bound to be some of Baldridge's men, up to no good."

"That's what I figure." Frank swung up into Goldy's saddle. "Come on."

They started trailing the two riders again. As they rode, Frank became aware of a low roaring sound coming from somewhere up ahead. He saw a rocky bluff looming about fifty feet in the air, ahead and to the left. A narrow, silvery thread ran over the edge of that bluff and dropped straight down.

A waterfall, Frank realized, and it was responsible for the sound he heard. There were probably springs atop the bluff that fed the waterfall and a tributary stream that ran across the valley and into Loco Creek.

That was where the two mysterious riders seemed to be heading. They cut across an open pasture that bordered the thick band of pines running along the base of the bluff.

"If we go across that pasture after 'em," Salty said, "all they'd have to do to see us is to look back."

"They don't seem to be paying much attention to what's behind them anymore," Frank said. "It's like they've almost reached their destination, and they're in a hurry to get there."

"Yeah, I reckon that's true," Salty said as the two men disappeared into the trees.

"We'll give them a minute and then go after them. Might be a good idea to leave Stormy and the packhorse here."

They tied the reins of the two extra horses to trees, then started after the gunmen. Dog started to lope ahead, but Frank snapped his fingers and the big cur fell back to trot alongside them.

A tense few moments passed as Frank and Salty crossed the pasture, but nothing happened except that the sound of the waterfall got louder as they approached it. When they reached the trees, Frank signaled to Salty that they should dismount and go ahead on foot.

Frank couldn't hear the hoofbeats of the other horses, couldn't hear anything except the roar of the waterfall and the splashing as it plunged into the pool it formed at the bottom of the bluff. Then, through the branches, he caught sight of the horses they had followed. Their saddles were empty.

Frank slid his Colt from its holster. Salty followed suit. They crept forward, not worrying too much about any small noises they might make because the waterfall's racket would cover them up. The two men they had followed were probably counting on that, too, as they snuck up on their quarry.

A bushwhacking was what those men had in mind, Frank thought. Somebody else was at that waterfall, and the two gunmen planned to slip up and open fire on them.

He didn't have that completely right, he realized as he and Salty reached a spot where they could look down at the pool formed by the waterfall. A few yards in front of them, the two men they had followed crouched behind some rocks and stared intently at the pool.

Or rather, they were staring at the beautiful young woman who stood there stark naked, knee deep in the water as she let the spray from the waterfall cascade over her. Dark, wet hair hung down her back.

Salty opened his mouth to exclaim in surprise. Frank's free hand clamped down hard on the old-timer's shoulder, silencing him before he could say anything. Salty ducked his head, brought his mouth close to Frank's ear, and whispered, "She ain't got a stitch on! It ain't proper us lookin' at her!"

"I know," Frank said. He had averted his eyes from the young woman's nude form, too. He watched the two gunmen instead, who were nudging each other and grinning as they spied on her.

Frank figured they had more in mind than just being Peeping Toms. He was right. After a few more moments, the two men rose from the concealment of the rocks and walked out boldly onto the gravelly stretch at the edge of the pool. The young woman had her back to them and obviously had no idea they were there until one of them called, "Hey, missy!"

She let out a startled cry and whirled around. Instinct made her try to cover herself, without much success. The pool was too shallow to do a much better job of concealment, so she backed off quickly until she was completely under the waterfall. The thick spray obscured her form, even if it didn't hide her completely.

"You men shouldn't be here!" she shouted. "Go away!"

The two gunmen laughed, and the one who had called out to her said, "No chance of that, darlin'. Not until you come out of there and treat us friendly."

In the trees and brush, Salty raised his gun and growled, "By God, I never back-shot nobody in my life, but I'm fixin' to start!"

"Hold on," Frank breathed. "I don't like what's going on, either, but if we start shooting, the girl's liable to get hurt."

"We can't just let 'em get away with this!"

"We won't," Frank promised.

He was every bit as outraged as Salty was. Western men were raised to treat respectable women with, well, respect. Most of the time a woman was safe around even the most hardened owlhoots.

But with gutter trash like these two gunwolves, there was no telling what they might do if they got the chance. Frank knew he and Salty had to put a stop to this.

He was wondering, though, who the young woman was and how the men had known she would be here, bathing in this pool.

"Come on, sweet thing," the second man urged. "We've already seen just about everything you got to show us."

"Yeah, but we want a closer look at it," the first man said. "A lot closer look."

"My father and my brother will kill you!" the woman shouted from under the waterfall. "You'll never leave the Boxed E alive!"

"Must be the Embry girl," Frank muttered to Salty. "I had a hunch that might be her."

One of the men confirmed that by saying, "Nobody knows we're here, Miss Embry. You just go along with what we say, and we won't hurt you. You got my word on that."

Frank saw the sly look that passed between the two men and knew the one who had just spoken was lying. They couldn't take a chance that Faye Embry would point them out later and accuse them of assaulting her. If that happened, both of them would wind up dancing on air at the end of hang-ropes, very quickly.

No, there was no doubt in Frank's mind that they intended to kill Faye when they were through with her.

He wasn't going to gun them down in cold blood, though. Instead he lifted his revolver, nodded to Salty, and stepped out of the trees. The old-timer was right beside him as they leveled their Colts at the two men and Frank said in a powerful, commanding voice, "Don't move!"

CHAPTER 8

The men started to reach for the guns on their hips, but at the same time, Frank and Salty both drew back the hammers on their Colts. The distinctive sound of the weapons being cocked made both interlopers freeze.

"Go ahead and twitch, you varmints!" Salty said. "It'd be a plumb pleasure for me to ventilate your mangy hides!"

Neither man moved. They seemed carved out of stone now.

"Miss Embry, you stay right where you are for a minute," Frank called to the young woman. "We'll get these men out of here."

"Don't worry, I . . . I'm not coming out!" she replied as the waterfall poured down around her. Frank could dimly see that she was hugging herself. Fed by snowmelt and springs from deep in the earth, that water was probably pretty cold. That was why Faye had been standing in the spray, not directly in the waterfall.

"I'll cover them," Frank said. "Salty, you get their guns."

"Can I use their own shootin' irons to plug 'em?" the old-timer asked. "Seems like that'd be, what do you call it, poetic justice?"

"I think you mean irony," Faye called from under the waterfall.

"Shootin' irony?" Salty said as he holstered his gun. "I never heard'a that."

"Just get their guns," Frank suggested.

"All right, all right." Salty moved up closer to the two men, being careful not to get in Frank's line of fire.

Faye said, "When my father finds out what you men have done, he'll horsewhip you and then hang you! Then he'll ride for the B Star and kill your boss and his gunslinging toady!"

"Settle down, miss," Frank told her. "We'll take care of these hombres, and if you want to press charges against them —"

"Press charges?" Faye broke in. "For what they threatened to do? It would be a waste of time, and besides, I don't want to have to stand up in court and say that they . . . they . . ."

She couldn't go on, but Frank knew what she meant. It would be a humiliating ordeal for her to have to testify that the two gun-

men had spied on her and seen her unclothed. And in the end the two would
probably be hanged anyway.

But Frank, despite the troubles he'd had
with the law over the years, believed in at
least giving the justice system a chance to
work. All too often, it broke down and folks
had to deliver justice on their own, but that
had to be a last resort.

Salty reached out to pluck the gun from
one man's holster. "I wouldn't want to be
in your boots," he said. "You fellas are done
for."

Pointing out the sheer desperation of their
situation might not have been the best thing
to do. The man Salty had just disarmed suddenly threw himself backwards and side-
ways, crashing into the old-timer. The hombre twisted around, grabbed for his gun,
and tried to wrench it out of Salty's hand.

As the two struggled, the other man took
advantage of the distraction and whirled
around as he clawed at the butt of his gun.
Frank fired, but the bullet narrowly missed
and smacked into the bluff instead. The
gunman darted behind Salty and the other
man as they staggered back and forth, fighting over the revolver.

Frank couldn't risk firing again with Salty
in the way. He slid to the side, trying to get

a clear shot. The second gunman wasn't worried about his partner. His Colt began to roar as he threw lead at Frank.

The first man finally succeeded in getting his gun away from Salty and smashed it against the old-timer's head. That was the worst thing he could have done, because when Salty pitched to the ground, stunned, that put him out of the line of fire. The man tried desperately to swing the gun toward Frank, but he was too late.

Frank's Colt blasted again. The slug drove into the man's chest and flung him backwards. The upper half of his body landed in the edge of the pool with a big splash that threw shining water droplets high in the air.

Frank pivoted as a bullet burned past his head. The other man was making a dash for the trees where they had left their horses when they snuck up on Faye Embry. He triggered his gun as he ran, spraying lead across the clearing.

Dropping to one knee, Frank tracked his sights after the man and squeezed off a shot. The man spun around like a top as the slug bored through his body. He caught his balance and tried to keep running, but he was mortally wounded and stumbling now. After a couple of steps, he pitched forward to land limply on his face.

The man lying half in the pool was closer. Frank checked him first and saw immediately that he was dead. Streaks of blood discolored the water around him. He lay on his back with water covering his face. His sightless eyes stared up through the pool.

Frank was worried about Salty, but he had to make sure the second man was dead, too, before he checked on the old-timer.

The man was still alive, but from the raspy, bubbling sound of his breathing and the way blood welled from the holes in his body, he wouldn't be for much longer. Frank picked up the gun the man had dropped when he fell, then hurried back to kneel beside Salty.

He was afraid that being pistol whipped like that might have resulted in a busted skull, but Salty was groaning and trying to come around. He had a bloody lump on the side of his head. Frank probed it with experienced fingers and didn't find any real damage, although with that swelling it was hard to be sure.

Salty opened his eyes and groaned again. "I didn't know any . . . train tracks ran through here," he said.

"Train tracks?" Frank repeated. Maybe the blow had addled Salty's brain.

"Yeah. That was a . . . locomotive . . . that

ran over me . . . wasn't it?"

A smile tugged at Frank's mouth. He had a hunch Salty was going to be all right.

He slipped an arm around Salty's shoulders and lifted the old-timer into a sitting position. Salty touched the lump on his head and winced.

"Got a damn . . . goose egg," he said. He looked up. "I'm sorry, Frank. I didn't think I was close enough . . . for that varmint to jump me like that."

"Don't worry about it," Frank said. He glanced at the second gunman and saw that the man's bloody chest had stopped rising and falling. "They're both done for. Now we can clear out and let Miss Embry get dressed."

He had already spotted Faye's clothes lying spread out on one of the big rocks around the pool. Even though he had been trying not to look at her and invade her privacy, when he spoke her name he couldn't help but glance in the direction of the waterfall.

It was a good thing he did because she was crumpled there behind the cascading water, apparently unconscious . . . or worse.

With alarm making his heart thud heavily in his chest, Frank leaped to his feet and charged past the dead gunman into the pool. Water flew up around his feet. Behind him, a startled Salty cried, "What in tarnation!" Then he said, "Oh, Lord! The girl!"

Water slammed down on Frank's broadbrimmed hat as he reached the falls. He couldn't worry about propriety now. He bent over and scooped Faye Embry into his arms. As he lifted her, he saw how her head lolled loosely on her neck. There was a raw streak on her forehead that started oozing blood again once she was out of the water.

Frank recalled how the second gunman had fired wildly across the clearing as he tried to flee. One of those stray bullets had struck Faye. The wound didn't appear to be a bad one, just a nick that must have stunned her. But if she had fallen under the water while she was unconscious, she might be drowned.

Salty was on his feet by the time Frank splashed out of the pool with Faye in his arms.

"Is she alive?" the old-timer asked as Frank carried Faye to the stretch of grass between the pool and the trees.

"I don't know," he said as he lowered her carefully to the ground. "Looks like a bullet creased her, but I don't see any other wounds."

Proper or not, he let his gaze travel along

her bare body, searching for bullet holes or other injuries. Except for the scratch on her forehead, she seemed to be unharmed.

And it was a mite embarrassing but pretty difficult to miss the fact that her chest was rising and falling as she breathed. If she had swallowed any water, it hadn't been enough to choke her.

"Get her dress and spread it over her," Frank told Salty, who hurried to obey. "She'll probably come around in a few minutes, and we don't want her waking up in a position like this. She's going to be upset enough just by everything that's happened so far."

"Better to be upset than dead," Salty said as he draped the gingham dress over Faye. "Those damn rannihans would've killed her when they were done with her, so she couldn't point no fingers at 'em later."

"I figured that, too," Frank said. The best thing to do for Faye now was to let her rest and wake up naturally, so he came to his feet and stepped back a little as he looked at Salty. "Are you all right? I wasn't finished checking you over when I saw what had happened to the girl."

Salty waved a gnarled hand dismissively. "I'm fine," he said. "It'll take more'n a wallop with a six-gun to dent this ol' noggin of mine. I ever tell you about the time a mule kicked me in the head?"

"I don't think so," Frank said. "But I'm not surprised."

"Yeah, that blasted jughead just hauled off and — Hey, wait a minute. What'd you mean by that?"

"Nothing," Frank said with a faint smile. He looked down at his clothes. "Reckon I'm soaked to the skin."

He took off his hat and slung water from it, then placed it on top of a rock to dry.

"I'll go get the horses," Salty offered. "You got some spare duds, don't you?"

"Yeah, but not any extra boots. The sun's pretty warm. Maybe it won't take them too long to dry."

He kept a discreet eye on Faye while Salty went to fetch the animals. He came back leading the four horses with Dog trotting ahead of him.

Frank got dry clothes from his saddlebags and went into the trees to change. When he got back, walking in sock feet and carrying his boots and a wadded mass of wet clothing, he saw that Faye still hadn't regained consciousness.

A worried frown creased his forehead. She was taking longer to come to than he had expected.

"I thought she'd be awake by now," he said as he spread the wet clothes on the rocks to dry.

"Reckon she'll have to take her own sweet time about it," Salty said. "You think we ought to drag these dead coyotes off so when she does wake up, she won't have to look at their ugly carcasses?"

"That's a good idea."

Salty went to grab the feet of the man lying at the edge of the pool, but Frank waved him off.

"You need to rest," he said. "I'll take care of this."

Salty grumbled some, but he stood aside and allowed Frank to drag the corpse into the trees. Frank did the same with the other dead man and then hunkered on his heels beside the bodies to check their pockets.

He didn't come up with much. Both men carried cigarette makin's, and they had more money than cowboys usually carried, upward of fifty dollars each. One had a deck of greasy, much-used cards, and the other had an envelope in his shirt pocket that had been folded over several times. This was the man who had fallen in the water, so the envelope was wet and whatever had been written on it had washed away. The same was true of the sheet of paper that Frank

90

carefully slid out of it. The ink had run, leaving only indecipherable blue smears.

The letter must have meant something to this man for him to have hung on to it. Even hired killers had families, sweethearts, friends. But whatever the letter contained was gone, just like the life of the man who had carried it.

Frank left the bodies there and went to bring in the horses the men had left in the trees. They were good animals, nothing fancy but solid mounts. He didn't recognize the brand on either of them. Untying the reins from the saplings where they had been fastened, he led the horses back to the pool.

When he got there, Faye Embry still hadn't regained consciousness, and Salty was starting to look worried, too.

"You reckon we better try to get her clothes on her and take her back to her pa's place?" he asked.

"We may have to," Frank said. "Maybe there's a doctor in Pine Knob —"

The crackle of brush alerted him. He turned toward the sound, his hand moving closer to his gun as he did so. But he stopped the motion as he spotted several rifle barrels poking out from behind nearby trees and a man shouted furiously, "What the hell have you done to my daughter?"

CHAPTER 9

Frank recognized Jubal Embry's voice. He stood there with his shoulders squared and said, "Take it easy, Embry. She's been wounded, but we didn't do it. We found a couple of men about to attack her and stopped them."

"Lies!" Embry bellowed from behind the tree where he pointed a rifle at Frank and Salty. "Again with the lies! I order you off my ranch, and what do you do? You come back and molest my daughter! By God, I ought to —"

"Pa, wait!" That was Hal Embry's voice, coming from the area where Frank had dragged the corpses. "There are a couple of dead men over here, and I think I recognize them. I've seen them with Brady Morgan."

"What?" Embry sounded confused, but he was so obviously sure of himself that the feeling didn't last long. "They must've all four come over here to our end of the valley and had a fallin' out amongst 'em when they found your sister like . . . like that. Good Lord, I've told Faye she was just askin' for trouble by comin' out here to swim in this pool, but she wouldn't listen to me. Your sister won't listen to nobody!"

"Especially not an . . . old buffalo bull like you," Faye said weakly from where she lay on the grass.

Frank looked around in mingled surprise and relief that the young woman had regained consciousness. Her father's roaring tone must have roused her from her stupor.

Faye lifted her head and pushed herself up on an elbow to look down at her body. When she realized that she was still nude, with only her spread-out dress covering her rather inadequately, she gasped and clutched at the garment as she tried to make it shield more of her from view.

"You men get out of here!" she cried. "Get out!"

"You heard her, damn you," Embry said. He jerked the barrel of his rifle. "Come on! And keep your hands away from those guns."

"We're not going to draw," Frank said as he walked toward the trees with his hands held in plain view. "We haven't done anything wrong."

As he and Salty entered the trees, several Boxed E hands closed in around them, brandishing Winchesters. Jubal Embry came up and jerked Frank's Colt from its holster. Another man disarmed Salty.

"I reckon I'll take a whip to you," the rancher said, "and then I'll tar and feather you, and then I'll string you both from the highest tree I can find. Buzzards who'd molest a respectable young woman don't deserve no better."

"We're not the ones who were trying to hurt your daughter," Frank said. He didn't know if it would do any good to argue with Embry. The man seemed to be as stubborn as a mule. But once Faye got dressed, maybe she would tell her father what had really happened.

They had another potential ally in Hal, too, who walked up and said, "Pa, didn't you hear what I told you?" He pointed over his shoulder with a thumb. "There are a couple of Brady's men back there in the trees with bullet holes in them. I've got a hunch Frank put those holes in them."

Salty said, "You'd be right about that, sonny. He drilled both those skunks, and it was one of them what fired the shot that creased your sister." The old-timer pointed to the swollen lump on his skull. "One of 'em gave me this, too, by wallopin' me with a gun while we were tryin' to corral 'em."

"I don't believe a word of it," Embry snapped. "I ordered you off my range. Men who would disobey an order like that would lie, too."

"Then why did Frank shoot those two?" Hal asked.

"I told you. They had an argument over what they were gonna do to your sister."

"Don't talk about me like I'm not here," Faye said as she strode into the trees, fully dressed now down to soft leather boots on her feet under the long skirt she wore. "And could you stop shouting, Father? My head hurts, and all the noise is just making it worse."

"I'm not surprised your head's sore, Miss Embry," Frank said. "One of those bullets flying around clipped you and knocked you out. You'd better take it easy for a few days. Sometimes head injuries like that can be tricky. I've had my share of 'em."

"Don't bother givin' my daughter any advice," Embry said. "I'll send for Doc Hutchison in Pine Knob. He'll tend to her health."

Faye said, "This man's just trying to help. And he and his friend have told you the truth. If it wasn't for them, there's no telling what might have . . . happened to me."

Embry frowned at her. "The four of them weren't all together?" he asked.

"No. That's what they've been trying to tell you. Those other two men came up first and . . . and accosted me while I was bathing. Then these two showed up and pointed guns at the others and tried to disarm them. That's when the fight started." Faye lifted a hand toward the scratch on her head. "And when I got hurt."

"That's what I figured," Hal said. "Frank and Salty were just trying to help."

His father glared at him. "You're still too damn trustin'," the elder Embry said. "It'll get you killed one of these days, if you ain't careful."

"Why don't you stop pointing those rifles at these two men?" Faye suggested. "This is getting ridiculous. I've already told you they didn't do anything wrong."

"They saw you . . . well . . ." Embry hesitated.

Faye flushed prettily. "That can't be helped," she said. "And I'd rather be a little embarrassed than dead."

That was the way Frank had hoped she would react. He nodded to her, smiled slightly, and said, "Salty and I are obliged to you for telling the truth, Miss Embry."

Jubal Embry finally lowered his gun, but he didn't stop glaring. "There's still the matter of you comin' back on my range when I told you to clear off and stay gone! What do you have to say about that?"

"We've been to Pine Knob and found out more about what's been going on around here," Frank said. He told them about the encounter with Brady Morgan and Gaius Baldridge at the Feed Barn, and also about their conversation with Katie Storm and Marshal Trask.

Frank noticed how Hal perked up at the mention of Katie. The two of them were interested in each other, that was for sure.

"So you talked to your son," Embry said with a sneer. "I don't see how that changes anything."

"I'll be honest with you, Mr. Embry. I don't know if Brady Morgan is my son. I suppose he might be. But like I told you before, I never saw or heard of him until today, and I'll stand by that."

"Then why did you come. back?" Hal asked.

"It looks to us like Baldridge has got you outgunned," Frank said. "And Brady Morgan's already got it in for us. Seems like the best thing for us to do would be to give you folks a hand."

Embry's bushy eyebrows rose in surprise. "You want me to hire you? As regulators?"

"As men who'll ride for the brand, whatever that takes." Frank grinned. "But I've done my share of cowboying when I was younger, and I'll wager Salty has, too. We can work the range if you need us to."

"I've got cowhands," Embry said. "But I don't have hired killers, and I don't intend to." He snorted in disgust. "I should've known, considerin' your reputation, mister. You're no better than that no-good whelp of yours."

"Pa, I think you've got it wrong," Hal said. "They saved Faye."

Embry rounded on his son and roared, "It ain't your place to do the thinkin' around here! I still do that . . . unless you figure you're man enough to take over the Boxed E and run it better than I can!"

Hal looked angry and frustrated as he replied, "I never said that, Pa, and you know it. But I got a right to tell you what I think."

"And I got a right to ignore it."

"What about me?" Faye asked. "Are you going to ignore my opinion, too, Father?"

Embry frowned at her. "What're you talkin' about?"

"You trust my business sense. Well, I think

it would be good business to hire Mister . . . ?"

She looked at Frank.

"Morgan," he told her. "Frank Morgan. And this is Salty Stevens."

Salty took off his hat and said, "We ain't been formally introduced 'til now, miss, but it's an honor and a pleasure to meet you."

Faye smiled a little. "I imagine it was, considering how I was dressed at the time."

"Blast it, girl, don't be so familiar with these men," Embry snapped. "Even if they're not workin' for Baldridge, they're just drifters. No-account saddle tramps. Hired guns."

Even though the riches sitting in various banks in his name meant very little to him, Frank couldn't help but think about how he could probably buy and sell Jubal Embry several times over, and throw in Gaius Baldridge for good measure.

But he didn't say anything about that. Instead he said, "You can think whatever you want about us, Embry, but you've got to admit it's come in handy having us around today. We helped Hal and those other three hands of yours get out of that bush-whacking without a scratch, and your daughter would have been a lot worse off now if we hadn't come along when we did."

"He's right, Father," Faye said. "We owe a debt to Mr. Morgan and Mr. Stevens."

"And I promised them a good meal earlier today," Hal put in, "a meal they didn't get because you ran them off. Why don't you let them come back to the ranch with us, have some supper, and spend the night? While they're doing that, we can figure out what to do next."

Embry still wore a dark scowl, but he was smart enough to know that at the moment, the game was running against him, Frank thought. After a few seconds, the rancher jerked his head in a curt nod.

"All right, we won't horsewhip you or tar an' feather you or string you up," he said.

"We're obliged to you for that," Frank said dryly.

"And I'll feed you and give you beds in the bunkhouse for the night. Nobody's ever said that Jubal Embry ain't hospitable, and they ain't gonna start now!"

"Appreciate that."

"But as for lettin' you hire on . . . don't count on it, mister. I still don't trust you as far as I could throw you. Even if you're tellin' the truth, you're liable to wind up on the opposite side from your own son, lookin' at him over the barrel of a gun. You thought about what you're gonna do if that happens,

Morgan?"

"I have," Frank replied honestly.

But he didn't have any answers yet, and that was the truth, too.

CHAPTER 10

The ranch hands who had ridden out here with Embry and Hal took charge of the extra horses. When everyone was mounted up, they started back toward the Boxed E headquarters.

Embry had returned their guns to Frank and Salty, which surprised Frank a little. He was grateful for that, though, because he never felt quite right without the weight of the Colt on his hip.

Not surprisingly, Embry took the lead, leaving the others to follow him. Frank suspected it was that way in most things the rancher did.

But he didn't mind, because it gave him a chance to talk with Hal.

"I'm curious about something," he said to the young man. "How did you and your pa happen to show up out there at that waterfall when there was trouble going on?"

"One of the hands heard the shots and

galloped back to the ranch house," Hal explained. "Headquarters is too far away for the sound to have traveled that far, but we've always got men riding in various parts of the spread. After all the problems with Baldridge, and especially after Morgan and his men jumped us earlier today, whenever there's any shooting we all come a-runnin'."

Frank nodded and said, "That makes sense. You believe what we told you about what happened at the pool, don't you?"

Hal looked at Faye, who was riding ahead of them, but not as far ahead as her father, and said, "My sister's a lot of things, Mr. Morgan, but she's not usually a liar. I can't think of any reason why she wouldn't tell the truth about what happened."

"I'm glad to hear you feel that way. By the way, why don't you call me Frank? The name Morgan sort of stirs up bad feelings around here."

"That's the truth," Hal agreed. "All right, Frank. Did you say you didn't tell the folks in town who you really are?"

"That's right. Seemed to me like it would just complicate matters."

"And you didn't want Brady to know, did you?"

"I'm still trying to figure that one out," Frank admitted. "Like I said, there's a chance he really is my son, even though I never knew about it until today."

"I reckon it'd be pretty hard to gun down your own flesh and blood."

"People have done it," Frank said. "I'd just as soon not be one of 'em, but I won't stand by and let Brady Morgan kill some innocent person."

"What if you're the one he's trying to kill?"

"I'm going to try not to let it come to that."

But he might not have any choice in the matter, Frank thought. He might have to make a decision . . . and if he did, he would have to do it in less than the blink of an eye.

He would have to do it in the time it took to draw a Colt and pull the trigger . . .

When they reached the Boxed E, the sun wasn't far above the horizon. Once again, the ranch dogs bounded out to greet the newcomers with raucous barks and growled at Dog, who ignored them except for a warning lift of his lip.

A woman stood on the front porch of the ranch house, obviously waiting for Embry and Hal and the other men to return from investigating the shots. She was middle-aged, with enough of the same sort of beauty in the lines of her face and her thick brown hair that it was equally obvious she was Faye's mother. She looked like she wanted to rush down from the porch and run to meet them, but she kept that impulse under control.

"The girl's all right, Mary," Embry said gruffly as he reined to a halt in front of the porch. "You can see that for yourself."

"But those two men aren't," Mary Embry said as she pointed to the two corpses draped over their saddles. The Boxed E hands had tied them to the horses. Frank wasn't sure what Embry planned to do with them. Mary went on. "What happened, Jubal?"

Faye dismounted and said, "I'll tell you about it in the house, Mother. We don't need to talk about it out here."

Mary put a hand to her mouth in alarm. "Oh, my God," she breathed. "Are you sure you're all right, Faye?"

"I'm fine. I just want to go inside."

Faye stepped onto the porch, where her mother put an arm around her shoulders and led her through the open door.

Embry turned to Frank and Salty and said, "You can put your horses in the corral and your gear in the bunkhouse. There are empty bunks out there. Claim a couple for the night." Embry looked at Gage Carlin.

"Gage, I'm puttin' you in charge of keepin' an eye on these two."

"Sure, boss," Carlin said with a nod.

Hal had already dismounted. Embry swung his lumbering bulk down from the saddle and handed his reins to his son. He went into the house.

"Don't take what he says too serious-like," Hal told Frank and Salty, keeping his voice low enough that his father wouldn't hear him inside. "He'll come around."

"We're obliged for the hospitality," Frank said, "and the offer to stick around and give you folks a hand still stands."

"Better listen to him," Salty advised. "This ain't the first range war he's been in the middle of. Now, as for me, I'd just as soon ride on, but I reckon I'll do whatever Frank says."

The hands headed for the corral and the barn. Frank and Salty followed suit, and Gage Carlin showed them where to put their saddles once they'd pulled the hulls off Goldy and the paint and turned the horses into the main corral.

Stormy and the packhorse went into the pen, too, and Frank and Salty carried their war bags and supplies into the bunkhouse. Carlin gave them a hand and lingered by the bunks where the newcomers dumped their gear.

"On behalf of me and the rest of the crew, I want to thank you fellas for helpin' Miss Faye," the cowboy said. "She can be a mite bossy at times, but most of us have watched her grow up and we're right fond of her."

"You believe us about what happened, then?" Frank asked.

Carlin shrugged. "I heard Hal tell you that Miss Faye's not a liar. I agree. Since her story jibes with yours, I reckon you're tellin' the truth."

"What's Embry going to do with those bodies he had you bring in?"

"He told some of the boys to wrap 'em up real good and put 'em down in the root cellar for the night. In the morning he's going to put them in a wagon and take them to town. He said Marshal Trask can turn them over to Baldridge. 'Let Baldridge take care of his own trash,' he said."

"That's liable to stir up even more trouble."

Carlin shook his head and said, "The trouble's already stirred up. Bushwhackin' Hal and the rest of us this mornin' was bad enough, but goin' after the boss's daughter . . . The storm's gonna break now, that's for sure."

Frank tossed his hat on the bunk, sat

down, and clasped his hands together between his knees.

"You don't think Baldridge sent those men over here to attack Miss Embry, do you?" he asked. "That wasn't the way it sounded to me. I think they showed up on their own."

Carlin thumbed his hat back and leaned a shoulder against the bunkhouse wall.

"Well, you've got to remember, I've been around here for quite a spell, and I remember how things used to be. I wouldn't go so far as to say that the boss and Baldridge were amigos, but they got along all right most of the time. Baldridge is sort of a stuffed shirt, but would he order a couple of gun-hawks to ride over here and rape a young woman?" Carlin shook his head. "I don't think he would. I just don't think so. But he hired the sort of skunks who'd do such a thing."

"That's a good point," Frank agreed. "He has to bear part of the responsibility. I've got another question for you. How did those men know that Miss Embry would be there at that waterfall this afternoon?"

"I don't have an answer for you, Frank," Carlin said. "I don't have any idea."

It was an intriguing question, Frank thought, and he had a feeling that the answer might be important. For the time being, though, there were other things to consider, and one of them was uppermost in Salty's mind.

"When's supper?" the old-timer asked.

As if someone had been waiting for the question, the sound of a dinner bell being rung floated through the evening air to the bunkhouse. The cowboys headed eagerly for the door.

"Mrs. Embry cooks for the whole crew?" Frank asked Carlin as they left the building and started toward the main house.

"That's right. The boss hires a chuck-wagon cook for roundup and when we drive the herd to Great Falls, but the rest of the time Miz Embry handles the cookin', and she's mighty good at it, like Hal told you."

"She'll have to go a ways to beat that fella Solomon at the Feed Barn in Pine Knob," Salty commented.

Carlin laughed and said, "Yeah, that crazy ol' coot can rustle up some mighty good grub. Miz Embry runs him a pretty close race, though."

"From what I can see, Hal's a little sweet on that Katie Storm," Frank said.

"Maybe," Carlin allowed, "but that gal's got a mind of her own, and she and Miss Faye don't see eye to eye on a lot of things, so I don't figure anything'll come of it. Hal generally listens to his sister's advice."

And that was one of the things Katie didn't agree with, Frank thought, recalling her comment about how Hal needed to stop listening to his father and sister all the time.

Mary Embry stood next to the iron triangle that hung from the porch roof. An iron bar was attached to the iron piece at the end of a cord. That was what she had rung to announce that supper was ready, running the bar around and around the inside of the triangle. The ranch hands took off their hats and nodded politely to her as they trooped in.

When Frank reached the porch, he asked, "How's your daughter doing, Mrs. Embry?"

"Faye is resting," Mary said. "She doesn't have much of an appetite tonight, so she's not coming down to supper. I'm sure you can understand that."

"Yes, ma'am."

Frank, Salty, and Carlin went inside. Carlin led the way to a large dining room dominated by a long table that practically filled it up. The center of the table was covered with platters heaped high with food. Frank saw fried chicken, roast, and ham, along with greens, potatoes, bowls of still-steaming biscuits, thick chunks of butter, gravy, molasses, and pots of stew.

Mary Embry must have cooked all day to put together a spread like this, Frank thought, although some of the food could have been left over from the midday meal.

Jubal Embry sat at the far end of the table, reminding Frank of pictures he had seen in books of English kings. The table wasn't round, and these rough cowboys weren't exactly knights, but the comparison wasn't that much of a stretch. Cattle barons like Embry ruled their spreads sort of like feudal monarchs.

Except for Embry, all the men stood up when Mary came into the room. She motioned them back into their seats and took the empty chair at the near end, opposite her husband. None of the men had started filling their plates yet, so Frank figured they were waiting for something.

Mary confirmed that guess by saying, "Will you please say grace, Jubal?"

Embry looked a little pained by the request, but he heaved himself to his feet as everyone else at the table bowed their heads.

"Lord," Embry intoned, "thank you for this bounty you've put before us and the good friends we're about to share it with. Bless us and this food, and thank you for watchin' over my children today when they were in danger."

Mary cleared her throat.

Embry made a face and went on. "Thank you for sendin' these strangers to share our hospitality . . ." He gave Frank and Salty a hard look. "And protect us from wolves in our fold. Amen."

Mary frowned at him as everyone looked up, but Embry seemed not to see her.

"Dig in, boys," he told the crew.

"That was a good prayer, Mr. Embry," Frank said as he reached for the fried chicken. "Especially that last part."

Embry grunted and said, "You think so, do you?"

"That's right," Frank said. "Of course . . . it helps if you know who the real wolves are."

CHAPTER 11

The night passed quietly on the Boxed E, and when Frank and Salty went into the ranch house the next morning, they found that Mary Embry was just as talented with breakfast as she was with the day's other meals. Salty waxed eloquent about how good the flapjacks were, and Frank thought the coffee was some of the best he'd had in a long time.

Jubal Embry was still surly, and Faye didn't come down for breakfast, although Mary mentioned that she had taken a tray up to her daughter and that Faye's appetite was back.

As the men were lingering over their coffee, Embry said, "Hal, I want you to pick three of the men and take those carcasses into town."

"You still intend to turn them over to Marshal Trask?" Hal asked. "Can't we just bury them here?"

Embry scowled and shook his head. "I'll not profane our buryin' ground by plantin' those two polecats in it," he rumbled. "They're Baldridge's men. Let Baldridge take care of 'em."

"They're probably getting a little ripe by now, even after being kept in the root cellar overnight," Hal pointed out. "They'll be worse by the time we get them to town."

"That's Baldridge's problem. Are you gonna do what I told you or not?"

Hal sighed. "Sure, Pa. I always do, don't I?" He looked around the table. "I should pick three men to go with me, you said?"

"That's right."

"Then I'll take Frank, Salty, and Gage."

"Blast it!" Embry burst out. "I meant three of our men, and you know it. Morgan and Stevens don't count."

"We'd be glad to go," Frank said. "And since I'm the one who shot those fellas, the marshal's liable to want to talk to me, even if it did happen outside his jurisdiction."

"Frank's right, Pa," Hal said. "Besides, if they come with me, that frees up two of the other hands for their regular work."

"All right, all right," Embry said with a curt gesture. "Take 'em. That means I won't have to look at 'em for a while."

The men went out to the corral a short

114

time later. Salty was grumbling about the way Frank had volunteered them for this grim chore.

"That's just how I wanted to spend my mornin', playin' nursemaid to a couple o' decomposin' gun-wolves," he said as he saddled his pony.

Since he'd been riding Goldy lately, Frank put his hull on Stormy to give the sorrel a chance to rest.

"Maybe we can stop and have dinner at the Feed Barn while we're in Pine Knob," he suggested.

That made Salty's spirits perk up.

"Seems like the bullets fly a hell of a lot in this part of the country," he said, "but I got to admit, there's good eatin' everywhere you look!"

Hal hitched a team of draft horses to the ranch wagon and drove it over to the root cellar's entrance.

"You three will be outriders," he told Frank, Salty, and Carlin. "I can handle the wagon."

Salty wrinkled his nose when one of the ranch hands lifted the cellar door. "Them varmints are a mite fragrant already," he said.

"Better get used to it," Frank said. "It'll get worse before we get to town. Is there an undertaker in Pine Knob, Hal?"

"Yeah, and I don't envy him his job," the young man replied. "Not one little bit."

They got the blanket-shrouded shapes into the back of the wagon. Hal climbed to the seat and took the reins again. He turned the team toward the settlement and got the horses moving. Frank and Salty rode on one side of the vehicle as it rolled along the trail, Gage Carlin on the other.

Since the Boxed E had been invaded twice the previous day by forces from the B Star, the four men kept a close watch on the rugged, beautiful landscape around them. Brady Morgan and some of the other regulators might try to set up another ambush.

Frank knew that if that happened, he would fight back along with the others without any consideration of whether or not Brady might be his son. Salty was his friend, and now Hal and Carlin were, too, and he would do his best to protect them.

Nothing happened on the way to Pine Knob, though, except that the bodies in the back of the wagon began to stink even worse, as Frank had known they would. Growing up on a ranch, he had experienced the smell of dead animals at an early age.

Not until he was in the war, though, had he encountered the stench of thousands of

116

dead men littering a battlefield. A man never forgot that experience, although the lucky ones were able to put it aside and not dwell on it.

In the more than three decades since then, death had followed Frank enough that, while not exactly friends, he and the Grim Reaper had to be considered close acquaintances.

When they reached the settlement, the citizens of Pine Knob who were on the street cast curious glances at them, then some of the townspeople grimaced as they caught a whiff of what was in the back of the wagon. The vehicle rattled across the bridge over Loco Creek. Hal brought it to a stop in front of a frame building with a sign on it that read FINNEGAN'S UNDERTAKING ESTABLISHMENT — OMAR FINNEGAN, PROP.

"Gage, ride on down to the marshal's office and let him know what we've got here," Hal said.

Carlin nodded and trotted his horse along Main Street.

Hal set the brake, looped the reins around the lever, and climbed down from the seat while Frank and Salty dismounted and tied their horses to a hitch rack. A mostly bald man with a fringe of graying red hair around his ears appeared in the doorway of the undertaking parlor and asked, "Is it some work ye have for me, young Embry?"

"That's right, Mr. Finnegan," Hal replied. "Two men." He didn't provide any details of how the men had died.

Finnegan pointed to the alley beside the building and said, "Take them around back, if ye would. We'll unload them there."

"All right. I, uh, never delivered any bodies before. I wasn't sure where we were supposed to take them."

Finnegan looked curiously at Frank and Salty, as if recognizing that they weren't regular Boxed E hands.

"I'm glad ye brought some help wi' ye. My assistant's not here right now, and we can use the extra hands."

Hal climbed back onto the wagon and drove it around behind the building. Frank and Salty walked along the alley rather than untying their horses and mounting up again. Finnegan went through the undertaking parlor and met them at the back door.

"I ain't too fond of this," Salty muttered as he and Frank lifted one of the corpses to carry it into the undertaking parlor. "Carryin' a dead body ain't very good luck."

"Better than being carried," Frank pointed out.

"Well, I reckon I can't argue about that. But I still don't cotton to it."

They took the corpses into Finnegan's spacious back room, which had several coffins stacked along the wall and a couple of tables where he did his work. They had just placed the bodies on the tables when Marshal Roy Trask came through the building from the front room, followed by Gage Carlin.

"What's all this about?" the lawman asked. "Who are these men?"

Hal pushed his hat back and said, "We don't know their names, Marshal, but I've seen them with Brady Morgan. Pretty sure they work for Baldridge."

"Let's take a look."

"Before I have a chance to prepare them, Marshal?" Finnegan asked.

"Right now," Trask said.

Finnegan shrugged and undid the lashings that held the blankets around the bodies. He pulled the blankets back to uncover faces that were gray and doughy in death.

Salty turned away, muttering and shaking his head.

Trask studied the dead men for a moment, then motioned for Finnegan to pull the blankets back into place.

"I've seen them before, too, and you're right, Hal, they were with Brady Morgan." Trask turned to the undertaker. "I guess that makes Gaius Baldridge responsible for the cost of burying them, Omar."

"I'll make a note of that," Finnegan said.

"Are you going to send a rider out to the B Star with the news?" Hal asked.

"First of all, I want somebody to tell me what happened to these men."

"I shot them," Frank said.

Trask frowned at him and said, "Don't think I didn't notice that you're back, Browning. I told you and that old pelican with you to get out of Pine Knob, and I don't like it when folks ignore me."

"We left like you told us," Frank said. "But you didn't say anything about not going back to the Boxed E. When we did, we found these two about to attack Miss Faye Embry. There's a good chance they would have killed her, too. When Salty and I stepped in to put a stop to it, they put up a fight."

"And you gunned 'em both down?"

"That's right."

Trask rubbed his heavy jaw and frowned in thought. "One of those hombres was called Royal, the other was Dodds. Supposed to be pretty slick on the draw, both

120

of them."

"Not slick enough," Salty said. He took off his hat and showed Trask the lump, which had gone down some overnight but was still visible. "One of 'em walloped me with a pistol and gave me this goose egg. You ask me, I'd say they got what was comin' to 'em."

Hal said, "I hope you're not thinking about causing trouble for Frank here, Marshal. I'm convinced he saved my sister's life."

"If this happened on the Boxed E, there's nothing I can do about it," Trask replied with a shake of his head. "I just wanted to get the facts straight for when I talk to Gaius Baldridge."

"You're going to send for him?"

"I don't have to. He's already in town. He's waiting for the stagecoach that ought to be rolling in pretty soon."

"He's leaving town?" Hal asked in surprise.

"I don't think so. He doesn't have any bags. It's more like he's waiting for somebody."

"More hired guns, prob'ly," Salty suggested.

"Could be. As long as they don't try anything in town, it's none of my business."

Frank understood why the marshal felt that way, but he thought it was unlikely that Trask would be able to maintain that stance of neutrality forever. Sooner or later — probably sooner — the hostilities between the Boxed E and the B Star would spill over into Pine Knob.

And once blood was in the streets, it was impossible to put it back.

"I'll go find Baldridge and let him know what happened," Trask went on. "Last time I saw him he was over at the stage station, waiting."

"Was Brady Morgan with him?" Hal asked.

Trask shook his head. "No, just a couple of the regular B Star hands brought the buckboard in. Baldridge drove his buggy himself."

The marshal left. Hal said, "I'm sort of curious to see who Baldridge is meeting on that stagecoach, if that's what's going on. You need us for anything else, Mr. Finnegan?"

The undertaker shook his head. The four of them walked through the undertaking parlor's front room and stepped onto the porch. The stagecoach station was located diagonally across the street. Marshal Trask was walking toward it, not getting in any hurry. Clearly, he wasn't looking forward to breaking the news to Gaius Baldridge.

In the middle of the street, Trask stopped short and looked toward the east. Frank heard the same thing the marshal had: the rumble of hoofbeats and the rattle of wheels. A Concord stagecoach being pulled by a six-horse hitch came into view, trailing a cloud of dust behind it.

"Does the stage road go right past the B Star?" Frank asked Hal.

The young man shook his head and said, "No, it comes up from the south through Granite Pass about halfway between here and Baldridge's headquarters."

"That's why he had to come here to meet the stage, then, instead of just having it stop at his ranch."

"That's right. After the road turns south, there's still a good trail onto the B Star, but not good enough for a coach."

Marshal Trask stayed back out of the way as the stagecoach pulled up in front of the station. Gaius Baldridge emerged from the building. Frank saw a fancy black buggy parked not far away, along with a buckboard, and knew those vehicles had to belong to Baldridge. The rancher had to be meeting someone, as Trask suspected. Baldridge would carry the new arrival out to the ranch in the buggy, while the cowhands he had brought with him would load up the person's bags on the buckboard.

After Frank had figured that out, he wasn't surprised when the stationmaster opened the coach door and helped a woman climb down from the vehicle. Baldridge waited on the boardwalk with a welcoming smile on his face.

"Laura, it's so good to see you again." Frank heard Baldridge's greeting clearly across the street. "You look as beautiful as ever. No, more beautiful."

The woman stepped onto the boardwalk and took both the hands Baldridge extended to her. She wore a blue traveling gown with a hat of the same shade perched on honey-colored curls. Frank couldn't see her face, but as he hooked his thumbs in his belt and leaned a shoulder against one of the posts holding up the awning over the undertaking parlor's porch, he thought that the woman had a nice shape in that blue dress.

Laura, Baldridge had called her.

Frank frowned. Something about that name and the woman's shape . . . something . . .

She leaned forward and let Baldridge kiss her cheek, then she stepped back and turned so she could look around the town.

As she did, she glanced across the street at the four men on Finnegan's porch. Her gaze started to move on, but she stopped short and looked back at them.

Frank felt the same shock of recognition. He straightened from his casual pose as the woman stepped to the edge of the boardwalk and called across the dusty street, "Frank? Frank Morgan? Is that really you?"

CHAPTER 12

Marshal Trask heard the words as clearly as Frank did. His head snapped around toward the undertaking parlor.

"Morgan!" he exclaimed. "You said your name was Browning! But you're . . . you're . . ."

Frank sighed and stepped down from the porch. "Stay here," he told Salty, Hal, and Carlin.

"Not hardly," the old-timer said again. "I want a ringside seat for this!"

He hurried to keep up as Frank strode across the street. Hal and Carlin came along, too.

"Sorry for lying to you, Marshal," Frank said as he reached Trask. "I just wanted to find out a little more about what was going on around here before I let on who I really am."

"Then you're really Frank Morgan, the gunfighter?" Trask asked. "Brady Morgan's father?"

"One of those things, anyway," Frank said. "Not sure about the other."

He walked on toward the stage station, where the woman called Laura smiled at him and Gaius Baldridge stood with a puzzled, surprised look on his face.

"Frank, I never expected to see you here," Laura said as he reached the boardwalk.

"That goes for me, too," he told her. "You're as lovely as you ever were."

"Oh, now, you're just being gallant. Not that I don't appreciate it!"

It was the truth, Frank thought. Laura Donnelly had been a breathtakingly beautiful young woman when he had known her, but the years had been more than kind to her. Her hair was still thick and lustrous, her blue eyes as bright and sparkling as ever, and her figure remained the sort that would make any man sit up and take notice. Time had added a few lines to her face, but they were the sort that merely enhanced her beauty and gave it character, rather than detracting from it.

"Laura Donnelly," Frank murmured. "I don't believe it."

"It's not Laura Donnelly any longer," she said. "I'm Laura Wilcoxon now. *Mrs.* Laura Wilcoxon."

"You're married?"

"Widowed."

Baldridge moved up beside her and lightly laid a hand on her arm in a possessive fashion as he said, "That's right. Mrs. Wilcoxon is here to visit my ranch . . . and her son."

Frank stiffened as the implications of Baldridge's words went through him.

"Your son?" he repeated quietly as he looked at Laura.

"That's right, Frank," she said. "Brady is my son . . . and yours."

San Antonio, Texas, 1872

"Lay your bets, gentlemen," Laura Donnelly said as she toyed with the deck of cards in her hands. She looked at the man seated directly across the table from her and went on. "Anything else you'd like to lay, cowboy?"

Frank Morgan leaned back in his chair and grinned.

"I've anted up, ma'am," he said. "I'll wait and see what the cards bring."

Laura returned his smile and dealt, her long, slender fingers spinning the cards to the players around the table with deftness and speed.

Frank had drifted into San Antonio a few

days earlier after a dust-up with some Mexican bandits down around Laredo, and from the moment he had stepped into the Caballo Rojo Saloon and seen Laura Donnelly dealing cards, he'd been interested in her. He had sat in on several games, introduced himself to her, and bought her a few drinks. She seemed to like him, but there was a certain coolness about her. A woman who looked like her, in her line of work, probably was accustomed to keeping most men at arm's length.

But he thought she was warming up to him, and he thought that maybe, just maybe, tonight would be the night she would consent to having a late supper with him in her room upstairs.

The Caballo Rojo was in downtown San Antonio, not far from the murky, twisting river and the old mission where a small group of stubborn Texicans had held off the Mexican army for almost two weeks before being slaughtered. Frank liked San Antonio. The town had a sleepy quality to it that was very restful, especially for a man who in a few short years had gotten used to the roar of guns and the acrid bite of powdersmoke in the air.

He was a conservative poker player, never winning or losing much but enjoying the game. Tonight, though, the cards seemed to be running his way, and even though he didn't place big bets, the pile of greenbacks in front of him kept growing. Other players came and went, but Frank and Laura continued playing, along with one other man who had been in the game from the start. He was a hawk-faced cattle buyer named Russell, and he lost about as steadily as Frank won.

The hour was growing late when Laura gathered in the cards at the end of a hand and murmured, "That'll be all for this evening, gentlemen. A lady needs her beauty sleep, you know."

"Not you, ma'am," one of the other men said. "If you were any more beautiful, us poor fellas'd be so overwhelmed we wouldn't stand any chance at all."

Laura laughed. "That's very sweet of you, but I still have to bid you good night."

They all stood up when she did, and except for Frank and Russell, the men began to drift away from the table, most of them heading for the bar and a fresh drink.

Since his growing reputation as a gunman had forced him to leave his home several hundred miles north of here and become a drifter, Frank had learned that when a man wanted something, he had to seize the opportunity to get it. Because of that, he said, "It would be my honor to have dinner with you, Miss Donnelly."

"It's pretty late, cowboy," she said, but her smile took any sting out of the words. "I don't think I feel like going out to some restaurant."

"I thought maybe we could have some food sent up to your room."

"Oh, you did, did you?" Her eyes sparkled even more than usual. "That sounds . . . intriguing."

Frank came around the table and held his arm out to her. She hesitated, but only for a second, and then linked her arm with his. They started toward the stairs, leaving Russell behind them at the table, where he stood watching them with a glare on his dark, narrow face.

They were halfway up the stairs when Russell said in a loud voice that instantly quieted the hubbub in the room, "Morgan!"

Frank stopped and turned as Russell walked quickly to the bottom of the staircase.

"You want something, mister?"

"You've got a lot of my money in your pocket," Russell said, "and what you don't have, that Jezebel with you does."

Frank moved down a step and positioned

131

himself so that he was between Laura and the cattle buyer. His face might have been carved from stone as he said, "I think you owe the lady an apology."

"I don't owe her anything, and I don't think she's a lady. I saw the looks you two have been giving each other all night. She's just a damn tinhorn in cahoots with a two-bit gunman to cheat all the honest men dumb enough to sit down at a table with her!"

Laura put a hand on Frank's shoulder as she stood behind him. He shrugged it off and came down another step.

One of the men who sat at a table near the bottom of the stairs said into the tense silence, "Mister, you best back off. That's Frank Morgan. He's not a two-bit gunman. He's the Drifter."

"I don't care who he is," Russell said. "They cheated me, him and that no-good slut!"

Men started to scramble out of the way, convinced that bullets would be flying any second now.

"Mister, we'll settle this —" Frank began.

"How?" Russell demanded. He pulled his coat back to reveal that he wasn't wearing a gun. "I'm not packing an iron. You shoot me, Morgan, and it'll be murder. With this many witnesses, the Rangers will hang you for sure."

Frank drew in a deep breath and let it out in an angry sigh.

"Forget it, Frank," Laura said from behind him. "He's not worth it. Let's go upstairs."

"That's right," Russell said with a sneer. "Go upstairs with your whore."

Frank knew what Russell was trying to do. The cattle buyer wanted to goad him into a fight. Russell was almost as big as Frank, with the heavy, powerful shoulders of a man who knew how to brawl. Normally, Frank would have been glad to oblige him, but tonight he had more pleasant things on his mind.

"Russell, you'd better be gone when I come back downstairs," he said. Contemptuously, he turned his back on the man and started up the stairs again toward Laura.

"Frank, look out!" she cried as he heard a rush of footsteps behind him.

Russell charged up the stairs and tackled him from behind as Frank tried to turn around again. They were big men, and as they rammed against the banister, it gave way under their weight with a splintering crash. They fell about four feet to land on a hastily vacated table that collapsed under them.

Russell hammered punches at Frank as the two men lay in the wreckage of the table. Frank blocked some of the punches and shrugged off the others as he got hold of Russell's shirt front. With an angry roar, Frank heaved him to the side and sent Russell rolling across the sawdust-littered floor. Both men came to their feet at the same time.

Russell charged in. Frank met him with a hard left that hooked into the cattle buyer's stomach. Russell grunted and started to double over, but Frank's right fist came around in a looping blow that was timed perfectly to coincide with the arrival of Russell's jaw. When the punch landed, it made a sound like an axe blade biting deep into a chunk of wood. Russell's head slewed around on his neck as his eyes rolled up in their sockets.

He toppled to the floor, landing facedown and not moving again.

As soon as it was obvious the fight was over, the saloon's owner, a short, slender Mexican with a mustache and an agitated air, rushed up, looked at the shattered table and the broken railing, and clapped his hands to his cheeks in dramatic fashion.

"Who's gonna pay for all this damage?" he wailed in dismay.

"Don't take on so, Pedro," Laura said from where she still stood on the stairs. "I'll pay for it. Mr. Morgan was defending my honor, after all."

"Oh." The saloon man was instantly all right again. "In that case . . ." He snapped his fingers and motioned for a couple of the bartenders to drag Russell's senseless hulk out of the place.

"Oh, and Mr. Morgan and I will need some supper, too, Pedro . . . in about an hour."

"I will take care of it, Señorita Donnelly," Pedro said, bobbing his head in a nod.

Frank picked up his hat where it had fallen on the floor, slapped it against his thigh a couple of times, and went up the stairs to join Laura again.

"Sorry about the commotion," he told her.

"You were just defending yourself — and me," she said. "I can't hold that against you." She linked arms with him again. "Shall we?"

"We shall," Frank said as they started up the stairs together again.

"Let me guess," Laura said as she looked at him from the boardwalk in front of the stagecoach station in Pine Knob, Montana. "You're remembering a certain night in San

Antonio. The Caballo Rojo Saloon."

"The red horse," Frank said.

"And it was quite a ride, wasn't it? Those were good times."

Good times indeed, Frank thought. He had spent several weeks in San Antonio with Laura, and they were passionate weeks, cut short only when a couple of young firebrands who wanted to prove how fast on the draw they were threw down on him in front of the old mission. Both of those young men had died there, leaking gore onto ground that might well have been watered by the blood of Texican patriots thirty-six years earlier.

Until that happened, the local authorities had been tolerating the presence of a notorious gunman in their town. Less than twenty-four hours after the fight, a large group of deputies armed with shotguns had called on Frank at his room in the Menger Hotel and suggested strongly that he leave San Antonio behind him. He had refused, even though he knew it might mean more trouble, and gone to the Caballo Rojo to warn Laura that all hell might be breaking loose.

She was gone. Her room was empty, and Pedro told Frank that she had cleared out earlier in the day.

She had heard about what was going to happen and decided that she couldn't afford to be involved with him anymore. That was the only explanation Frank could think of. And with Laura gone, there was nothing to hold him there.

He rode out less than an hour later. In the years since then, he had been back to San Antonio many times.

But he had never seen Laura Donnelly again.

Until now.

CHAPTER 13

"Why didn't you tell me?" he asked. "Why didn't you tell me about the boy?"

Her lips tightened a little in response to the harsh note that had come into his voice, despite his best intentions.

"I didn't know when I left San Antonio, Frank," she said. "You can choose whether to believe me or not, but it's the truth. Later, when I realized . . ." Her shoulders rose and fell in an eloquent shrug. "I didn't know where you were. Over the years, I heard stories about you many times, and yes, I probably could have looked you up. But there didn't really seem to be any point to it."

"Except that I had a —"

Frank stopped. This was like what had happened when he was reunited with Vivian Browning after many years apart and found out about Conrad.

And how did that work out? he asked

himself.

At first Conrad had refused to believe that Frank was his father. When he finally accepted that fact, reluctantly, he'd had nothing but hatred and contempt for Frank. He had turned his back on his true father, and if he hadn't needed Frank's help desperately a few years later, the two of them probably never would have seen each other again.

The circumstances that had brought them together had resulted in the beginning of friendship and mutual respect. But even though the Drifter and Kid Morgan would each lay his life on the line for the other now, there was still a barrier of years between them and probably always would be. Nobody's fault, just the way things were.

If he had met Brady Morgan years ago, there was no way of knowing how the young man would have reacted. Laura knew Brady a lot better than Frank did; maybe she had been right not to seek him out and introduce them.

Anyway, it was in the past. There was nothing Frank could do now to change it.

He had to wonder, though . . . In his one real encounter with Brady, the young man had struck Frank as being cruel, arrogant, and ruthless. Would things have been different if he'd had a stronger hand than Laura's helping him grow up?

Gaius Baldridge stepped into the brief, awkward moment by saying, "My dear, we really should be going. It will take a couple of hours to reach the ranch. I'm sure you're already tired from your journey and would like to settle in and freshen up."

Laura turned to him and said, "You're right, Gaius. I *am* tired. Too tired to go on to the B Star today, I think. I know it means changing our plans, but if there's a decent hotel here in Pine Knob, I believe I'll take a room there and rest for a day or two before I go on out to your ranch."

Baldridge didn't look happy about that at all. "But I brought my buggy, and men with the buckboard for your bags," he said.

"I'm sorry," Laura told him. "I didn't know I would be quite so exhausted by the trip so far."

Baldridge looked at Frank. His eyes burned with anger and resentment.

"I don't believe it's exhaustion that's caused this change in your plans," he said.

"Are you calling me a liar, Gaius?"

Baldridge took a deep breath and shook his head as he controlled his emotions with a visible effort.

"Of course not," he said. "And of course I respect your decision. The men can come back with the buckboard tomorrow."

"I may not have recovered enough by then," Laura cautioned.

"They can come every day, if necessary," Baldridge said. "As for myself, I'll be here, ready whenever you are."

"You're not going back to the ranch?"

"I'll take a room at the hotel as well. The Territorial House isn't the sort of fine accommodations to which you're accustomed, I'm sure, but it's reasonably comfortable."

"All right," she said with a smile. "If that's what you want to do."

"It is," he said, his voice flat and emotionless.

Frank wondered if the reason Laura had decided to stay in Pine Knob was because he was here. That was possible, he supposed, and he wasn't sure how he felt about that.

She seemed to indicate that his hunch was right by turning back to him and saying, "I'm sure I'll see you around town again, Frank."

Marshal Trask spoke up, saying, "No offense, ma'am, but I wouldn't be so sure about that. I don't think I much like the idea of having a gunman like Frank Morgan in my town."

"That's not fair, Marshal," Hal said. "You

141

let Brady Morgan come into town any time he wants."

Trask scowled. "That's different," he insisted.

"I don't see how. Brady's a hired killer."

Baldridge said sharply, "I'll thank you to keep a civil tongue in your head, Embry. Remember, this lady is Brady Morgan's mother."

"I'm sorry, ma'am," Hal said with a nod to Laura. "I mean no offense to you, but facts are facts."

"And who are you?" she asked coolly.

"Hal Embry, ma'am. My father owns the Boxed E."

"What he means is, his father made a spurious, illegal claim on land that belongs to me," Baldridge said.

Hal's jaw tightened and he stepped forward. Trask moved to get in front of him and held up both hands.

"All right, that's enough of this," the lawman said. "Hal, you've taken care of the business that brought you to town. Why don't you head on back out to the ranch?"

"That's right, the business that brought us to town," Hal said as he continued to look at Baldridge. "Dropping off the bodies of two dead B Star gun-wolves at the undertaker's."

Baldridge drew in a sharp breath. "What are you talking about? Two of my men are dead?"

Trask grimaced, looking like he sure wished this subject hadn't come up. "Royal and Dobbs," he told Baldridge. "They're over at Finnegan's. I expect you'll be getting a bill from Omar for their planting."

"My God! What happened?"

Trask inclined his head toward Frank. "Morgan shot them."

Looking outraged, Baldridge said, "Then I expect you to do your duty, Marshal, and arrest this man immediately. I want him charged with murder!"

"First of all, it happened out of my jurisdiction, so I'm not arresting anybody."

"And Frank killed them because they were about to rape my sister," Hal said. Grudgingly, he added, "Sorry about speaking so plain, ma'am."

Laura nodded but didn't say anything.

"Well, I simply don't believe it," Baldridge said. "Dobbs and Royal were good men. They wouldn't have done such a thing."

Salty said, "Sounds like he's callin' you a liar, Frank."

"He's calling my sister a liar, too," Hal said. "Faye backed up everything Frank and Salty told us. The question is, did you order

143

them to do it, Baldridge?"

The urbane exterior Baldridge cultivated vanished as he clenched his hands into fists and took a step toward the edge of the boardwalk.

"If I was twenty years younger, I'd answer that impudent question with a thrashing, Embry!"

"Settle down, settle down," Trask said. "Everybody just stay calm. Mr. Baldridge, why don't you show Mrs. Wilcoxon to the hotel? Hal, you and your men go on back to the ranch. There's been enough squabbling for now."

"This is more than a squabble, Marshal," Baldridge said. "I consider the killing of my riders an act of war!"

"I don't care what you consider it, you'd better keep it out of town," Trask warned. He looked at Hal. "That goes for the Boxed E, too."

"We're not going to start any trouble," Hal said, "but we'll damn sure defend ourselves." He gave Baldridge a hard look. "You can count on that."

Trask stood between the two sides, looking back and forth at them and glowering until Baldridge took Laura's arm and said, "Come with me, my dear. I'll show you to the Territorial House."

"Pa will be expecting us back," Hal said to Frank, Salty, and Carlin. "We might as well head that way."

Frank looked at Laura walking away arm-in-arm with Gaius Baldridge. She glanced back over her shoulder at him.

"You fellas go ahead," Frank said to Hal. "I'll be along later."

Salty snorted and shook his head. "No such thing," the old-timer insisted. "I ain't leavin' you here in town with nobody to watch your back, Frank. Not when there's a snake under just about every rock."

Hal said, "I thought you were going to throw in with us, Mr. Morgan. Your gear and your other horses are still out at the ranch." He paused. "But I guess since it looks like Brady Morgan really is your son, and he's working for the other side . . ."

"That's not it," Frank said. "I still don't have any use for hired guns."

Marshal Trask said, "That sounds a mite strange coming from you, Morgan. And I don't want you here, either. You're just trouble waiting to happen."

Frank's voice was hard and flat as he said, "I haven't broken any laws in your town, Marshal, and the last I heard, this was still a free country."

"And we ain't et dinner yet, either," Salty put in.

"That's right," Hal said. "I could do with a surrounding before we start back to the Boxed E. How about you, Gage?"

"Whatever you say, boss," Carlin replied, but from the faint smile that lurked on his face and in his eyes, it was obvious he was enjoying this confrontation. Trouble wasn't exactly welcome, but it sure helped break up the usual monotony of frontier life.

"All right, fine," an obviously frustrated Marshal Trask said. "Go get your dinner. But if any ruckuses start while you're here in town, you're gonna be damned sorry you didn't listen to me."

"We're not going to start any ruckuses, Marshal," Hal said.

"But we might finish one or two if we have to," Salty added.

Trask glared at them, then walked away shaking his head.

"That last comment probably didn't help any," Frank said to Salty.

"I can't abide a fence-sitter," the old-timer said. "Sooner or later that fella's gonna have to figure out which way he wants to hop."

The four men started toward the Feed Barn. There wasn't any question about where they were going to eat.

It was a little early for the midday meal, but the café was already busy, which was a testament to Solomon Storm's cooking and Katie's abilities as a hostess.

She didn't smile in welcome when the four of them came in and jingled the bell over the front door, though. She locked gazes with Hal for a second, then glanced away. When she looked at them again, she had regained her composure.

As they took seats at the counter, Hal said, "Hello, Katie. You look mighty nice today."

"Save the flowery talk," she told him briskly. She looked at Frank and went on, "And you . . . no gunfights today."

He laughed and said, "Unless I'm forgetting something, there weren't any gunfights in here yesterday."

"No, but there could have been. I'm just warning you, my uncle and I won't put up with any trouble."

"Won't be no trouble today," Salty said. "That Brady Morgan fella ain't in town."

Katie looked past them, her gaze evidently drawn by something she had spotted through the front windows. She paled as she said, "You're wrong about that, Mr. Stevens. He just rode in."

CHAPTER 14

Frank turned to look past the yellow curtains that were pushed back over the front windows. He caught a glimpse of several men riding past the café but didn't really get a good look at them, so he stepped over to the closest window.

"Blast it!" Salty said behind him. "I had my stomach set for some more o' that good grub!"

Brady Morgan rode at the head of four other men, Frank saw. They clattered across the Loco Creek bridge into the western part of town and pulled rein in front of Corrigan's Casino. They dismounted and went inside, with Brady still in the lead slapping aside the batwings.

As the gunmen disappeared into the saloon, Frank turned away from the window.

"You're still going to get your dinner, Salty," he told his friend. "They're not looking for us."

That might change, though, Frank thought as he returned to the counter and took a seat on one of the stools. Salty sat to his right, Gage Carlin to his left, with Hal Embry on Carlin's left.

Rivalries between ranches such as the Boxed E and the B Star were common, Frank knew, and any time a settlement like Pine Knob sat perched in between two rival spreads, loyalties inevitably developed among the townspeople. He was sure that Gaius Baldridge had his supporters here in Pine Knob, and Jubal Embry probably did, too.

A number of people had been on the street and on the boardwalks when the stagecoach rolled in and Laura Donnelly — Laura Wilcoxon now — climbed out of the Concord. Those people had seen and heard the confrontation that had taken place. They had heard that two of Baldridge's men, Royal and Dobbs, were dead, shot down by the notorious gunfighter Frank Morgan.

Frank figured that by now at least one hombre who wanted to curry favor with Baldridge had gone scurrying down to Corrigan's place to tell Brady Morgan all about it.

So it was only a matter of time before something else happened, but until it did,

Frank wasn't going to worry about it. He thumbed his hat back, smiled across the counter at a worried-looking Katie Storm, and said, "We'll have four plates of whatever your uncle's got on the bill of fare today."

"Four bowls, you mean," Katie said. "Irish stew."

"Bring it on," Salty told her with a whiskery grin.

Katie nodded and went out to the kitchen. When she was gone, Salty leaned closer to Frank and said quietly, "The condemned men are gonna get a hearty meal, anyway. You know Brady Morgan's gonna hear about what happened, and when he does, he ain't gonna be happy about it."

"I know," Frank said solemnly.

"Appears to me you got some thinkin' to do, Frank."

Frank shook his head and said, "Nope. If Brady starts anything, we'll handle it. Whatever it takes."

Was that true, though, he asked himself? If it came to a showdown, would he hesitate for a fatal split-second before pulling the trigger? Would the knowledge that he was facing his own flesh and blood cause him to wait?

Could he kill not only his son but Laura's as well, with her right here in town?

There was no way this was going to end well, Frank mused. No way in hell.

Katie came out of the kitchen carrying two bowls of Irish stew, as well as plates with large chunks of cornbread on them. She set the food in front of Hal and Carlin, then returned to the kitchen for the other two meals.

"Your uncle's outdid himself today, miss," Salty said after the first couple of bites. "This is mighty good."

"Thank you," Katie said, but she seemed distracted. She kept glancing toward the windows and the front door, and Frank knew why.

There was nothing he could do about it until the time came, though, except enjoy his dinner, so that was what he concentrated on doing.

Suddenly, one of the men seated at a table near a window stood up and said in a loud voice, "Uh-oh. Brady Morgan's headed this way, and he don't look happy."

Those words started a mass exodus. Katie's lips thinned as she watched the customers disappear out both front and back doors.

"No offense, Mr. Browning . . . I mean, Mr. Morgan . . . but you're bad for business," she told Frank. "Unless it's Omar

Finnegan's business, that is."

"I'm sorry about that, Miss Storm." Frank took a double eagle out of his pocket and slid the twenty-dollar gold piece across the counter to her. "Maybe this'll help make up for it."

She took the money without hesitation this time, saying, "I guess I'd better collect while I still can."

Salty, Hal, and Carlin frowned at the comment, but a grin split Frank's face.

"That's the practical way to look at it, all right," he said. He dipped a piece of cornbread in the stew and took another bite, then pushed his stool back and stood up. "We'll do this outside. No point in risking a lot of damage in here."

The other three men were right behind Frank as he headed for the door. Pausing with his hand on the knob, he looked back at them.

"This is my fight, fellas, not yours."

Salty let out a snort and said, "You know better'n that, Frank."

"Yeah, I suppose I do."

Frank opened the door and stepped onto the café's porch. Brady Morgan and his men had mounted up again and were at the eastern end of the bridge. They rode on until they came to a stop in front of the

Feed Barn.

Brady and the other men stayed on their horses. They were all the same sort of lean, cold-eyed gunslingers Frank had seen many times before. Brady's face was flushed, as if he had been drinking before they ever got to Pine Knob and went to Corrigan's place.

"I hear you're my pa," he said to Frank in a challenging voice. "I reckon that means you lied to everybody yesterday when you said your name was Browning."

Frank stood in an apparently casual pose, but his right hand was close to the butt of his Colt . . . just as Brady's was.

"I figured it wouldn't hurt anything to be a mite careful until I knew what was going on around here," he said. "Now I know."

"And what is it that you know?" Brady demanded with a sneer.

"That Gaius Baldridge has some mighty sorry hombres working for him. Two of them were about to molest a young woman yesterday until I stopped them."

Brady's face darkened with anger. "We've got only your word that happened!" he shot back. "Dobbs and Royal wouldn't do such a thing!"

Hal said, "My sister tells the same story as Mr. Morgan here. I heard her with my own ears. Faye wouldn't lie."

153

"Sure she would," Brady snapped, "if she was actin' like a slut and lured those two fellas over there to get killed."

The skin around Hal's mouth turned white. He might have reached for his gun, but Frank said sharply, "Hold it."

"Why, Frank?" Hal demanded through clenched teeth. "These varmints have been wanting a showdown. I say we give them one."

There was a good reason not to let this turn into a gunfight if it could be avoided: all five of the men on horseback were professional killers. Of the four on the porch, Frank knew he was the only one who could be counted on to get a shot off. Salty, despite his loyalty and fierce tenacity, was no gunman. It would take too long for him to haul out the old hogleg on his hip. Frank didn't know how fast Hal and Carlin might be, but he felt certain they couldn't match the speed of Brady and his men.

"There's not going to be any shooting," Frank said in a harsh voice. "Brady, you may not know this, but your mother is in town."

The young man was unable to completely conceal the look of surprise that flitted across his face.

"She is?" he said. "I knew she was coming, but I saw the buggy and the buckboard and figured the stage hadn't gotten here yet."

Frank glanced down the street at the stagecoach station. The Concord was gone. It had already rolled out of Pine Knob on its return trip to Great Falls.

"She's here," he said. "She's decided to spend a day or two at the Territorial House before going out to Baldridge's ranch."

"I wonder why," Brady grated.

"You'd have to ask her that. She said she was tired, and I don't have any reason not to believe her."

Brady sat there stiffly in his saddle, obviously torn about what to do next. He wanted to kill the man who had gunned down Royal and Dobbs. The killings were a direct challenge to the man who ramrodded the crew of gun-wolves Baldridge had hired.

But Brady now knew that the man responsible for those deaths was his own father. Frank knew better than to delude himself into thinking that Brady might have any affection for him; they had only seen each other twice, and before yesterday Frank hadn't even known of Brady's existence.

But to look at your father over the barrel of a gun . . . that had to give a man pause.

Just like the thought of looking at your

155

own son that way did.

Also, Brady might not want to get mixed up in a gunfight with his mother in town, because then there was the possibility that she would emerge from the hotel to see his bloody corpse lying in the street. Frank didn't know how close Brady and Laura were, but he figured no son would want to subject his mother to that.

The silence stretched out until one of the other hired guns asked, "Brady, what are we gonna do about this?"

Brady took a deep breath. "Where are the bodies?" he asked.

"Over at Finnegan's," Frank told him.

Brady turned his head to look at the other men. "Go talk to the undertaker," he ordered. "Make sure he understands that Royal and Dobbs get the best treatment he can give them, got it? And Baldridge is paying."

"Brady, we've got to do something about this," one of the other men said.

"I've told you what you're gonna do, damn it!" Brady burst out. "Now move!"

The men didn't look happy about it, but they turned their horses and rode slowly toward the undertaking parlor, leaving Brady to face Frank and his three companions alone.

"Don't think I give a damn that you're my father," Brady bit off as he glared at Frank.

"The thought never crossed my mind," Frank said.

"I don't know you, and I don't want to know you. All you ever gave me was a rep to live up to. I've done it, too. Maybe I haven't killed as many men as the famous Frank Morgan, but my day's coming, old man. My day's coming!"

Frank didn't say anything.

After a few more seconds, Brady jerked his horse around and cruelly raked its flanks with his spurs. The horse leaped into a pounding gallop that carried Brady toward the hotel where his mother and Gaius Baldridge had gone earlier.

Salty sighed and said, "Frank, you're gonna have to kill that boy sooner or later."

"I'm afraid you may be right, Salty." Frank took a deep breath and let it out in a sigh. "Right now, though, let's go finish that stew before it cools off anymore. Don't want Miss Storm having to feed us twice every time we come in."

The four men turned toward the front door of the café, but they hadn't reached it when more hoofbeats suddenly pounded in the street. Frank looked around and saw that the four men who had come to town with Brady hadn't gone to the undertaking parlor after all.

Instead they were charging toward the Feed Barn with guns in their hands, and as the citizens scattered in fright, tongues of flame began to stab from the muzzles of those guns.

CHAPTER 15

Some of the slugs that whipped past Frank's head struck the café's front window and shattered it into a million pieces. Frank knew that shards of glass must have sprayed across the inside of the building, and he hoped that Katie hadn't been standing anywhere near the window.

There was no time to check to see if she was hurt, though. Frank's Colt was already in his hand. He hadn't had to think about drawing it. Instinct had taken care of that. The same instinct brought the gun up with blinding speed, lined the sights on the man who was in the forefront of the attackers, and pulled the trigger.

As if swatted out of the saddle by a giant hand, the man went backwards off his horse as Frank's bullet drove into his chest. One of the other men reacted automatically and jerked his horse aside to keep the animal from trampling the fallen man.

That sudden swerve caused the horse to lose its footing. With a high-pitched whinny of alarm, the horse tumbled to the ground in a welter of flailing legs and hooves. The rider sailed out of the saddle and vanished in the cloud of dust that boiled up around the panic-stricken horse.

Hal and Carlin had their guns out by now and were returning the fire, but Frank didn't think they were hitting anything. He half-turned, aimed at one of the two men still on horseback, and pulled the trigger. The Colt roared and bucked, and the gunman dropped his revolver and slewed around as he clutched at a bullet-shattered shoulder.

That left just one man mounted, and by now he was probably wishing he and his companions hadn't decided to disregard Brady's orders and try to avenge Royal and Dobbs anyway. He tried to pull his horse around, but Hal and Carlin finally found the range and drilled him, the two bullets passing through his body only a second apart. He threw up his arms and slid out of the saddle, but his foot caught in the stirrup and his body dragged behind the horse as it bolted along the street.

That left the man who had been thrown clear when his horse fell, and as Frank turned to look for him, he heard Salty's heavy old revolver boom. The man who had just emerged from the swirling dust with a gun in his hand clawed at his chest, doubled over, and collapsed.

"That'll teach ya," Salty said as gray smoke curled from the barrel of the hogleg.

Frank stepped down from the porch and moved quickly between the gunmen on the ground, kicking their weapons out of reach if any of them proved not to be dead. That didn't appear to be the case, however. All of them lay limp and lifeless, including the man whose foot had finally slipped from the stirrup, leaving him sprawled in the street about fifty yards from the café.

The man with the busted shoulder sat slumped in his saddle, clutching the injury and whimpering in pain. Frank caught Salty's eye and nodded toward the man, indicating that the old-timer should watch him to make sure he didn't try anything.

Everyone who'd been out in the open had ducked for cover as soon as the shooting started. Now that the echoes of the gunfire were dying away, people began looking out of windows and doors again to assess the results of the violence.

Hal suddenly whirled around and cried, "Katie!" He plunged toward the door of the

Feed Barn, obviously having just realized the bullets that had shattered the windows might have gone on to do some damage inside.

"Gage, go give him a hand," Frank said.

The cowboy nodded and hurried into the café as if the fact that Frank had given him an order didn't bother him at all.

"Got comp'ny comin' from two directions, Frank," Salty warned.

"I see them," Frank said. He had already spotted Roy Trask trotting toward the café from the marshal's office. Trask had the double-barreled shotgun in his hands again.

Brady Morgan emerged from the Territorial House, and when he saw his men lying in the street, he broke into a run.

"Damn it, what did I say . . . about startin' a ruckus?" Trask demanded as he came up, slightly out of breath from hurrying.

"We didn't start it," Frank said.

"But like I told you we would, Marshal, we durn sure finished it!" Salty added.

Brady Morgan reached the scene of the gunfight and shouted, "What the hell happened here?"

Frank still had his gun in his right hand. He used his left to gesture toward the man whose shoulder he had broken with a bullet and said, "Maybe you better ask your men

162

about that, Brady. They're the ones who opened the ball."

Brady glared at the wounded man. "What is this, Lew?" he asked. "I told the four of you to go to talk to the undertaker."

"Yeah, but Peevey wouldn't stand for it, Brady," the man whined. "He said we had to even the score for Royal and Dobbs. Nobody around here would respect us anymore if we didn't, he said."

"So now three more men are dead," Brady said disgustedly. He looked at Trask. "These killings took place in town, Marshal. What are you gonna do about them?"

Trask looked like he wished he was somewhere, anywhere, else, as he said, "I guess I'm gonna have to arrest these fellas until we can straighten everything out."

"There's nothing to straighten out, Marshal," Frank said. "Those men came at us shooting, and we fought back. It's as clearcut a case of self-defense as you'll ever see, and if you ask around town, I'm sure you can find plenty of witnesses who agree."

"Yeah, but I could probably find just as many who'd say you and your friends started the whole thing, Morgan."

Frank knew Trask was alluding to the situation he had thought about earlier, the splitting down the middle of Pine Knob's citizens between Baldridge and Embry.

Trask went on. "Besides, there's no gettin' around the fact that if the four of you had ridden out of town when I told you to, none of this would have happened."

The marshal was right about that, Frank supposed . . . but that still didn't mean he was inclined to give up his gun and go sit in a jail cell just because he had defended himself.

"Where are the Embry boy and Gage Carlin, anyway?" Trask asked as he looked around.

"Right here, Marshal," Hal answered from the open doorway of the café. He led Katie onto the porch with an arm around her shoulders. She looked pale and shaken, and she had a bloodstained cloth wrapped around her left hand. Gage Carlin and Solomon Storm followed them out.

"Good Lord!" Trask exclaimed. "How bad are you hurt, Miss Storm? Do we need to fetch Doc Hutchison?"

Katie shook her head. "It's just a little cut from the flying glass, Marshal. It could have been a lot worse. I was standing fairly close to the window when the shooting started and it broke. So I saw those gunfighters attack these men, if you need a witness to what happened."

Trask frowned and said, "So you saw the whole thing, did you?"

"That's right, she did," Solomon said, "and so did I! It happened just like Katie told you, you no-good, two-bit tin badge! Why, if you were any sort of a lawman, you'd hang that whole bunch of killers who work for Baldridge, startin' with that one!"

He pointed at Brady Morgan.

Trask didn't seem bothered by the abuse Solomon heaped on his head. He was probably used to the way the mentally disturbed old man acted.

Brady didn't react so well. He took a step toward the porch and said, "Why, you mangy buzzard! I'll —"

"You won't do anything, Morgan," Trask snapped. He moved the shotgun slightly, so that the barrels pointed in Brady's general direction. "You won't do anything except take your man down to the doc's office. That shoulder's gonna need a sawbones to patch it up."

Brady was white around the mouth with anger as he stood there stiffly, but after a moment he nodded. "All right. But what about the ones who were killed?"

"I'll see to it that they're taken over to Finnegan's and things are handled properly," Trask promised.

"Fine." Brady turned away and took hold of the injured man's reins. He started leading the horse along the street.

Frank watched him go. He didn't trust Brady not to spin around with no warning and slap leather.

But that didn't happen. It looked like the violence was over for the time being.

Trask said to Frank and Salty, "I'd be much obliged if you fellas would holster those guns."

"You're not going to try to take them away from us?" Frank asked as he pouched the iron.

Trask sighed and shook his head. "I believe you about what happened. But there'll have to be an inquest, and you'd better be there." The lawman looked at Hal and Carlin. "All four of you. So plan on riding back into town tomorrow morning."

"And if we don't?" Hal asked.

"Then there'll be a warrant out for your arrest the next time you set foot in the town limits," Trask said. "So unless you plan on never coming to Pine Knob again, Embry, I'd suggest you do like you're told."

Hal glanced at Katie, and Frank knew what the young man was thinking. Hal couldn't stay away from Pine Knob. Not as long as Katie was here.

166

Hooking his thumbs in his gunbelt, Frank said, "We'll be here, Marshal. You've got my word on it."

Trask nodded, evidently satisfied. "Fine. *Now* will you get out of town like I asked you to an hour ago before all this hell broke loose?"

"We might as well," Frank said. "I'm sure our dinner is cold by now, and I don't reckon Miss Katie needs to be worrying about dishing up some more for us."

Salty opened his mouth, probably to say something about not being so hasty, but a look from Frank made him fall silent before any words came out.

"Are you going to be all right?" Hal asked Katie.

"Of course," she told him. "It's my left hand. I can bandage it just fine. Solomon can help me if I need him to. We'll be open again for supper."

"Well . . . if you're sure. But you need to take care of yourself. That cut bled pretty bad."

"I'm more worried about getting that window replaced," Katie said with a sigh. "A new pane of glass will have to be freighted up from Great Falls or maybe even Helena. In the meantime I guess I can get Danny Kyle to board it up." She glanced at

167

Frank and Salty and added by way of explanation, "He's the town handyman."

"You ought to make Baldridge pay for it," Hal said. "When you get right down to it, he's responsible for what happened here. He's the one who brought those gunmen into the valley."

Seemed like somebody always brought snakes into paradise, Frank mused a few minutes later as he and his three companions rode out of Pine Knob. He glanced toward the Territorial House as they turned west, and he thought he saw a curtain over one of the windows in the hotel lobby move and then fall back, as if someone had looked out at them.

Was it Laura? he asked himself. Just how much did she really know about what was going on in this valley?

And although he hated to think about it, he had to wonder if she'd had anything to do with it.

CHAPTER 16

"Come away from there, my dear," Gaius Baldridge said as he rested a hand lightly on Laura's shoulder. "You shouldn't concern yourself with such terrible things."

"Perhaps you're right, Gaius," she said as she let the curtain fall closed over the window in the hotel lobby. They hadn't gone up to their rooms yet when the shooting erupted down the street, but by the time Laura reached the window, it was all over. Her son, who had been talking to her when the gunplay started, had already rushed out to see what was happening.

Brady was alive, she thought as she turned away from the window. He hadn't been in the middle of this battle.

But there would be others.

She had long since learned to accept the fact that Brady was in a violent, dangerous profession. His life was at risk nearly all the time.

That was the way it had to be, if they were both going to get what they wanted. And they were so close now . . .

It wasn't like she could strap on a gun, stride into the street, and seize what she desired. Lord knew, she would if she could, and there had indeed been times in the past when she had taken direct action. In this world, though, a woman had to work behind the scenes for the most part. She had to find a man to do her bidding and provide her with the things she wanted and needed.

Or, in her case, she had to give birth to one.

Baldridge put a hand on her elbow and steered her gently across the lobby toward the stairs. The Territorial House wasn't fancy. There were rugs on the floor, some comfortable overstuffed armchairs, a writing desk, and a few potted plants, but that was the extent of the amenities in the lobby. The rooms upstairs would be much the same, Laura knew: comfortably furnished but on the plain side. A person couldn't expect any more than that in a Montana cowtown.

"So that was Frank Morgan," Baldridge mused as they started up the stairs. "I wonder what his real reason was for lying about his identity at first."

"I'm sure what he said about his reason was the truth," Laura replied. "Frank isn't in the habit of lying."

"He lied about who he is."

"That's true," Laura murmured, "but I'm sure he thought it was necessary. Frank can be a very practical man in some ways." She smiled. "In others he's wildly romantic and idealistic."

"I don't think I'd care to know the details that prompted that statement," Baldridge said dryly. They reached the landing, and he took her along the corridor to the adjoining rooms he had gotten for them. He opened one of the doors, swung it back, and said, "Here we are."

Yes, it was just as she had expected, Laura thought as they went inside. A sturdy four-poster bed, a wardrobe, a dressing table with a basin and pitcher on it, a ladderback chair, and a single, blue-curtained window that looked out on the decorative balcony running along the front of the building.

"I'll see to it that your bags are brought over shortly from the stage station," Baldridge said. "We can eat in the dining room downstairs, or I can have something sent up."

"It might be better to have something sent

up in a while," Laura said. "I really am tired."

"Of course." Baldridge paused. "I'm sorry there's been so much trouble since your arrival. This business with Embry is coming to a head. Did you bring any new word from our lawyers?"

Laura unpinned her hat and took it off, setting it carefully on the dressing table. She shook her head and said, "No, they're still working on the case down in Helena." She managed not to smile at the way Baldridge referred to them as *our lawyers.* It was her money that paid them, not his.

Well, her late husband's money, to be precise, she thought. Or it had been.

But it was *hers* now, and it always would be as it continued to grow.

Frederick Wilcoxon had been a decent man, a widower in his sixties who had been canny enough — and lucky enough — to amass a considerable fortune in the railroad business. He had built a number of spur lines across the country, and all of them were quite profitable.

But with his wife gone, he was lonely, and when he had met a beautiful society widow who was wealthy in her own right, it hadn't taken much effort at all on Laura's part to get him to fall for her and convince him that it had all been his idea, not hers.

Of course she wasn't a widow — she had never been married until she wed Frederick Wilcoxon, in fact — she wasn't a member of society, and she had just enough money to put on a good act. Frederick hadn't discovered any of that during the six months they'd been married. Then he had died, quite conveniently, in fact, and she hadn't even had to ease him out of this life, although she had considered the idea. She had never actually killed anyone, though, and didn't particularly want to start down that path.

That was one reason she had Brady, after all. He was quite good at killing and didn't seem to mind doing it. Laura was sure he would have gotten rid of Frederick if she'd asked him to, but fortunately her husband's heart had given out one night when he was paying one of his occasional visits to her bedroom in his Denver mansion.

Frederick Wilcoxon died happy, and the money and power she inherited from him made Laura happy, so everything had worked out well all around.

But there was always more money to be made, more power to be seized, and once she had talked to Frederick's lawyers and business managers about his plans, she had seen that she could carry them out, probably even better than he would have been able to. Because Frederick, may he rest in peace, had had scruples.

Laura had known for decades just how useless those things were.

"You really must be tired," Baldridge said. "You look like your mind is a million miles away."

She turned to him with a smile. "I'm sorry, darling. I think I'll rest for a bit, then if you want to have some dinner sent up, we can eat together."

"I'd like that very much," Baldridge said. He had taken off his hat. Now he settled it back on his head, and Laura thought, not for the first time, that he really was a handsome, distinguished-looking man, not at all the sort you'd expect to be a Montana cattle baron who had spent years fighting Indians and outlaws. Gaius Baldridge had a certain class about him that he clung to stubbornly, refusing to allow the rude lifestyle of the frontier to take it away from him.

But now he had met his match. He just didn't know it yet.

Baldridge left the room. Laura didn't know if he went downstairs or to the adjoining room. She made sure the corridor door and the door between the rooms were locked, then loosened the collar and top button of her traveling gown, opened the window to let in some fresh air, and stretched out on the bed. Although she often used tiredness as an excuse when she didn't want to do something, she really was weary after the stagecoach journey from Great Falls.

It would be so much easier once the railroad came through here, she thought. And *she* was the one who was going to make that happen.

She had been resting for only a few minutes when a soft knock sounded on the door. She sat up, swung her legs off the bed, and stood up.

"Who is it?" she asked quietly through the door.

"Me."

Recognizing her son's voice, Laura turned the key in the lock and opened the door. Brady looked furious as he came into the room.

"Where have you been?" Laura asked as she closed the door. "I saw Frank leave town with those other men a while ago, so I expected you back sooner."

"I had to take one of my men to the doctor's office. Morgan busted his shoulder with a bullet, but at least he'll live. The others are dead. Then that damned marshal cornered me and started reading me the riot act again," Brady said. He took off his hat and threw it on the dressing table next to his mother's hat. The contrast between the expensive chapeau and the dusty black Stetson was striking. "It would have been easy to put a bullet in his ugly face. It was mighty damned tempting, too."

"We're not going to kill any lawmen unless we have to," Laura said sternly. "I have work to do here, and having my son be a wanted murderer would make it a lot more difficult."

"Well, I wouldn't want to do anything that would interfere with your business."

Laura felt her face flushing with anger at the contemptuous tone of his voice.

"Don't forget that my business is about to make us rich," she reminded him.

"You're already rich."

"It'll make us *very* rich," she said. "Once we bring the railroad through to those mines in the mountains northwest of here, there's no limit to the profits we can make."

Brady shrugged and said, "I don't care that much about the money."

Laura knew that was true. What Brady liked was the killing. Standing in front of another man and knowing you were about to end his life, looking into his eyes and seeing the fear there that told you he knew it, too . . . That was what mattered most to Brady, proving himself in the most elemental fashion there was.

"You're certainly your father's son," Laura said quietly as Brady stepped to the window. "Frank never cared that much about money, either."

He whirled back toward her. "Did you know he was going to be here?" he asked fiercely. "Did you?"

"Brady, I swear to you I had no idea Frank Morgan was anywhere in this part of the country. When I stepped off that stagecoach this morning and saw him standing across the street, it was a complete surprise to me."

He frowned, and for a moment she thought he didn't believe her even though this was one of the times she was actually telling the truth. But then he shrugged and nodded and said, "I guess we just got lucky."

"I'm not sure it's all that lucky. He seems to be on the opposite side. And Frank Morgan is a formidable enemy, Brady. Never forget that."

Brady grunted and waved off the warning. "You'll just work your magic on him and bring him over to our side."

Laura shook her head and said, "I don't

know if that's going to be possible."

"Then I'll kill him if he gets in our way." Brady's face, normally so savage and brutal, softened slightly as he went on. "It's what he deserves, anyway, for what he did to you."

Laura smiled. So many times when he was a baby, she had thought about abandoning him somewhere. She had heard that if you left a baby on the steps of a church, the preacher or the fools who attended services there would find a home for it. Someone would always take in a baby.

But she hadn't done that, and later, as he began to grow, even though she still thought from time to time about trying to pawn him off on somebody, she had come to realize just how valuable he really was. He was hers, to mold and shape any way she wanted to. To fill his head with stories about how his father was Frank Morgan, the famous gunfighter, and how Frank had deserted them because he didn't love either of them. To carefully cultivate the hatred that began to blossom inside the boy, watching it grow stronger and stronger until it was part of him, the thing that drove him, the thing that made him who he was.

Of course, all that effort would have been wasted if it turned out Brady was weak. But he wasn't. He was strong, and he was fast on the draw, and he had whatever it took to make a man laugh when he pulled the trigger and blew the guts out of another man . . .

Laura stepped closer to her son, lifted a hand, and rested it lightly against his cheek.

"Sooner or later, Frank Morgan will get what's coming to him," she promised.

CHAPTER 17

It was late in the afternoon before Frank, Salty, Hal, and Carlin reached the headquarters of the Boxed E. The ranch dogs pitched a barking fit, as usual, but Dog just sauntered out of the barn, parked his haunches on the ground, and gave Frank a look that seemed to ask when they were going to get out of here and back on the trail again.

The commotion brought Jubal Embry out of the house. He stalked across the yard to the barn as Frank and the others led their mounts inside.

"Took you long enough to deliver a couple of corpses," Embry snapped.

"We stopped for dinner at the Feed Barn," Hal said. "And then . . . well . . ."

"What is it?" Embry asked. "Dadblast it, I can tell something happened. None of you seem to have any bullet holes in you, anyway."

"Yeah, but the same thing can't be said of the other hombres," Gage Carlin put in.

"Damn it! There was another shootin'?"

"Brady Morgan and four of his men rode in while we were in town," Hal explained. "They found out what happened to the two who tried to attack Faye."

"Tell me one of you killed Brady," Embry breathed. "Please tell me."

Hal shook his head. "He stayed out of it this time. But three of the other men are dead, and the other one is wounded bad enough he won't be doing any gunfighting for a long time, if he ever does again."

"Well, that's three more of the buzzards gone under," Embry said. He looked at Frank. "I'll bet you did for most of them."

"I don't keep count," Frank said. "Killing's never been anything I'm proud of."

"That ain't all," Salty said. "Brady's ma is in town. She come in on the stage, and ol' Gaius Baldridge met her. Looked to me like he's sweet on her." The old-timer glanced over. "Sorry, Frank."

"Don't worry about it," Frank said as he shook his head. "Whatever was between Laura and me was over a long time ago. More than twenty years ago."

Embry tugged at his beard and frowned. "So Baldridge is mixed up with this lady who's Brady Morgan's ma," he said. He looked at Frank. "And you *are* the boy's pa. But you still claim you're on our side."

"It's not just a claim," Frank said. "I am on your side, Mr. Embry. I've thrown in with you, and I'll stick. So will Salty."

"Life sure can get in a tangle, can't it?"

Frank nodded slowly. "You can say that again."

Faye Embry emerged from her room for supper that night and seemed to be back to her usual self, which didn't surprise Gage Carlin, according to what the cowboy told Frank and Salty in the bunkhouse after the meal.

"Figured she'd bounce back pretty quick," Carlin mused. "I've been ridin' for the Boxed E ever since she was a little girl, and she's always been full of fire. Never bothered her a bit standin' up to her pa and her big brother. Maybe I'm a mite out of line for sayin' so, but I don't think Miz Embry ever knew quite what to make of her."

"I'm just glad she's gotten over being shaken up by what happened," Frank said.

Carlin glanced toward the other end of the bunkhouse, where a card game was going on between half a dozen of the punchers. With a nod toward them, Carlin went on quietly, "Miss Faye went 'round and 'round with her folks and Hal when she got it in her head that her and Bill Kitson were sweet on each other. The boss said there was no way his daughter was gonna take up with some forty-a-month-and-found cowpoke. Miss Faye was so mad about the whole thing, I halfway expected her and Bill to run off to Great Falls together and get hitched, just to spite the old man. But she changed her mind, and that was the end of that. You can't *force* Miss Faye to change her way of thinkin', but once she does it on her own, she won't budge any more than a mountain does."

Frank listened to the story with interest. It might be nothing more than idle gossip, but he had learned over the years that it was best to know as much as you could about whatever situation you found yourself in.

They turned in not long after that, and early the next morning rose to eat breakfast and ride back into Pine Knob for the inquest, as Marshal Trask had insisted. Frank put his saddle on Goldy this time and told Dog to stay there and keep Stormy company. The big cur didn't look happy about it, but he followed Frank's orders, as always.

When Hal came out of the ranch house, his father was with him. Jubal Embry was dressed for riding, and as Frank saw the cattleman approaching the corral, he guessed that Embry planned to attend the inquest, too.

That wasn't all Embry had in mind. In his usual bellow, he started calling out names of the ranch hands. When a dozen of them had assembled, Embry said, "Saddle up. We're all goin' to Pine Knob this mornin'."

Hal frowned. "I knew you were coming along, Pa," he said, "but you didn't tell me you figured on taking most of the crew with us."

"Baldridge's bunch of gun-throwers are all liable to be in town," Embry said. "I ain't takin' any chances. They might be plannin' to bushwhack the four of you when you show up for that sham of an inquest!"

Frank said, "That doesn't seem very likely to me, Mr. Embry. Baldridge acts like he wants to keep the peace in town."

"No man who hires a bunch of cold-blooded killers wants to keep the peace," Embry snapped. "Sooner or later things'll bust wide open."

Frank suspected he was right about that, and it was hard to predict when the explosion might occur. But it seemed to him that

184

taking most of the Boxed E hands to town and confronting Baldridge's men was sort of like lighting the fuse.

Hal obviously felt the same way, because he said, "This is a bad idea, Pa. It'll make it seem like you're looking for trouble. I agree with Frank. Brady Morgan won't try anything in front of the marshal, the coroner, and everybody else in town who shows up for the inquest."

He might as well have been talking to a stone wall. Embry turned to look at the men he had assembled and said, "Didn't you hear me? Get your horses, damn it! We're goin' to town."

Hal looked at Frank and Salty and shook his head. There was nothing he could do, he seeming to be saying.

Frank went back to tightening his saddle cinches on Goldy.

They rode out a short time later, leaving a skeleton crew at the ranch. That worried Frank. If Baldridge really did want to attack the Boxed E, this would be the time to do it.

On the other hand, if Embry was right and Brady Morgan and the rest of Baldridge's hired guns showed up for the inquest, at least the odds would be closer to even if trouble broke out.

When the group reached Pine Knob, Frank noticed quite a few horses tied at the hitch racks in front of Corrigan's Casino. Even the Popular Saloon, which usually wasn't, seemed to be doing a brisk business today despite the fact that the hour wasn't noon yet. With that many men in town, Frank thought there was a good chance Embry had been right about Brady and the others coming to attend the inquest.

They crossed the bridge into the eastern part of the settlement. Frank turned to Hal and asked, "Where will they hold this thing?"

"At the town hall," Hal replied. "It's the only place big enough except for the saloons, and Judge Woodville is a teetotaler. He doesn't even like to be around where they serve liquor."

"Woodville's the local magistrate?"

"That's right. Deputy coroner, too. He was appointed to the job so the real coroner wouldn't have to come all the way up here every time there was a killing."

Salty said, "Yeah, in this part of the country a fella would be on the road all the time just tryin' to keep up with the dead men."

"That's the way it used to be," Hal agreed, "but things have settled down quite a bit in recent years, according to Pa. At least, they had until here lately."

Hal looked at the Feed Barn as they rode past. Frank figured he wanted to stop and see how Katie was doing today, but Embry glanced over his shoulder and said sharply, "Don't lag behind, son! We don't want to be late."

Frank didn't think that was likely. Judging by the number of horses tied up at the saloons on the other side of the creek, Brady and his men were still down there. They would be along before the inquest started.

Jubal Embry drew rein in front of a large wooden building with a high front porch. Some of the townspeople were already waiting there, eager to sit in on the proceedings and enjoy a break from their everyday routines, even though the cause of it was the deaths of three men.

The riders from the Boxed E dismounted and spread out to tie their horses at hitch racks in front of the town hall and the adjacent buildings. As Frank was looping Goldy's reins around the rail, Salty nudged him in the side and said quietly, "Baldridge just come outta the hotel, and the lady's with him."

Frank looked up and saw Baldridge and Laura walking arm-in-arm toward the town hall. They seemed mighty companionable, he thought.

And Laura looked as pretty as ever, in a green dress and hat this morning. No matter what was going on around her, she always looked cool and unruffled. She had been that way back in San Antonio, and the years since then hadn't changed her.

"I reckon they're planning on attending the inquest, too," Frank said. "Baldridge has got a right to be there. Those three men worked for him. He was in town when it happened, too."

Since Frank, Salty, Hal, and Gage Carlin had the most riding on the outcome of these proceedings, the rest of the group from the Boxed E moved aside for them. With the exception of Jubal Embry, who clenched a fist and pounded on the locked door of the town hall.

"Open up in there!" he shouted. "Let's get this damned thing started!"

"Take it easy, Pa," Hal advised. "There's no point in putting a burr under the judge's saddle before he even calls the inquest to order."

"This is all a waste of time," Embry grumbled. "Any son of a buck who rides for Gaius Baldridge deserves to be shot!"

Baldridge's British-accented voice said, "I

don't believe you'll find that written any-where in the statutes, Jubal."

The crowd had parted again to let Bald-ridge and Laura approach the hall's front door. Embry glared at his longtime rival, but Baldridge just regarded Embry levelly with a cold-eyed stare.

Laura smiled and said, "Good morning, Frank."

Without thinking about what he was do-ing, he reached up and took off his hat. "Hello, Laura. I hope you're not feeling as tired today."

"No, I've been able to rest and I feel much better now," she said.

Baldridge frowned, and so did Embry. It appeared that neither of them particularly liked the idea that Frank and Laura were carrying on a conversation.

A key rattled in the lock, and the door swung inward. But before the crowd could press forward into the hall, Marshal Roy Trask stepped onto the porch. The double-barreled shotgun in his hands made people step back instead. Some of them stepped back in a hurry. The twin muzzles of the weapon had that effect on folks.

"The judge will be calling the inquest to order soon," Trask announced, "but before he does, I've got something to say. The town council got together early this morning and passed a new ordinance. From now on, no guns are allowed inside the town hall."

A few of the townspeople exclaimed in surprise, and some angry, defiant muttering came from the Boxed E cowboys. Embry put a stop to it with a sharp sweep of his hand.

"You don't have the authority to do that," he challenged Trask.

"You weren't paying attention, Jubal. *I'm* not doing it. The town council is. And since the town hall belongs to Pine Knob and those gents run things around here, I reckon they've got every right in the world to say whether or not folks can bring in guns. The answer now is no. They can't."

From the corner of Frank's eye, he spotted movement from the western end of town. Brady Morgan and a number of other men had emerged from the saloons and were swinging up in their saddles. They turned their mounts and trotted toward the town hall.

"What about Brady and his bunch?" Frank asked. "Does the same rule apply to them?"

"Applies to everybody," Trask said. "No exceptions."

"In that case," Frank said to Embry, "I

suggest we abide by it. But I'd leave half your men out here, if I was you."

"That's what I was thinkin'," Embry said with a note of grudging respect. He pointed out half of the men he'd brought with him. "You fellas take your guns off. You're comin' inside with me. The rest of you stay out here."

Trask said, "Put your gunbelts in the back of that wagon over there. I parked it there for just that reason."

Reluctantly, the men who had been picked to be disarmed unbuckled their gunbelts and placed them in the back of the wagon Trask had pointed out. Frank, Salty, Hal, and Carlin did likewise.

"You, too, Jubal, if you're goin' in," Trask said to Embry.

The rancher drew himself up. "I didn't figure the rule applied to me."

"No exceptions," Trask repeated dryly. "Take off that smokepole, or stay out here with the rest of your boys."

"All right, blast it, but I don't like it."

Trask didn't have to explain the new ordinance to Brady Morgan and the other gunmen. Baldridge said, "Excuse me, my dear," to Laura and walked out into the street to intercept Brady. He spoke in low tones as Frank watched. Frank saw the flash of anger in Brady's eyes, but Baldridge was insistent. After a moment, six men dismounted, including Brady, and started removing their guns to place them in the wagon.

The delegations were going to be the same size, Frank thought, then amended that slightly. The Boxed E would actually have superior numbers, once you counted him, Salty, Hal, and Carlin. Embry and Baldridge countered each other.

And Frank still wasn't sure exactly how Laura figured in all of this.

"All right," Trask said at last as he moved back from the door. "Anybody who's not carrying a gun can go on inside, and just as soon as we can, we'll get this inquest started."

CHAPTER 18

The crowd filed into the town hall in an orderly fashion, probably because Marshal Trask was standing beside the door glaring and holding the shotgun. Nobody in his right mind was going to argue with a Greener.

The chairs in the hall were arranged in two sections with an aisle between them. When Baldridge, with Laura on his arm, took a seat on the front row of the section to the left, Brady Morgan and his men followed suit, filling the first two rows of that section. Embry and the men from the Boxed E went to the right.

Six chairs stood by themselves along the right-hand wall at the front of the room. The jury would sit there, Frank knew. A table for the judge, with a chair at the end of it for witnesses, faced the audience. A small man with wispy white hair and a round, unlined face, so he looked like a cross between a baby and an old man, emerged from a room at the hall's rear and came to the table. He wore a black suit and string tie.

From the back of the room, Trask called, "Everybody settle down! All —"

People started to get up. The judge waved them back into their seats.

"This is an inquest, not a trial," he said. "We don't have to be too formal." He picked up a gavel that lay on the desk and rapped it. "Come to order."

The spectators all settled back in their seats. Judge Woodville sat down behind the table and took a pair of spectacles from his vest pocket. He put them on and peered around the room.

"Madam," he said as his gaze landed on Laura and stayed there. "You appear to be the only lady in attendance today. Some of the details in the matter at hand may be quite unpleasant. Are you sure you wouldn't prefer to withdraw, in order to protect your feminine sensibilities?"

Frank grunted and tried not to grin. He had a hunch Laura wouldn't react too well to that suggestion.

"With all due respect, Your Honor," she said, "my sensibilities are quite sturdy, even though they are feminine. So I'll decline your kind offer." Then she gave Woodville a dazzling smile that robbed her previous words of any sting. "Though I do so appreciate your chivalrous consideration."

Woodville glanced down at the papers on the table in front of him, obviously flustered but pleased at the same time.

"As you wish, ma'am." He straightened the papers, picked them up, and looked them over even though he had almost certainly read them before now. Then he cleared his throat and continued, "We are here to render a verdict as to the cause of death of three individuals, and the appropriateness of same. For that a jury of six good men and true is required."

The judge picked up the gavel, used it to point out half a dozen townsmen among the spectators, and called their names.

"Line up here in front of me while I question you as to your suitability for this panel," he told them.

The questioning was quick and simple. None of the men Woodville had selected worked for or had any connection with either Jubal Embry or Gaius Baldridge, or so they claimed. Frank supposed it was possible some or even all of them leaned one way or the other. It was almost impossible not to in a small town like Pine Knob.

One by one, the judge waved the men into the chairs along the wall. When the jury was seated, he went on. "As I said, this is a legal proceeding but not a trial. There will be no opening or closing statements. I will call witnesses and ask questions, and then the jury will render its verdict. As the first witness, I call Hal Embry."

Looking slightly uncomfortable, Hal stood up, set the hat he had been holding in his lap on his chair, and went to the table where Woodville swore him in. When Hal had settled into the witness chair, the judge said, "Tell me in your own words what happened yesterday morning in front of the Feed Barn café, Mr. Embry."

"Well, sir, Your Honor, we brought in a couple of dead men and delivered them to Mr. Omar Finnegan's undertaking parlor —"

"Who were these dead men to whom you refer?"

"I believe their names were Royal and Dobbs."

"Who do you mean when you say 'we'?"

"There was me, Gage Carlin, one of the hands from the Boxed E, and Frank Morgan and Salty Stevens."

Several people in the crowd murmured at the mention of Frank's name. By now

196

everybody in Pine Knob probably knew that the notorious gunfighter known as the Drifter was in their midst, but Frank Morgan was a famous name and brought a response from folks anyway.

"Do Mr. Morgan and Mr. Stevens work for the Boxed E as well?"

Hal tilted his head to the side and said, "That's sort of hard to say, Your Honor. They're staying at the ranch and riding with us, but I can't say that my pa has actually hired them."

"So they're visitors?"

"I reckon you could say that."

"Go ahead," Woodville said, nodding solemnly.

For the next several minutes, Hal ran through the story with the judge stopping him from time to time to ask a question. Frank watched Brady while the testimony was going on, and he could see that his son was seething with anger inside. Other than his skill with a Colt, a gunman's pride was really the only thing he had, and when that was challenged, it was very difficult not to respond with hot lead.

Frank knew the feeling. He had experienced it as a young man. But he had conquered it years ago.

"Do you have anything else to add?"

Woodville asked when Hal was finished with the story.

"No, Your Honor, that's all I remember about what happened."

"Very well. Step down." Woodville looked at the audience. "Gage Carlin, please step forward and be sworn."

When Carlin was seated in the witness chair, the judge asked, "Do you have anything to add to Mr. Embry's testimony, Mr. Carlin?"

"No, sir, Your Honor," the cowboy said. "Hal told you what happened, and that was the straight truth of it."

"All right. Step down, please. Call Frank Morgan to the stand."

Frank rose slowly to his feet. He had been in court before, and even though Judge Woodville had said a couple of times that this wasn't a trial, it sure felt like one.

"Mr. Morgan, do you swear to tell the truth, the whole truth, and nothing but the truth, so help you God?"

"I do," Frank said.

"Please be seated, and tell me, do you have anything to add to Mr. Embry's testimony?"

"I don't, Your Honor. That's the way it happened."

"Very well."

Frank started to get to his feet, grateful that it was over so quickly.

"Wait just a moment, Mr. Morgan. I have another question or two for you."

"Oh," Frank said as he settled back in the witness chair. "Sorry, Judge."

"Is it true that you are also known as the Drifter?"

Frank took a deep breath and nodded. He said, "Some folks call me that. It's not a name I gave myself."

"And you're a gunfighter?"

"Well . . . I think I like drifter better, Your Honor."

"But you have killed a number of men in gun duels?"

"Yes, sir," Frank said heavily. "I have. More than I like to think about."

"Were you hired to come to this valley?"

"No, sir, I was not. I didn't even know there was trouble in this valley until Salty and I got here."

Woodville looked like he was about to ask something else, but then he said, "All right, that's all. Step down."

Frank did so, gladly.

"I'm going to call Marshal Trask to testify now," the judge said.

As Frank sat down by Salty again, the old-timer leaned over and whispered, "He didn't ask me any questions. How come?"

"I guess he figured he has the facts established."

Salty snorted quietly and said, "I think he just don't want nobody as dignified as me sittin' up there next to him. He's afraid I'll steal all his legal thunder."

"That's probably it," Frank agreed with a nod.

When Trask had been sworn in, Woodville said, "In the interests of simplicity and efficiency, Marshal, let me ask you if you questioned any witnesses to the events of yesterday morning."

"I did, Your Honor," the lawman said. "I talked to at least a dozen townspeople, including Katie Storm and her uncle Solomon, who saw the whole thing from inside the café. Miss Storm even has a cut on her hand from flying glass to show for it."

"And did these witnesses tell you anything that differed substantially from the testimony of Mr. Embry, Mr. Carlin, and Mr. Morgan?"

"No, Your Honor, they didn't. Everybody I talked to backed up their story."

"Since this isn't a trial, I'm going to ask you for an opinion, Marshal. Do you believe those men are telling the truth?"

"Yes, sir, I do."

"Thank you, Marshal. That's all." As Trask left the witness chair and walked to the back of the room again, Woodville turned to the jury and said, "You've heard the testimony, gentlemen, so now I'll ask you to confer and render a verdict in the deaths of . . ." He had to look at the papers on the table to remember the names. "Carl Peevey, Jed Wallace, and Lester Chapman."

"Wait just a blasted minute!" Brady Morgan said as he shot to his feet.

Baldridge jerked around in his chair and shook his head at Brady, who ignored him and went on angrily, "What kind of a trial is this? You haven't called anybody to testify except those killers!"

"You're Mr. Morgan, too, aren't you?" Woodville asked.

"That's right."

"Then sit down, Mr. Morgan," the judge said. "This isn't a trial, as I've made perfectly clear."

"But it's not fair! You haven't asked me or any of my boys what happened!"

"Did you witness the events, Mr. Morgan?"

"Well . . . no. I was in the hotel —"

"And I can't very well call Mr. Peevey, Mr. Wallace, or Mr. Chapman to the stand, because they're all dead. My understanding is that the only other member of your group who was on hand is now at Dr. Hutchison's house, too seriously wounded to testify. What would you have me do?"

Brady opened his mouth to say something else, but Baldridge got to his feet and interrupted.

"My apologies, Your Honor," he said. "My employee Mr. Morgan is understandably upset. Three of his good friends were killed, and he believes that they haven't received a fair hearing."

"There's no way to hear them, Mr. Baldridge. They're dead."

"Yes, of course. But you should be aware that this matter is directly related to the legal case concerning the false claim that Jubal Embry filed on the western half of the valley —"

"False claim!" Embry roared as he bounced to his feet as well. "There's nothin' false about that claim! The only thing false around here is that snake in the grass Baldridge, who used to say that he was an honorable man!"

Shouts broke out all around the courtroom as men on both sides started yelling angry words at one another. Woodville pounded wildly with the gavel, making a lot of racket for such a small man, but even so, it took him several minutes to restore order.

"By God, I'll have Marshal Trask clear this courtroom at the point of a shotgun if I have to!" Woodville threatened. He was on his feet now like everybody else in the room. He turned to the jury and asked, "What's your verdict?"

One of the men stepped forward and said, "We've already talked about it, Your Honor! Self-defense!"

"Verdict so rendered!" The gavel slammed down again. "We're adjourned! Take it outside!"

CHAPTER 19

Both sides turned toward the door at the same time, and Frank figured there would be a logjam there. That could lead to trouble in a hurry if Brady and his men found themselves at close quarters with the Boxed E hands.

Marshal Trask was prepared for just such a thing. When he stepped down from the witness chair, he had moved quickly to the door and posted himself there with the shotgun. As the still yelling crowd surged toward the door, Trask lifted the Greener and shouted, "Settle down!"

The powerful, commanding voice and the presence of the shotgun caused a sudden silence over the town hall.

Trask motioned with the twin barrels and ordered, "Boxed E goes out first. Baldridge, keep your men where they are."

Brady Morgan started to object, but Baldridge lifted a hand and stopped him.

"Very well, Marshal. We shall remain patient . . . for now."

The implied threat was clear. Trask flushed angrily and jerked the shotgun toward Embry.

"Move your men out, Jubal," he said.

"Let's go," Embry growled. He clapped his hat on his balding head and took the lead. The rest of the Boxed E men followed him, including Frank and Salty.

Frank stopped when he heard Laura call his name. He looked back at her and she asked, "Can I talk to you for a minute?"

Baldridge didn't look happy about that at all. Maybe because he was feeling contrary, or maybe because he was just curious what she wanted, Frank said, "Sure." He turned to Salty for a second. "Go on outside with Embry's bunch. I'll be there in a minute."

"Be careful, Frank," Salty said.

Frank knew what the old-timer meant. Laura was involved somehow with Gaius Baldridge. Baldridge seemed to think it was romantically. Frank wasn't so sure about that, but he couldn't be certain.

By the time Frank reached Laura's side, holding his Stetson in his left hand out of habit even though he wasn't wearing a gun, all the Boxed E men were outside. Brady and his men began to follow them. Laura turned to Baldridge and said, "I'll just be a moment, Gaius. I'm sure you understand."

"Of course," Baldridge said, although his puzzled and disturbed expression indicated that he didn't understand at all. He left the two of them standing near the judge's table. Judge Woodville had already gone back into the small room at the rear of the hall, which was probably his office.

"What can I do for you, Laura?" Frank asked. "Or should I call you Mrs. Wilcoxon?"

She smiled. "I don't think there's any need for formality between us. Not when we're such old friends. And that's what I wanted to talk to you about."

"Go ahead," he told her when she paused.

"I wanted to make sure that just because you appear to have befriended those people from the Boxed E, that's not going to cause any hard feelings between you and me."

"Why would it do that?"

"Well, I *am* visiting with Gaius, and there's no denying the hostility that exists between the two ranches . . . so even though Gaius is just a friend . . ."

"Is that all he is?" Frank asked. "I got the feeling it's more than that. At least *he* thinks it is."

"I'm not responsible for what Gaius

thinks," Laura said. "I'm acquainted with him because my late husband had some potential business dealings lined up with him, that's all. When Gaius asked me to come here and see his ranch, I thought it would be polite to do so."

"As well as good business?"

"I'm just a poor woman struggling to make sense of everything that's been dumped into my lap, Frank. I can't afford to burn any bridges."

Frank nodded slowly. The idea of Laura Donnelly Wilcoxon being just a poor woman out of her depth in the world of business made him smile to himself. Laura knew exactly what she was doing all the time, or at least she had when he had been with her in San Antonio.

"I don't hold any grudges against you because you're friends with Baldridge," he said.

"I hope you don't hold any grudges against me at all," Laura said as she rested a hand lightly on his arm. "I'm sorry about what happened with Brady, Frank. I . . . I see now that I was wrong not to find you and tell you about him. I denied you the chance to know your son, and perhaps more importantly, I denied your son the chance to know his father."

"You did what you thought was best," Frank told her. "I can't fault you for that."

He might fault her for not doing a better job raising Brady, he mused, but he wasn't cruel enough to say so.

Her touch on his arm became firmer as she pressed her fingers against him.

"Fate has a way of helping things work out, don't you think?" she asked. "Even though sometimes it takes a long time, maybe even years. But now we've come together again, Frank. You and I can mend all those old fences, and more importantly, you and Brady finally have a chance to get to know each other."

Frank shook his head and said, "That's not very likely. Not with Brady working for Baldridge and Salty and me throwing in with the Boxed E."

Laura leaned closer to him, still gripping his arm. "But, Frank, you said yourself that you didn't know any of these people until you rode into the valley a few days ago. There's no reason you have to take Embry's side in this. For all you know, he's in the wrong, and his claim on the western half of the valley is fraudulent."

"He seems like an honest man to me," Frank said.

"Perhaps he is. Perhaps he's well intentioned. That doesn't mean he's not wrong anyway. And I can tell you without a doubt that Gaius Baldridge is an honest, honorable man, a true pioneer in this part of the country."

The pioneer part was true, no doubt about that, Frank thought. And maybe Baldridge had been honest and honorable back in those days. Everything Frank had seen and heard so far seemed to indicate that he had been.

But that didn't change the facts now. Frank couldn't stop a harsh note from creeping into his voice as he said, "Some of those men Baldridge has hired are nothing but professional killers."

Including his and Laura's own son.

Anger flashed in her eyes as she said, "I've heard the same thing said about you many times, Frank. Whether you ever wanted it or not, you have the same sort of reputation that Brady is starting to acquire. Are you saying that you're better than him?"

Frank had had enough of this.

"I'm saying that I'm not going to abandon Embry and the Boxed E and come over to Baldridge's side," he told her. "I figured out pretty quick that's what you were after with this conversation."

Her nostrils flared as she drew in a deep,

sharp breath and took a step back from him.

"Frank, you have this all wrong —"

"I don't think so. You believe that if Baldridge had both me and Brady on his side, there's no way the Boxed E could win. Baldridge would get what he wants, and so would you . . . although I'm not sure yet exactly what that is."

Her voice was cold and angry as she said, "I wanted you to get to know your son, and I thought maybe you and I could recapture something we lost a long time ago. Something we never should have let get away from us. That's all."

"Well, if that's true, I'm sorry," Frank said. "But I'm sticking with Embry."

"I'm sorry, too," Laura said, although her expression said she was much more angry than she was regretful. "I think you're making a big mistake —"

A sudden commotion from outside made her stop. Both of them looked toward the door of the town hall, which still stood open. Shouts and curses filled the air. Frank started for the door.

He expected to hear shots ring out at any second, but by the time he reached the porch there hadn't been any gunfire.

There was plenty of trouble, though. A big knot of men slugging and punching at each other filled the street in front of the town hall. It was a full-fledged brawl between the ranch hands from the Boxed E and Baldridge's crew of gunmen.

"Oh!" Laura gasped as she stepped onto the porch behind Frank. She moved up beside him and clutched his arm. "They're going to kill each other if somebody doesn't stop them!"

"Not likely as long as nobody goes for a gun," Frank said. He glanced along the street. Marshal Trask was nowhere in sight, and neither was the wagon where all the guns had been placed. Frank spotted the vehicle parked in front of the marshal's office. Moving that armament away from the town hall while the inquest was going on was probably a good idea . . . but some of the men from both sides who hadn't gone into the hall still had their guns. All it would take was a single shot from somebody to turn this ruckus deadly.

Baldridge stood at the edge of the porch, shouting, "Stop it! Stop it, I say!"

But no one paid any attention to him. This was more than a fight. It was fast becoming a riot.

Jubal Embry was right in the middle of it, despite his age. His hat had been knocked off and one eye was swelling and darkening, but he continued trading punches with one of the B Star riders. A few feet away from him, Hal Embry and Gage Carlin were locked up in their own battles with a couple of Baldridge's men. The two sides seemed to be evenly matched as they whaled the tar out of each other.

Frank looked for both Salty and Brady, and he found them at the same time. That was because Brady was behind the old-timer with an arm locked around Salty's neck under the jutting white whiskers. A hate-filled grimace twisted Brady's face as he bore down hard on Salty's throat. The old man's face was turning purple.

Brady was going to choke the life out of Salty if somebody didn't stop him.

Frank didn't hesitate. He didn't think about the fact that Brady was his son. All he knew was that Brady was about to kill his friend, and Frank didn't intend to let that happen.

Frank pulled his arm free from Laura's grip, and with a bound, he was off the porch and plunging into the melee. His powerful shoulders brushed men aside as he plowed through the struggling crowd toward Salty and Brady.

Brady didn't seem to see Frank coming. He was concentrating on choking Salty, and a gleeful expression appeared on his face as the old-timer's struggles grew feeble. Another minute or two and Salty would be dead, and Brady was eager for that to happen.

When Frank reached them, he roared, "Brady!" The young man finally looked up . . .

Just in time for Frank's fist to smash into his face with the force of an explosion. Frank had put all his considerable strength behind the haymaker.

Brady let go of Salty and flew backwards. He collided with a couple of struggling men and bounced off them to fall to the ground. In the middle of the battle like this, he was in danger of being trampled, so Frank stepped forward, leaned down, and grabbed his shirt front. Frank hauled the stunned young man to his feet. Blood welled from Brady's nose, which had been flattened by the impact of Frank's fist.

Frank slung Brady clear of the battle. Brady fell, rolled over a couple of times, and came to a stop against the town hall porch. Frank didn't pay any attention to him after that. Instead he moved quickly to the side of Salty, who had collapsed, and dropped to a knee next to the old-timer.

Sliding an arm around Salty's shoulders,

Frank lifted him to a sitting position. Salty was gagging and coughing as he tried to drag enough air back into his lungs, and his face was still red, but at least he was alive. Frank figured he would be all right once he caught his breath.

"I . . . I'm . . . much obliged . . . Frank," Salty managed to say between hacking coughs and rasping breaths. "I couldn't get loose . . . from the varmint."

"You just take it easy, Salty," Frank told him. "You'll be fine."

"Yeah, I reckon . . . I will be . . . thanks to you."

Frank looked over toward the town hall. He saw that Laura had come down from the porch and was kneeling next to her son, heedless of the dust she was getting on her expensive dress. She had Brady's bloody head resting in her lap. He appeared to still be in a stupor.

He came out of it, though, with a sudden start. He lurched up into a sitting position. His mouth worked furiously. Frank figured Brady was cursing, although he couldn't hear the words over the uproar around him.

There was no doubt about what happened next. Ignoring his mother's clutching hands, Brady levered himself to his feet. As two men who were punching at each other reeled close to him, he reached out and plucked out the gun that rode in one man's holster. Lifting the weapon, he thumbed back the hammer and pointed the gun right at Frank.

CHAPTER 20

With blood from his broken nose covering the lower half of his face, Brady strode toward Frank. Men saw the blood and the gun and got out of his way.

"Look out, Frank!" Salty exclaimed as he saw Brady coming.

Since Salty had recovered a little from almost being choked to death, Frank stood up and moved in front of the old-timer. He regarded Brady with a hard, level stare as the young killer stalked toward him. The fight came to an end around them as men hurried to get out of the way of any flying bullets.

"You bastard!" Brady yelled in a blood-thickened voice as he came to a stop in front of Frank and threatened him with the gun. "You broke my nose!"

"And you almost killed my friend," Frank said. "I reckon you got what was coming to you."

"I ought to blow your brains out!"

Frank wondered how Laura was taking this confrontation, but he didn't take his eyes off Brady to look toward her, not even a glance. The gun Brady held was a single-action Colt, and with the hammer pulled back like that, all it would take to fire it was a little pressure on the trigger. Frank didn't know how much; the gun's owner could have filed it down to hair-trigger sensitivity.

"I'm unarmed, Brady," he said. "You shoot me in cold blood in front of a hundred witnesses and you'll hang. Baldridge won't be able to help you, and neither will your mother."

From off to one side, Jubal Embry said loudly, "If he shoots you, he won't live to hang, Morgan! My men will gun him down like the dog he is!"

Frank's jaw tightened. Embry just couldn't seem to help himself when it came to making a bad situation worse. If the Boxed E hands who were armed started shooting at Brady, then the B Star hired guns would return the fire. In the blink of an eye, this confrontation in the street would become a bloodbath.

"Put the gun down, Brady," Frank said quietly. "This isn't the time or place for you and me to settle things."

Brady's lips drew back from his teeth in a snarl. "It's as good as any. You've been hanging around too long, old man. This is my time now!"

Frank had been easing closer, a fraction of an inch at a time. He could see the craziness, the urge to kill, lurking in Brady's eyes, and he knew he couldn't afford to wait any longer.

With the same sort of speed that made him feared and respected from the Rio Grande to the Canadian border, from the Mississippi to the Pacific Ocean, he sprang forward and lashed out with his left arm. His forearm came up under Brady's wrist, which caused the gun to jerk toward the sky as it blasted.

At the same time, Frank brought his right fist flashing up and hit Brady again, this time on the jaw. Brady's head jerked to the side and he flew off his feet. Frank went after him. He reached down and plucked the revolver from Brady's hand, then stepped back quickly with the gun ready in his own grip in case any of Brady's men opened fire on him.

No shots rang out. The crowd watched in stunned silence. The only sound was a low whimper from Brady as he lay in the dusty street with blood still dripping from his nose.

Then Laura cried shrilly, "Let me through! Let me through!"

Men got out of her way. She reached Brady and dropped to her knees at his side. For the second time in a matter of minutes, she lifted his head into her lap.

This time, though, she lifted her head, fixed cold, angry eyes on Frank, and said, "I hope you're happy. Beating your own son to within an inch of his life. You should be proud of yourself, Frank."

Frank opened the Colt's cylinder, shook out the cartridges that remained in it, then dropped the empty gun in the dust next to the bullets.

"What was I supposed to do, stand there and let him choke my friend to death? Tell him to go ahead and shoot me, that it was all right?"

"Go to hell," she whispered through clenched teeth.

Marshal Trask broke into the tense scene by striding up and shouting, "Break it up! Break it up! The next man who throws a punch will spend a month in jail! Clear the street! Clear the street!"

"You're about ten minutes too late, Marshal," Salty told him. "Where were you when all this ruckus broke out?"

"Where I was is none of your business, old man," Trask snapped. He was still carrying the shotgun. He brandished it and went on. "Clear the street, I said! I'll arrest anybody I see out here ten minutes from now!"

"Boxed E, with me!" Jubal Embry ordered. He stomped off toward the Feed Barn. Hal and Gage Carlin and the other men followed him.

Baldridge stepped up to Laura and Brady and said, "Let me help you with him, my dear."

He bent to take hold of one of Brady's arms. Laura got on her son's other side, and between them, they lifted Brady to his feet. He was still only semiconscious, but he was able to shake his head and mutter incoherently. Finally, he said, "Lemme go . . . lemme go!" and tried to pull away from them.

Baldridge used his free hand to motion curtly to some of the other hired guns from the B Star.

"Take him to the doctor's office," he ordered. "That nose will need medical attention. Then put him on his horse, and all of you go back out to the ranch. Stay there until I tell you otherwise."

Two men stepped forward, slung Brady's arms over their shoulders, and half-carried him down the street toward Dr. Hutchison's place. The rest followed, with plenty of snake-eyed stares directed toward the Boxed E crew along the way.

Baldridge put a hand on Laura's shoulder and said, "I think I should have the horse hitched to the buggy so we can go on out to the ranch as well."

She glared at Frank as she nodded and said, "I believe you're right, Gaius. There's nothing here in town for me."

Baldridge put his arm around her and led her away. As they walked off, Salty stepped up beside Frank, still rubbing his abused throat, and said hoarsely, "If you had any hopes of patchin' things up with that gal, Frank, I reckon they're pretty much done for now."

"That was never my plan," Frank said. "I hoped we could be friends, but that's all."

"Hard to believe any son of yours could turn out to be so low-down mean and rotten."

"Yeah, it is," Frank agreed. Conrad Browning had been arrogant and abrasive when Frank first met him, but he had been able to see a spark of decency in the boy, a spark that had since been fanned by life's tragedies into a flame that had tempered Conrad and transformed him into a fine young man.

There was no such spark in Brady Morgan, and Frank didn't know whose fault that was. He supposed it didn't really matter.

"Let's go on over to the Feed Barn with the others," he suggested.

Salty nodded and said, "Yeah, some coffee might help this poor ol' throat of mine."

Still alert for an attack, they walked over to the café and went inside. The place was crowded with the extra customers from the Boxed E, and Katie Storm was busy behind the counter pouring coffee and placing plates full of food in front of the men on the stools.

One of those men was Hal Embry. He looked like he wanted to talk to Katie, but the way she was bustling around, he had no chance to do so.

Solomon Storm was doing more than cooking right now. He went back and forth from the kitchen in his stained white apron, carrying plates of food that he delivered in surly fashion to the tables. None of the men seemed to mind Solomon's less-than-friendly demeanor. They were used to it, and they were hungry as well, so they dug into the food.

"Dang, the place is full up," Salty complained.

"Morgan!" Jubal Embry called from one of the tables. "Come on over here!"

"There's two empty chairs at Embry's table," Frank pointed out to Salty. "Let's go."

They joined Embry, Gage Carlin, Bill Kitson, and another of the Boxed E hands Frank didn't know. As Frank and Salty sat down, Embry went on. "I reckon maybe I was wrong about you and this old pelican, Morgan."

"Old pelican, is it?" Salty challenged.

Frank and Embry both ignored that remark. Frank asked the cattleman, "What do you mean about being wrong?"

"I mean I had you pegged as a hired killer at best, or a spy for Baldridge at worst," Embry said. "I ain't sure about the hired killer part, but if you're really workin' for Baldridge, you're playin' the deepest game I ever did see. The way you busted Brady Morgan's nose, it looked like the two of you just plumb don't get along. And it damned sure looked like he wanted to kill you. Came pretty doggoned close, I'd say. If that was an act, it was a mighty good one."

"It wasn't an act," Frank said, and he couldn't stop a note of regret from sneaking into his voice. "He came close to pulling the trigger as soon as he pointed that gun at me."

"If he had, there would have been a hell of a lot more blood spilled out there in the street."

Frank nodded and said, "That's why I'm glad he didn't. As for me being a hired gun or a regulator, whatever you want to call it . . . I'm not, Embry. I've told you that before."

"So I can't pay you to get rid of Brady and the others?"

"No." Frank's answer was flat and hard, with no room for compromise. But then he said, "I'll ride for you, though, and back your play against Baldridge. I just won't take money to do it."

Embry frowned in confusion. "Why risk your life to help us, then?" he asked.

"Because I think you're in the right."

Embry stared at him for several seconds, then slowly nodded.

"I remember when a lot more people felt that way about things," he said. "It's a shame more of 'em don't these days."

Solomon came up to the table with plates of fried chicken, potatoes, and greens.

"Here," he said as he set them in front of the men.

"We didn't even tell you what we wanted

yet," Embry said.

"You'll eat what I give you and like it," Solomon snarled. He turned and stalked off.

Embry grinned and said, "I like that old fella. He's the only man I know who's more cantankerous than I am." He grew more serious as he continued, "I'm glad to have your help, Morgan. Can't be easy for you, bein' on the opposite side from your boy like that. Those two punches you landed on him were real honeys, though."

Frank picked up a piece of fried chicken. "From what I've seen of Brady Morgan, I'm not sure I'd want to claim him. I know that's a harsh thing to say, but he came mighty close to killing Salty."

"That's the truth," the old-timer rasped. "I reckon it's gonna take a few glasses of tonsil varnish later on 'fore my throat stops hurtin'."

"Once we're finished with dinner, we'll head down to one of the saloons. I'm buyin'," Embry declared.

They all ate in relative silence for the next few minutes. Then Marshal Trask came into the Feed Barn, and absolute quiet fell over the room as the lawman stood just inside the front door with the shotgun tucked under his arm.

"Baldridge and his men are all gone," Trask announced. "I watched them ride out of town with my own eyes. When you're done here, you can come down to my office and reclaim your guns. Once you've done that, I expect you to clear out as well."

"We got a right to be here," Embry insisted.

Trask sighed and said, "Give me a break, Jubal. After this morning, the town could use a little peace and quiet and a chance to catch its breath. We've known each other a long time, and I'm asking you as a favor to go back to the Boxed E."

Embry scowled, but finally he nodded reluctantly.

"All right." He turned to Salty. "Stevens, I'll buy you those drinks some other time."

"I'll hold you to that," Salty croaked.

Chapter 21

Hal finally got a chance to lean over the counter and talk briefly with Katie, Frank noted as he finished his meal. He couldn't tell what was being said between them, of course, but the conversation, though brief, seemed like a pleasant one.

When everyone from the Boxed E had finished eating, they left the Feed Barn and walked up the street to the marshal's office. Trask was sitting in a ladderback chair on the porch with the shotgun across his knees. He nodded toward the wagon and said, "All right, you can get your guns and then head back to the ranch."

Frank's eyes narrowed slightly as he looked at the marshal. Trask's face seemed grayer than it had been before the inquest. Frank supposed that the strain of being caught in the middle of the looming range war between the Boxed E and the B Star might be getting to the lawman. Sometimes it was harder *not* to take a side in a dispute like this.

When Salty had strapped on his gunbelt, he slapped the heavy pistol on his hip and said, "Sure does feel good to have this old hogleg draggin' me down again on this side. I been carryin' iron for so long I walk slanch-wise without it."

Frank buckled his gunbelt and nodded. "I know just how you feel."

The men got their horses from the town hall, mounted up, and rode out. As they passed Omar Finnegan's undertaking parlor, Frank thought about how much more work Finnegan had almost had. If a shootout between the Boxed E and the B Star had erupted on Pine Knob's Main Street, it would have been horrific.

The bad thing was, Frank had a nagging worry in the back of his brain that the gundown had only been postponed, not prevented.

The white plaster across Brady's broken nose stood out in sharp contrast to his tanned skin. Black circles had appeared around both eyes, giving him a raccoon-like appearance and making his eyes seem to be set even deeper than they really were. He didn't look good at all, Laura thought.

The doctor had set Brady's nose as best he could, but Frank's punch had done considerable damage. Also, it was just lucky that Frank's second blow hadn't broken Brady's jaw, the doctor said. Hutchison had warned Brady and Laura that the nose would probably never look the same as it had before the injury.

However, Brady's appearance was the least of Laura's worries right now. Brady's vanity might be wounded along with his nose, but it was much more important that Frank Morgan was lined up solidly on the side of their enemies. That threatened all of their plans.

The buggy rattled along the trail to the B Star with Baldridge skillfully handling the reins. Brady rode alongside the vehicle, swaying a little in the saddle. The doctor had given him a little morphine to dull the pain of the broken nose and suggested that it might be a good idea for Brady to stay at the hotel at least until the next day.

But Brady had insisted that he was capable of riding, and since his mother and Baldridge were heading back to the ranch, he was coming along, too. Laura had never been able to argue successfully with Brady or persuade him to do anything he didn't want to do. She always gave in. He was her son, after all, and she wanted him to be happy.

Now the only thing that would really make him happy, she mused, was for him to kill Frank Morgan.

And that might not be a bad idea at all.

The other hired gunmen were strung out behind the buggy, with the ranch wagon that was loaded with Laura's bags bringing up the rear. The two cowboys riding on the wagon had to eat some dust that way, but being actual cowboys instead of gunslingers, they were used to the misery.

"I hope the ride isn't too uncomfortable for you," Baldridge said to Laura. "This is a fine buggy, but still, this trail is rather rough in places."

"It's nothing to worry about, Gaius," she told him. "After riding in that terrible stagecoach all the way from Great Falls, this isn't bad at all."

"Traveling here will be much easier and better when the railroad comes through," Baldridge said. "I plan to have my own station near the ranch headquarters, so only a short ride will be required to reach my home. You'll be able to visit with much more ease and comfort." He paused and glanced over at her. "Unless, of course, you've already become a permanent resident of the

B Star by then. We've talked about —"

"I know what we've talked about. It's still too soon to consider such things seriously," she told him in a gently chiding tone.

"Of course. Of course, my dear. My apologies."

"Besides, this has been a very upsetting day. Brady has been injured, and it could have been even worse."

"That's true. Anything the young man needs, I'll take care of it immediately, of course." Baldridge raised his voice over the rattle and squeak of the buggy wheels. "Did you hear that, Brady? If there's anything you need, you just let me know."

"Bring me Frank Morgan and let me shoot the son of a bitch," Brady rasped. "I think I'd blow his knees off before I killed him. That way he'd have to come crawling to me to beg for his life."

Laura loved her son, but there were times when Brady let his emotions get the best of him and just didn't think straight. If he believed that Frank Morgan would ever beg for anything, even his own life, Brady was sadly mistaken.

Laura didn't bother to point that fact out to him. Instead she said to Baldridge, "I'm as eager for the railroad to arrive in the valley as you are, Gaius. I just worry that once

231

it gets here, the line won't be able to go any farther. I don't think Jubal Embry will be very cooperative about letting it cross his land."

"It's not *his* land," Baldridge said. "You know what the lawyers told us. I will prevail in court, and I very much want the railroad to cross the entire valley."

Laura sighed. "That's all well and good, but you know how long court cases can take. And lawyers tend to say what they think their clients want to hear. Besides, even if you win, Embry will probably appeal the decision, and that will stretch things out even longer. We run a real risk of having the railroad's financial backers get impatient and decide they can't wait. Men with that sort of money like to keep it working for them all the time."

"I thought you were providing most of the funds for the line," Baldridge said.

"I am, but I can't do it alone. I need help from those other backers, or I can't proceed. I would truly hate to see this entire deal collapse, Gaius."

Visibly agitated, he slapped the reins against the buggy horse's back and made the animal trot faster.

"It won't collapse," he said. "It can't collapse. But I don't see what I can do to make things go any faster. The legal system has to work at its own pace."

"When you first came out here, Gaius, did you depend on the courts to solve all your problems for you?"

"The courts?" Baldridge repeated. He let out a disdainful laugh. "When I settled in this valley, there was no courtroom within two hundred miles! The only way to solve a problem was for a man to pick up a pistol or a rifle and deal with it himself. No one relied on lawyers in those days."

"It was certainly simpler back then, wasn't it?"

"Simpler and much more effective. When I was a young man, if something stood in my way, I just —"

He stopped short and stared over at her instead of watching the trail. After a moment, he asked, "What are you saying, Laura?"

"I'm saying that you're in the right, and even though your body may not be young anymore, Gaius, I know the same fire still burns inside you that burned back then. Anyone who stands in your way is taking his chances, and he deserves whatever happens to him."

"My God," Baldridge breathed. "You think I should kill Jubal Embry."

"I think you should deal with the problem that's facing you in the same way you would have forty years ago. Some things never change. A man has the obligation to take what's rightfully his."

Baldridge swallowed hard and looked at the trail again.

"Yes, yes, I know you're right," he said. "But the world *has* changed —"

"No. People would like to believe that. They'd like to think that civilization will protect the weak from the strong. But in the end, the strong will always win. Like you, Gaius. You're strong, and you deserve this valley, and you deserve to become a very rich man when the railroad runs from one end to the other of it and on to the mountains beyond."

Laura was looking at him intently as she spoke, and his eyes kept flicking over toward her. She tried to catch his gaze and hold it, and when she finally did, she added softly, "That's not all you deserve, Gaius. You deserve something else, too, and you can have it . . . if you're man enough to seize it."

"I . . . I don't know . . ."

"Are you, Gaius? Are you man enough?"

His hands tightened on the reins and slapped them against the horse's back again.

His back stiffened, and he said, "I'm the same man I always was."

Laura leaned back against the seat and smiled. "That's what I thought."

"I'll have to figure out something to do, some way to get what we want."

"Talk to Brady when we get back to the ranch. He's good at this sort of thing. We have a little time to plan. We can let him recover some from what happened today, and by waiting we'll make Embry think that everything has blown over. Then when we make our move, it'll be that much more effective because it will come as a surprise."

"Yes," Baldridge muttered. "When we make our move . . ."

She slid closer to him and linked her arm with his, pressing against him so that she was sure he felt the soft warmth of her breast against his side.

"You won't regret working with me, Gaius," she said softly. "You have my word on that."

"No, of course not." A smile slowly formed on his face. "Some people are just destined to rule. Some men are born to be kings . . . and to have beautiful queens at their side."

She rested her head on his shoulder as the buggy rocked along, and the fierce glow of satisfaction filled her eyes.

CHAPTER 22

Frank wasn't too surprised when the next few days passed quietly on the Boxed E. Brady was probably laid up, recuperating from that busted nose, and Frank didn't figure Baldridge would make a move until Brady had recovered enough to take charge of the attempt.

He and Salty and Gage Carlin held an unofficial council of war in a corner of the bunkhouse the evening they returned to the ranch after the inquest. Even though Hal Embry was the foreman, Carlin had been riding for the Boxed E longer than any of the other hands. He knew the ranch, and he knew the men who worked here. That was why Frank sought his advice.

"We need to make sure that nobody's ever riding the range alone," Frank said. "Any time somebody goes out to do some work, it'd be a good idea if he took two or three other men with him. And at least one of those men needs to be standing guard the whole time, not tending to chores."

"That sounds good to me," Carlin agreed with a nod. "What about posting guards here at the ranch? If we put a man with a rifle up in the hayloft, he could see for a long way all around."

"I don't think Baldridge will order an out-and-out attack on the ranch headquarters," Frank said, "but we can't completely eliminate the possibility. So that's a good idea, too, Gage. Better to be too cautious than careless."

Salty said, "You've seen those gun-wolves, Frank. They're killers, pure and simple. I wouldn't put nothin' past 'em."

"They jumped me and Hal and Ike and Bill the other day," Carlin pointed out. "And they were on Boxed E range when they did it."

Frank rasped a thumbnail along his jawline as he frowned in thought. "I'm wondering if Brady did that on his own, without orders from Baldridge. He strikes me as the impatient sort. He could've gotten tired of waiting for Baldridge to tell him to make a move. He knew his mother was on her way to Pine Knob. Maybe he wanted things settled before she got here."

"Tryin' to impress his ma, you mean?"

Salty asked. "He reckoned she'd be proud of him if he killed a bunch of folks?"

"She wouldn't look at it that way," Frank said heavily. "She'd just be glad he got rid of some obstacles that stood in the way of her getting what she wanted."

Carlin let out a low whistle. "No offense, Frank . . . I mean, I know you were involved with the lady before . . . but it'd take a hell of a cold-blooded woman to look at the situation like that."

Frank nodded slowly and said, "No offense taken, Gage. I know just what you mean. But after seeing some of the things I did in town today, I'm starting to think you're exactly right about what it would take."

Nothing else was said about Laura. They figured out a schedule for guards to be posted there at the ranch headquarters, and Carlin tapped one of the men to go ahead and climb into the hayloft, taking a Winchester with him.

"If you see anything that looks threatening, you start makin' some noise," Carlin told the cowboy. "You'll need to wake the ranch up in a hurry."

The man nodded in understanding and left the bunkhouse carrying a rifle.

Nothing happened that night, though, and

the same held true for several days. Frank and Salty rode out with groups of punchers who needed to move cattle from one pasture to another and check on other chores around the ranch. They didn't do any work other than watching for trouble that failed to materialize.

One evening after supper, Jubal Embry said to Frank, "You and Stevens wait a minute before you go back out to the bunkhouse. I want to talk to you."

Frank didn't know what this was about, but he could tell that Embry was worried. So he nodded and said, "Sure. Come on, Salty."

They followed Embry to a large room in the rear of the house that served as the rancher's library and office. Frank was a little surprised to see Faye already waiting there.

After the trouble with Royal and Dobbs at the waterfall, Faye had been rather subdued for a few days, even after she resumed taking her meals with everyone else. Today, though, she seemed fully herself again, her eyes sparking with intelligence and stubbornness.

"I'm going to town," she announced as Frank and Salty followed Embry into the room.

Frank's eyebrows rose. "Tonight?" he asked.

"Of course not," Faye replied. "Tomorrow."

Embry said, "I've been tryin' to tell her it ain't a good idea. We can protect her a lot better if she stays right here on the ranch, close to the house."

"I haven't set foot *out* of the house in almost a week," Faye said. "I'm going crazy cooped up like this, and there are things I need from the store. I know Mother needs some supplies, too, so I'm going to take the wagon to Pine Knob tomorrow."

Her tone of voice made it clear that the decision had been made and nothing was going to change her mind. Frank glanced at Embry, thinking about the old saying involving apples not falling far from their trees.

"Your father's right, Miss Embry," he said. "You'll be a lot safer here at the ranch. I reckon if you give Gage Carlin a list of what you and your mother need from the store, he'd be glad to go in and get it. Salty and I could even go with him to make sure there was no trouble."

"But that wouldn't get *me* out of the house," Faye objected. "And if you and Mr. Stevens could protect Gage, why can't you come along and protect me?"

That was a fair question, Frank thought, but he said, "Carlin can fight back if somebody was to jump us."

Faye's chin jutted out defiantly. "And I can't?" she demanded. "I can handle both a pistol and a rifle. My father and Hal taught me. Actually, I think I'm a better shot with a rifle than Hal is."

Frank glanced at Embry, who shrugged with the same sort of helplessness he usually displayed in an argument with his daughter.

"That's true," the rancher said. "She's a good shot with a long gun."

"Shooting at targets and shooting at men are different," Frank said, and he didn't bother to keep the hard note out of his voice. "It's a bad idea, Miss Embry."

"I'm going, and you can't stop me!"

"No, I reckon I can't." Frank looked at Embry again. "I'm not your pa."

Embry sighed and said, "Frank, you told me you'd throw in with me and back my play. I want you to go with Faye to Pine Knob tomorrow, you and Stevens and whoever else you think ought to go along."

"It'll be perfectly safe," Faye insisted. "I'll have a famous gunfighter with me, after all."

Frank's eyes narrowed. He thought Embry should have put Faye across his knee and paddled her the first time she started acting like such a spoiled brat . . . but that wasn't his decision to make and it was much too late for that, anyway. He could hardly hold himself up as an example of being a good parent, either, since he hadn't participated in the raising of any of his two, maybe three, children.

"If that's what you want, Mr. Embry, we'll do it," he said. "We'll take along another of the hands. Not Carlin, though. He ought to stay here to keep an eye on things around the ranch."

"Fine. Take Bill Kitson."

Frank saw Faye's mouth tighten a little at the mention of Kitson's name. He recalled what Carlin had told him about the brief romance between Faye and Kitson that hadn't gone anywhere. Faye might not like the idea of traveling in close company with a former suitor, but now that she had gotten her way about going to Pine Knob, it didn't appear that she was going to object.

"That's all right with me," she said.

"It's settled, then," Embry said. "You'll tell Kitson?"

Frank nodded. "I'll tell him. Come on, Salty."

As they left the house, the old-timer said, "That little gal is sure used to gettin' her way. I'd say she's got Embry wrapped around her little finger more'n once."

"You're right about that. There's Kitson."

The cowboy was standing near the front door of the bunkhouse smoking a quirly. He was a lean, fair-haired young man in his midtwenties, a little older than Faye. As Frank and Salty came up to him, he nodded to them.

"We've got a job for you, Bill," Frank said.

"I generally get my orders from Mr. Embry or Hal," Kitson said. He didn't sound obnoxious about it. He was just stating a fact.

"This one comes from Mr. Embry, and you can check with him about it if you want. Miss Embry is taking the wagon to town tomorrow, and Salty and I are riding along with her. You're coming along, too."

In the light coming through the open bunkhouse door, Kitson looked surprised. "Faye . . . I mean, Miss Embry . . . went along with that?"

"She did," Frank said.

Kitson flicked away the butt of his quirly and shrugged. "Well, then, I reckon if she doesn't mind, I don't, either."

The cowboy turned and went into the bunkhouse. Frank and Salty lingered outside.

"Were we ever as young as him and Miss Faye, you reckon?" Salty asked.

"I'm not sure," Frank said. "I don't think I can remember back that far."

Sometime during the night, Frank's eyes snapped open. Over the long, dangerous years, like a lot of other frontiersmen, he had developed the ability to go instantly from being asleep to being fully awake. Out of habit, his hand moved toward the butt of the Colt where it hung in its holster close to his head.

The bunkhouse was dark and quiet, except for the snores coming from several of the bunks. Frank sat up and looked around. No one was moving.

He reached down. Dog had been sleeping on the floor next to his bunk, and when he touched the big cur he realized that Dog's head was lifted in alertness. Something had happened to disturb the animal's sleep, too.

Frank slipped the Colt from the holster and swung his legs off the bed. In bare feet, wearing only the bottom half of a pair of long underwear, he stepped silently to one of the windows and pushed back the flour-sack curtain that hung over it. From there he could see the ranch house. No lights were burning there, as far as he could tell.

All the windows were open to let in fresh air. Frank breathed in deeply. No smell of smoke. For a moment he had wondered if some of Baldridge's men had snuck up to set the barn on fire, or something like that. Barn-burning was an often used tactic in range wars.

But the night air didn't smell of anything except pine trees, horse flesh, and manure, a common mixture of scents around a Montana ranch like the Boxed E.

Frank frowned and let the curtain fall back. It seemed that whatever had roused him from sleep, it was gone now. Maybe a wolf had howled somewhere up in the mountains, or an owl had hooted as it swooped over the ranch looking for prey.

Frank didn't know, but an uneasy feeling continued to nag at him as he went back to his bunk, holstered the revolver, and stretched out on the mattress. He reached down to scratch Dog's head and whispered, "Go back to sleep."

He tried to take his own advice, but it was quite a while before he dozed off again.

CHAPTER 23

Frank had a look around the bunkhouse when he got up in the morning, but as far as he could tell, nothing was missing or out of place. If it hadn't been for the fact that Dog's slumber was disturbed, too, he might have thought that he had dreamed the whole thing, although he wasn't given to such flights of fancy.

At breakfast, Faye said that she would be ready to go in another half-hour or so. When they had finished eating, Frank, Salty, and Bill Kitson went out to the corral to get their horses ready to ride.

Hal Embry followed them with a worried frown on his face. "If Faye had said anything to me about this loco idea, I would have tried to talk her out of it," he said.

"Going to town to buy supplies isn't that loco," Frank pointed out. "It's just the circumstances that make it a risky thing to do."

"We could get by without the supplies," Hal said. "It's just that my sister gets bored easily. She always has."

Bill Kitson let out a little snort as he tightened the cinches of his saddle, then looked around and said, "Sorry, Hal. I shouldn't have done that."

"Don't worry about it," Hal said, although it was obvious he was a little irritated by Kitson's reaction. He turned to Salty, who hadn't saddled his pinto yet, and went on. "Do you mind handling the wagon team? Have you ever driven one before?"

"Have I ever driven a wagon before?" Salty repeated. He answered the question with a snort that was a lot louder than the one Kitson had given a minute earlier. "Son, I've handled every kind of wagon from a buckboard to a prairie schooner! I've rassled stagecoaches thousands of miles over every sort of terrain you can think of! I've fought Injuns and road agents and mudslides and snowstorms and tornadoes! There ain't any kind of a four-wheeled vehicle I can't handle!"

Hal smiled and said, "I'll take your word for it. But you never drove one with my sister sitting beside you telling you everything you're doing wrong."

Salty scratched at his beard and shrugged.

247

"I like a good challenge."

"You'll get one," Hal promised.

Frank had his saddle on Goldy, and Dog was waiting with him when Faye emerged from the house. She wore a long-sleeved white shirt, a brown, divided riding skirt, brown boots, and a flat-crowned brown hat with its strap tight under her chin. Frank thought she was as pretty as she could be.

Judging by the expression on his face, so did Bill Kitson. But the young cowboy turned his head and looked away as he sat on his horse waiting to leave for Pine Knob.

Hal said, "Are you bound and determined to do this, Faye?"

"Of course I am," she answered without hesitation. "It's going to be fine. Nothing will happen to me as long as I have Mr. Morgan with me."

"Give me a minute and I'll saddle up and come with you —" Hal began.

"That's not necessary. Father needs you and the men to start moving the stock down from the higher pastures. You know that."

"It can wait," Hal said stubbornly. "Anyway, Gage and the boys don't need me to handle a chore like that."

"You know what Father wants done better than anyone else," Faye insisted. "Just go on and do your work. Stop worrying about me."

"That's easier said than done."

But Hal stepped back with his hands in his hip pockets as Faye climbed to the wagon seat next to Salty.

"You're going to handle the reins?" she asked him.

"Yes'm, if that's all right with you. Your brother asked me to."

"I suppose that's fine. I could do it, but I don't really care."

Frank swung up into the saddle.

"Is your dog coming with us?" Faye asked.

"I thought I'd take him along." Frank added, "He doesn't like being cooped up, either."

"Well, if he gets tired, he can ride in the back of the wagon."

Frank didn't point out that Dog could lope along all day without getting tired. He just said, "Thanks, miss."

Mary Embry stepped onto the porch to wave good-bye as they rode away. Frank thought the woman looked worried, and with good cause. Faye had a wild streak in her to go along with her stubbornness, and that was a combination that would put plenty of gray hair on a parent's head.

And there he went again, thinking about

what it was like to be a parent even though he had very little actual experience in that area, he told himself with a wry, inward smile.

Frank rode to the right of the wagon, Kitson to the left. Dog bounded ahead. The trail to Pine Knob passed through several thick stands of trees and along stretches cut through low, rocky ridges. Frank was especially watchful while they were traveling along those places because they were good spots for an ambush.

Nothing happened, however, and by late morning the small group was approaching the settlement. Frank thought that maybe Faye had been right about there not being any danger.

But he wasn't convinced of it yet.

The wagon rolled into town, flanked by the two riders and the big cur. The saloons on the western side of Pine Knob weren't busy at all. A few horses were tied in front of Corrigan's, and the hitch racks in front of the Popular Saloon were empty. Evidently the crew from the B Star wasn't in town today.

After the wagon rattled across the bridge, Salty angled the vehicle toward the Pine Knob Emporium, and at Faye's direction, he pulled up in front of the store's high

250

porch that also served as a loading dock.

"You men can do whatever you want," Faye told them as she stood up and stepped from the wagon seat to the porch. "Mr. Crandell's clerks can load the supplies. When I'm finished with the shopping, I plan to have dinner at the Feed Barn. You can join me if you'd like, or I'll meet you back here in a couple of hours."

"Thanks, miss," Salty said. "Drivin' is thirsty work, so I might take on a little lubrication while we're here."

"Don't get drunk," Faye warned. "I'll leave you here if you're soused."

Salty's eyes widened with wounded dignity. "I never said nothin' about gettin' drunk," he insisted. "I can handle my liquor. Anyway, I don't plan on downin' more'n two or three mugs of beer. That ain't enough to get a horsefly drunk."

"Just remember what I told you," Faye said. She turned and went into the store.

"If that don't beat all," Salty muttered. He tied the reins around the brake lever, then climbed down from the wagon, grunting a little because of muscles that had grown stiff during the ride to town. Frank knew the feeling all too well. He seldom climbed out of bed these days without a few grunts and groans.

Bill Kitson swung down from his horse easily, though, and said in a voice low enough not to be overheard in the store, "She tends to be a mite bossy. Sometimes more than a mite. But I guess when you're the boss's daughter, you get used to people hoppin' when you say jump."

Frank figured Kitson's attitude was one reason things hadn't gone any further than they had between him and Faye. But that was none of his business, Frank reminded himself.

"Somebody needs to keep an eye on her anyway," he said. "I'll do that. Dog, stay with the wagon. Salty, you go on and get those beers you wanted. Bill, you can go with Salty or stay here with me."

Salty licked his lips and said, "Dadgum it, now I got me a dee-limma. Miss Faye said she was gonna have dinner at the Feed Barn, and you know how much I like the grub at that place, Frank. But I sure am thirsty, too."

"Why not go get a drink, then come back to the Feed Barn for dinner?" Kitson suggested with a grin. "I'll come with you."

Salty looked amazed. He slapped Kitson on the shoulder and said, "By golly, if that ain't a brilliant idea! I like this young fella,

Frank. He's got a head on his shoulders, by gum!"

Frank chuckled. "You two go ahead, then," he said. "Miss Faye and I will be over at the Feed Barn later."

Salty and Kitson set off toward the western side of town, with the old-timer asking which of the saloons down there was better. Frank turned and went into the Emporium after telling Dog to sit on the porch.

He hooked his thumbs in his belt and ambled along the aisles between shelves of merchandise. A general store in a cowtown like Pine Knob had to carry a little bit of everything, and Crandell's place was no exception. From castor oil to lilac water, from ten-penny nails to delicate bows, from Colt revolvers to bottles of ink, the Emporium had it all, along with barrels full of crackers, pickles, sugar, flour, and salt. Farm implements, saddles, and hats hung from hooks on the walls. There was even a small butcher shop tucked into a rear corner of the store.

A couple of local women were browsing in one of the aisles. They gave Frank sidelong glances of disapproval, as if this was their domain and a grizzled old gunfighter had no place in it. They were probably right about that, he reflected.

But he wasn't the only one who didn't meet with their approval. They cast the same sort of veiled looks at Faye, who stood at the rear counter talking to a short, bald-headed man in an apron. Frank figured he was probably Crandell, the proprietor. For a moment, Frank was puzzled about why the ladies from Pine Knob would be glaring at Faye like that; then he remembered how gossip spread in small towns. More than likely, the women had heard about how Faye liked to bathe naked in that waterfall and had been caught at it by Royal and Dobbs, and small-mindedly blamed her for letting the men see her unclothed.

The women were watching Faye and muttering something between themselves when Frank came up behind them, moving quietly for such a big man. He cleared his throat, which made them jump a little. As they looked back at him, he touched the brim of his hat, nodded, and said, "Ladies."

They didn't return the greeting. Instead they went around him and hurried out of the store, fluttering and clucking like a couple of old hens. Frank tried not to grin.

Then Faye glared at him, too, and said, "I'm perfectly fine in here, Mr. Morgan. Why don't you go back outside? I'll call you if I need you."

Frank looked around. The Emporium had a back door, but with the front doors open, he figured he could wait right outside and get back inside in a hurry if there was any trouble.

"All right, Miss Embry," he said.

When he stepped onto the porch, he looked both ways along the street as he rubbed Dog's ears. Marshal Roy Trask was coming toward him along the boardwalk in front of several other businesses. Trask stopped to cough and took a handkerchief from his pocket to wipe his lips. He put it away and continued on to the Emporium, climbing the three steps to the high porch.

"Morgan," the lawman said by way of greeting. "What are you doing in town?"

Frank nodded toward the wagon parked in front of the store. "Miss Embry needed some things for her and her mother. Salty and one of the hands and I came into town with her."

"Bodyguards, eh?"

"Just keeping an eye on her."

"Probably not a bad idea," Trask said. "Even though I haven't seen your son or anybody else from the B Star in the town for the past few days."

"What about Baldridge and Mrs. Wilcoxon?"

Trask shook his head. "Nope. I reckon they're sticking pretty close to the ranch. I suppose it's too much to hope for that both sides in the feud have decided to wait and let the courts sort it out."

"It's possible," Frank said.

"But you wouldn't count on it."

Frank thought about it and shook his head. "No. I wouldn't count on it."

"Well, keep it out of my town." Trask started to cough again but managed to suppress the impulse. He gave Frank a curt nod and moved on.

Faye came out of the store a few minutes later carrying a small bag. Frank started to take it from her, but she shook her head and placed it in the back of the wagon herself.

"Mr. Crandell and his clerk will load everything else in a little while," she said. "We can go on over to the Feed Barn."

"Salty and Bill said they'd meet us there later."

"What Bill Kitson does is no concern of mine," Faye said crisply. She went down the steps and started toward the café.

Frank called for Dog to come with them, then caught up to her easily. Dog trailed along behind, then found some shade to curl up under after Frank told him to stay.

A few townspeople sat at the counter when they came in, but Salty and Kitson weren't there yet. Frank assumed that Faye would want to sit at one of the tables, but she went straight to the counter and took one of the stools. She and Katie Storm greeted each other coolly. Frank knew that Katie thought Hal ought to stand up more often to his sister. Maybe Faye knew that, too.

Frank sat down on the stool beside her and thumbed back his hat. "Hello, Miss Storm," he told Katie.

"Mr. Morgan, how are you?"

"Fine, thanks. Ready for some of those fine vittles that your uncle dishes up."

Katie smiled and said, "I'll tell him to fix a couple of plates for you and Miss Embry."

She went through the swinging door into the kitchen. Frank turned his head to say something to Faye, but before he could open his mouth, he heard a crash and a scream from the kitchen.

Without even thinking, Frank was on his feet and heading for the door. He rammed it open with his shoulder and drew his Colt at the same time. As he charged into the kitchen, his keen eyes instantly saw Katie struggling in the grip of a man who looked vaguely familiar, while nearby on the floor lay Solomon Storm, his head covered with blood.

Frank's gun came up, and he was about to shout at the man to let go of Katie when the whole world came crashing down on the back of his skull. Blackness exploded all around him. He felt his knees hit the floor as he pitched forward, but he was out cold by the time the rest of him crashed down on the boards.

CHAPTER 24

Frank welcomed the pain in his head because it told him he was still alive. He had been knocked unconscious before, so he knew the stabbing agony would soon subside to a dull ache. He could live with that.

As he began to stir, a familiar voice exclaimed, "He's comin' around! Dadgum it, Frank, you had me scared for a minute there that you was dead!"

Frank pried his eyes open and saw the worried, whiskery face of Salty Stevens looming over him. He glanced the other way and saw Bill Kitson.

But he didn't see Faye, and concern for her safety prompted him to haul himself upright, into a sitting position. He was groggy, but Salty's arm around his shoulders steadied him.

"Where's Miss Embry?" he asked. Now that he was sitting up, he could see that he was in the kitchen of the Feed Barn. He hoped Faye was out front.

Salty dashed that hope by saying, "She was gone when we got here, Frank. So was Katie. And poor Solomon there's been walloped bad on the head."

Frank looked over and saw Solomon still lying senseless on the floor near the stove. Frank could see now what he hadn't caught in that brief glimpse. There was a cut on the old man's head above his ear where someone had hit him.

Maybe the injury was bloody but not too serious. Head wounds had a tendency to bleed a lot even when they were minor. But whoever had clouted Solomon could have busted his skull, too.

"Who was it, Mr. Morgan?" Kitson asked tensely. "Did you get a look at them?"

"One of them," Frank replied. "The other one was behind the door and hit me with what felt like an anvil."

"More'n likely the butt of a gun," Salty said. "Or a chunk of stove wood."

"Doesn't matter what it was," Frank said. "He knocked me out and then the two of them must have grabbed Faye and Katie. The one I saw was familiar, and now I remember where I saw him before. He was with Brady Morgan and the rest of the B Star bunch the day of the inquest."

"Jehosophat!" Salty exclaimed. "What in blazes does Baldridge think he's gonna accomplish by kidnappin' Miss Faye?"

"I don't know," Frank said grimly, "but I sure as hell intend to find out. Help me up."

Salty and Kitson each gave Frank a hand and helped him to his feet. Kitson picked up Frank's hat and handed it to him. Frank looked at how the Stetson's crown was dented and knew the hat might have saved his life by blunting some of the treacherous blow's force. Otherwise it might have crushed his skull.

As the three men came out of the kitchen, Marshal Trask hurried into the café through the front door. He said, "I heard there was a heap of trouble down here. What's going on?"

"Somebody attacked Solomon Storm and abducted his niece and Faye Embry," Frank said.

"Abducted?" Trask repeated. "You mean kidnapped?"

"That's exactly what I mean," Frank said. "There were at least two of them. They must've snuck into the kitchen through the alley door and knocked out Solomon. Then when Katie came in, she let out a scream and I charged in after her. One of the varmints walloped me, and that's the last I

261

knew until I woke up a couple of minutes ago."

"You couldn't have been out long," Trask said. "It's only been a few minutes since one of the customers who was in here ran into my office and told me there was trouble. I got here as fast as I could. The man said he heard Katie scream, then you ran in there, and then Miss Embry went through the kitchen door after you. That's all he knew because he lit a shuck out of here and went to fetch me."

Frank grimaced. Faye should have run for the marshal herself, rather than charging blindly into trouble.

But that was exactly what he had done, he reminded himself. And he had paid the price for it, too.

He just hoped that price didn't include the lives of two young women.

Trask went on. "Did anybody see who did this?"

"Baldridge's men," Frank said. "At least the one I saw rides for the B Star, so I reckon the others do, too."

Trask's eyes widened. "That's a mighty serious accusation, Morgan," he said. "No matter how Gaius Baldridge feels about the Boxed E, I can't imagine him ordering the kidnapping of two young women."

262

"They probably weren't after Katie," Frank said. "Maybe they just grabbed her to use as an extra hostage if they needed her. But I know for sure the man I saw struggling with her was one of Baldridge's gun-wolves."

"What are you gonna do about it, Marshal?" Salty demanded. "You can't let Baldridge get away with this. He sent his men into your town to kidnap Embry's daughter!"

Trask's face was as gray as mud, and he looked like he was so weary he just wanted to sit down somewhere. But he said, "He's not going to get away with this. I'll ride out to the B Star and get to the bottom of it."

"You won't go by yourself," Frank said. "I'm coming along, too."

"And me," Salty added.

"Me, too," Kitson said.

"All right, but I'm in charge, damn it," Trask snapped. "No going off half-cocked, understand?" He turned to the gaggle of townspeople who had crowded around the café's open front door. "Somebody go fetch Doc Hutchison! Solomon Storm needs help."

"He's already on his way, Marshal," one of the townsmen said.

Trask pointed to one of the other men and

said, "Bert, you've got a good horse. Ride out to the Boxed E as fast as you can and let Jubal Embry know what's happened." The lawman sighed. "That's probably not a good idea. This whole valley's about to blow up, and telling Embry that Baldridge kidnapped his daughter will just make it happen faster. But Jubal's got to know about it, in case we don't come back from the B Star."

The crowd around the door parted, and the doctor hurried in carrying his black bag. "Where's Solomon?" he asked.

Trask pointed to the kitchen door. "In there. I don't know how bad he's hurt."

"Somebody hit him on the head," Frank said. "I couldn't tell how bad it was, either."

The sawbones hustled past them and through the swinging door. Trask said, "The doc's got this under control. I'll go saddle my horse, and we'll head for Baldridge's place."

"Bill, go give the marshal a hand," Frank told the young cowboy. Kitson nodded and hurried out of the café behind Trask.

In the momentarily quiet room, Salty said, "You know this is about to turn into an all-out shootin' war, don't you, Frank? When Embry hears what's happened, he won't stop until he's wiped out Baldridge's bunch . . . or got wiped out himself."

Frank nodded and said, "I know."

"Miz Wilcoxon is still out on the B Star."

"I know that, too. She'll be all right."

Laura would always find a way to survive, he thought, no matter what happened.

Laura was at the window of her room on the second floor of the B Star ranch house when she saw Brady riding fast toward the house. Early this morning, he had ridden out with three men to put their plan into action.

That plan had been conceived hastily after their visitor had been here the night before, but Laura had gone over it in her mind numerous times, and as far as she could tell, it was solid and ought to work.

Now Brady was returning, and Laura hoped he brought news of the plan's success. If he did, they were one step closer to getting what they wanted.

Laura left the room and hurried down the broad staircase to the first floor. The B Star ranch house was a huge affair made of rocks, timbers, and thick beams. Inside, its sumptuous furnishings had been brought from far-off cities like Denver, St. Louis, and San Francisco. Gaius Baldridge was a man who liked his comforts.

She found Baldridge waiting on the wide gallery that ran all around the house. He stood tensely, his hands gripping the rail at the edge of the porch. When he heard her soft footsteps, he looked over his shoulder at her and said, "Brady is coming back."

"I know," Laura said. "I saw him from upstairs."

Her room was next to Baldridge's. She knew that he had expected them to be sharing a room by now, but she had fended him off successfully so far. She might not be able to for much longer, but she would do whatever was necessary.

Brady reined his lathered horse to a stop in front of the house and swung down from the saddle. He still had the plaster over his broken nose, but the black eyes had faded and he didn't look as grotesque as he had a few days earlier when they came back from Pine Knob.

He wore a savage grin as he came up the steps to the gallery, and when Laura saw that her heart leaped. She knew he wouldn't be grinning if things hadn't gone well.

"Is it done?" Baldridge asked. His voice was tight from the strain he was feeling.

Brady nodded and said, "Cotter, Felton, and Kern have the Embry girl at the line shack. They brought Katie Storm along, too."

Baldridge's bushy white eyebrows shot up in alarm. "Katie Storm!" he repeated. "They weren't supposed to take her, just Faye Embry."

"The Storm girl caught them right after they knocked out the old man," Brady explained. "She put up a fight, and Kern had to knock her out before they grabbed Faye. They figured they might as well bring her along, too. Actually, that works out pretty good for us. Hal Embry is sweet on Katie. He'll be even crazier when he finds out that both his sister and his sweetheart have been carried off."

"Well . . . I suppose that's all right. Anyway, it's too late to do anything about it now, isn't it?"

"Damn right it's too late," Brady said. "There's no turning back. By nightfall, Jubal Embry and his son and all the men who ride for them will be dead."

"What about Frank?" Laura asked.

Brady grimaced and said, "That's the only place where Cotter and the others fell down on the job. Cotter knocked him out in the kitchen of the Feed Barn. He might have busted the old man's skull, but he's not sure because Katie and Faye got spooked and he hustled out of there without checking to make sure Frank was dead."

"But he might be?" Laura pressed.

"Yeah, sure. That was the idea, wasn't it?"

Laura felt a sudden, unexpected twinge. She had no reason to mourn Frank Morgan's death, she told herself. Whatever had been between them was a long time ago and hadn't meant that much to start with. She had never allowed herself to care too much about any man, with the exception of her son.

But still she felt that brief moment of sadness. It wasn't too difficult to ignore, though.

Baldridge was pale and shaken after hearing Brady's report. He had known what the plan was, but even so, hearing about what had happened clearly bothered him.

"The young women aren't to be harmed," he said. "Your men are aware of that, Brady?"

"Sure," Brady answered easily. "I'll see to it myself, boss."

Baldridge sighed and nodded. "I wish it hadn't been necessary to take these steps."

"But it is," Laura said. "Soon we'll have everything we want, Gaius. Everything."

Because Brady hadn't been lying when he said that he would see to Faye Embry, and now to Katie Storm as well, Laura supposed. Once Jubal Embry and his son were dead, the girl had to die as well. That would leave Embry's widow alone, and she wouldn't be able to stand in their way. She would clear out, leaving the valley to Baldridge.

That was the only way, Laura told herself, because Baldridge was never going to win that legal case. Her lawyers had made that clear to her. There was nothing wrong with Embry's claim to the Boxed E. It would stand up in any court in the land.

But with the Embrys gone, no one could stop Baldridge from seizing the entire valley, and then he would take a wife to go along with his new riches.

A wife who would soon be an even richer widow, Laura thought as a faint smile curved her lips. She would make that happen.

One way or another.

CHAPTER 25

"I'd feel better about this if there were forty of us, not four," Marshal Roy Trask said as he approached the B Star headquarters with Frank, Salty, and Kitson.

"We could have waited for Embry and the rest of the Boxed E crew," Frank said.

Trask shook his head. "I was in no mood to wait. Were you, Morgan?"

"Not hardly," Frank answered honestly. Faye and Katie were in danger, and he wanted to locate them as quickly as possible.

This was the first time he had been to the B Star. It was a fine-looking spread, with plenty of good grazing land, and it was big enough for Baldridge to run a large herd. What Baldridge had here ought to be enough for any man, Frank thought. He had never understood why some men always had to have more, whether it was land, cattle, money, or women.

But obviously Frank was the one who was out of step by being satisfied with what he had, because greed seemed to be one of the main things that drove the world.

The ranch house was big. Not fancy, at least on the outside, but very impressive. As were the barns, the corrals, the blacksmith shop, the bunkhouse, and all the other outbuildings. The B Star was no greasy-sack outfit. It was as fine a spread as Frank had seen in this part of the country.

No one challenged them as they rode up to the house. Frank knew they had been spotted approaching, though, because as soon as they reined in, Gaius Baldridge and Brady Morgan stepped out and onto the porch. Brady still had the plaster on his broken nose, and the murderous glare he directed toward Frank said that he was still packing a grudge, too.

"Good afternoon, Marshal," Baldridge said. "What brings you out here?"

Trask took a deep breath, sighed, and leaned forward, resting his hands on the saddlehorn. He looked haggard.

"I reckon you know why I'm here, Mr. Baldridge," he said. "We've come for Miss Embry and Miss Storm. Turn them over to us now, unharmed, and maybe there won't be as much trouble over this as there will be

271

otherwise."

Baldridge frowned and shook his head in apparent confusion. "I'm afraid I don't know what you're talking about. I assume you're talking about Faye Embry, but I know of no reason why she would be here. And Miss Storm? You're talking about the young lady who runs the café in town?"

Salty burst out, "You know dang well who —"

Frank lifted a hand to stop him. "One of your men knocked out Katie's uncle in the kitchen of the Feed Barn earlier today and attacked Katie. I saw him with my own eyes."

"You must not see very good anymore, old man," Brady said with a sneer. "Nobody's been off the B Star all day. Isn't that right, Mr. Baldridge?"

Baldridge nodded and said, "That's the truth. All of my men are accounted for."

"You're lying," Frank snapped. "The man I saw has shaggy brown hair, a drooping mustache, and a scar over his left eye. He was with you at the inquest, Brady."

Baldridge and Brady looked at each other in apparent surprise. Brady said, "That's Vince Cotter. You're right. He rode for the B Star . . . but he doesn't anymore. He quit yesterday, along with two other men, Felton and Kern." Brady laughed. "They said it was getting too damned boring around here. They were tired of waiting for some action."

"You're sure about that?" Trask asked. "These men left the ranch?"

"They drew their pay and rode out," Baldridge said. "I have no idea where they are now, or what they might have done since then."

"You expect us to believe a cock-and-bull story like that?" Salty demanded.

Brady eased forward, his hand moving toward the butt of his Colt. "I think that old mossback just called you a liar, boss," he said. "And I know the other old mossback did."

"Take it easy," Trask said. "We're just trying to get to the bottom of this. You're saying these men rode into Pine Knob today and kidnapped those women?"

"I have no idea what they might have done, Marshal," Baldridge said. "But it makes sense. They didn't get the payoff they wanted out of this job. Perhaps they decided to kidnap Miss Embry and hold her for ransom. You say the abduction occurred at the café?"

"That's right."

"Then taking Miss Storm along was probably just a spur-of-the-moment thing."

273

Baldridge stroked his chin as he frowned in thought. He turned to Brady and said, "Do you have any idea where Cotter and the others might have gone?"

"Wait just a damned minute," Brady said. "Do you intend to *help* these varmints?"

"I don't want any harm to come to those two young women," Baldridge snapped. "If we can help these men find them, I think we should."

"I rode with Cotter and Felton and Kern before," Brady objected. "I'm not gonna send some posse breathing down their necks!"

Baldridge glared at him. "If you know where they might have taken those women, tell me! That's an order, Brady."

The atmosphere on the gallery was charged with tension. Brady looked like he was ready to draw on Baldridge. Frank didn't think that was going to happen, but he kept a close eye on the young man anyway. He wasn't going to stand by and allow Brady to gun down the old rancher.

After a few strained seconds, Brady grimaced and shrugged. "Fine, if that's the way you want it. I don't know if that's where they went or not, but I remember Cotter saying something about an old line shack up in the mountains north of here that your crew doesn't use anymore. He said it would make a good hideout if anybody ever needed one. I thought he was just making conversation."

"Maybe he was . . . then," Baldridge said. "But if he and the others are on the run, perhaps he remembered it." Baldridge turned to face Frank and the others again. "I think I know the line shack Brady and the others are talking about. I can tell you how to find it. Better yet, I'll send Brady and some of the men with you to show you."

Frank didn't like that idea. He didn't trust Brady Morgan, not for a second.

"Do you know those mountains, Marshal?" he asked Trask.

The lawman shook his head. "I'm afraid I don't. I didn't grow up in these parts, and since my jurisdiction ends at the town limits, I've never explored the rest of the valley that much."

"You'll need a guide," Baldridge insisted. "I'll go myself if that will make you feel better, Marshal."

Trask hesitated in answering. Finally he said, "Jubal Embry and his men are probably on their way here already. We need to wait for them."

"That's not a good idea," Frank said. "There are four of us. We can handle three kidnappers."

"Blast it, if Embry comes charging in and we're not here to tell him what's going on, he's liable to shoot first and ask questions later!" Trask said. "We're trying to prevent a war, not start one, Morgan."

"That's a good point, Marshal," Baldridge said. "If Jubal were to attack the B Star, my men would fight back, I assure you. If we wait and are able to talk some sense into him, then a combined force will be so overwhelming that Cotter and the others will have no choice but to surrender and release the young women without harming them."

Salty growled, "If they ain't been harmed already, you mean."

"I'm sure they're all right. As long as those men believe they can collect a ransom for Miss Embry, they won't hurt her."

Frank supposed that made sense, but the whole business still gnawed at him and made him uneasy. Brady and the other gunmen hadn't greeted them with hot lead, though, so maybe there was a chance he and Baldridge were telling the truth.

"It's settled, then," Trask said. "We'll wait here for Jubal, then head for that line shack and see if those varmints are there."

"Why don't you come inside and get out

of the sun?" Baldridge suggested. "No one has ever said that Gaius Baldridge is inhospitable, and I don't intend for them to start."

Trask looked over at Frank, who shrugged and said, "Might as well."

The delay grated on his nerves, but Trask was right about what Jubal Embry might do. Faye and Katie were probably all right, so it made sense to wait and defuse the situation as much as possible.

The four riders dismounted, tied their horses to a hitching post in front of the gallery, and went up the steps into the shade.

"Please come inside," Baldridge invited. "I'll have something cool to drink brought to you."

Salty and Kitson looked uneasy as they stepped into Baldridge's house, Frank noted. It was sort of like venturing into the lion's den, he thought. Although he didn't really think they were walking into a trap, he made sure that his hand didn't stray far from the butt of his gun.

As they entered the living room, Laura came toward them, looking cool and beautiful in a cream-colored dress. Her face wore a concerned frown.

"I heard what you were talking about out there on the gallery," she said. "Is it true,

Gaius? Some of your men kidnapped Faye Embry?"

"Men who worked for me until recently," Baldridge corrected her. "I had nothing to do with this, my dear. I can't be held responsible for what someone does after he leaves my employ."

"No, I suppose not," she said. "I just hate to see all this violence going on in such a beautiful place as this valley."

"It will be over soon," he promised. "You have my word on that."

Trask grunted and said, "I hope you're right about that, Mr. Baldridge. This trouble has gone on long enough, and if you and Jubal Embry weren't so blasted hardheaded, it could have been settled by now."

"You speak bluntly, Marshal, but you speak the truth."

As Baldridge spoke, a Mexican woman entered the room carrying a tray with several glasses of what appeared to be lemonade on it. The servant handed them out. The liquid was cool and crisp and tasted good as Frank downed a long swallow. He had never been much of an alcohol drinker. A good cup of coffee or something like this lemonade was much more suited to his tastes.

"To the successful recovery of those

unfortunate young women, and to the end of the hostilities in this valley as well," Baldridge said he lifted his glass. "Perhaps if we can help bring Miss Embry home safely, her father will see that we don't really need to be enemies after all."

"I'll drink to that," Trask muttered.

Frank would have, too . . . if he thought Baldridge really meant it. But something was still nagging at him, a sense that this just wasn't right. Every instinct in his body warned him that danger hung over him and his companions, and it would as long as they were on the B Star.

Baldridge's offer to help, though, was the only real lead they had to the whereabouts of Faye and Katie, so they had no choice but to trust the man . . . for now. Frank lifted his glass along with the others . . .

But he couldn't help but notice that Brady didn't.

CHAPTER 26

Frank found himself sitting in a comfortable armchair while they waited for the rest of the Boxed E crew to arrive. Laura came over and took the chair beside him. Baldridge and Trask were on the other side of the room, talking quietly together near the massive stone fireplace, while Salty and Bill Kitson were checking out the collection of animal heads mounted on another wall.

From the looks of it, Baldridge must have been quite a hunter in his earlier days. The wall was adorned with heads from grizzly bears, antelopes, bighorn sheep, and mountain lions — an impressive display of death.

"Are you all right, Frank?" Laura asked. "I heard the marshal say that you were attacked as well when Miss Embry was kidnapped."

"I'm fine," he told her. "I was knocked out, but just for a few minutes. My head's too hard to get a permanent dent from a gun butt."

She smiled and said, "I remember just how hardheaded you can be when you want to. I know you didn't mean it exactly like that, but it still applies."

Frank returned the smile. "I suppose it does." He glanced around the room. "Where did Brady go?"

"I think he's upstairs." Laura sighed and shook her head. "I hate to admit it, but he's not very comfortable around you, Frank. I should have done things differently while he was growing up, I know that. I still wish things were better between the two of you, but I suppose there's no hope for that."

"Not much," Frank said.

In fact, there was no hope. Brady Morgan was a brutal, cold-blooded killer, and Frank didn't think that would ever change. Brady would stay just as bad as he was until someone ended his life with a bullet or a hangrope.

He didn't say that to Laura, though. There was no point in hurting her even more.

After a moment she went on. "I hope you can see now that Gaius isn't the terrible man everyone makes him out to be. He's really worried about Faye Embry, even though her father is trying to steal Gaius's range from him. When this is over, I'm sure that if you asked him, he could find a place for you here —"

"That's not going to happen," Frank broke in, not letting her finish. "I'm playing out the hand the way it was dealt, and when it's over, Salty and I will be moving on. We never intended to stay in this valley."

"Where are you going?"

"Mexico," Frank said with a slight smile as he thought about the old-timer's determination to reach that land of warm sun, warm señoritas, and spicy hot food. "We're taking our time about it, but we'll get there."

"I hope you do, Frank," she said softly. "I hope you do."

It wasn't long after that that a rumble of approaching hoofbeats was heard through the open door. Frank stood up and joined the other men who started for the gallery.

"Stay inside, my dear," Baldridge told Laura. "Just in case Jubal won't listen to reason."

"He'll listen," Trask said. "He's not going to open fire on a lawman."

Frank wasn't so sure about that. Jubal Embry could be mighty hotheaded at times. But as he moved out onto the porch with the others, he hoped that his presence, along with that of Salty and Kitson, would cause Embry and his men to hold their fire.

A cloud of dust rolled up behind the galloping riders. From the looks of the packed mass of horsemen, Embry had brought every member of the Boxed E crew he could find. There were close to two dozen men charging toward the B Star ranch house.

Marshal Trask went down to the bottom step and held up a hand in a signal for the riders to stop. They were close enough now that Frank could make out the grim faces of Embry and Hal in the lead. They hauled back on their reins and brought their mounts to skidding halts.

"Get outta the way, Trask!" Embry roared. "We're gonna turn that house into a damned sieve!"

"Hold your fire!" Trask bellowed back in a surprisingly strong voice that matched Embry's tone. "Settle down, Jubal!"

"Settle down! By God, how can you tell me to settle down? Those no-good skunks have stolen my daughter!"

Hal said, "Frank, what are you and Salty and Bill doing up there with them? Are they holding you hostage?"

"You see this gun on my hip?" Frank asked. "Nobody's holding me hostage, Hal. You and your father had better listen to what Trask has to say."

"Mr. Morgan is right, Jubal," Baldridge said.

Embry pointed a blunt finger at Baldridge and said, "You shut up, you damned range hog! There wouldn't be any trouble in this valley if it wasn't for you!"

"Just listen to me for a minute," Trask pleaded. "Tell your men to take their hands off their guns and listen."

It was true that the Boxed E punchers were ready for a fight. Some of them held rifles, and others rested hands on gun butts. If they started shooting, the men on the gallery would be cut down in a matter of seconds.

After a moment fraught with impending violence, Embry lifted a pudgy hand and ordered, "Relax, boys. Hold your fire . . . for now. But Trask, if you've got somethin' to say, you'd better talk fast!"

"All right," the marshal said. "We know who took your daughter and Katie Storm."

"So do we!" Embry thundered. "Baldridge's men!"

"No," Baldridge said. "Men who worked for me, but they don't now. They quit and rode off yesterday, Jubal. They weren't acting on my orders when they kidnapped poor Faye. I give you my word on that."

Trask added, "As best we can figure, they

kidnapped Miss Embry thinking they would hold her for ransom. And we have a pretty good idea where they're holed up, too."

Embry frowned darkly and shook his head. "That's loco!" he said. "I don't believe it!"

"It's true," Baldridge insisted. "Think about it, Jubal. These men . . . well, I have to admit, even though I hired them to help protect my ranch, some of them proved to be less than trustworthy. To put it bluntly, they're little more than outlaws."

Embry snorted. "Now you realize that!"

Baldridge pressed on, saying, "Those three men drew their time and rode on yesterday. I'm not responsible for what they might have done today —"

"You're responsible for 'em bein' here in the valley in the first place!"

With a visible effort, Baldridge kept a tight rein on his temper. "That's true," he admitted, "and that's why I'm going to help you get Faye back safely, along with Miss Storm. I and some of my men will ride with you and take you to the line shack where we think those men are hiding with their prisoners."

"And we're supposed to trust you?" Hal asked. "Why in blazes should we?"

"Because I think I know where your sister

is, Hal, and I'm willing to take you to her. I wouldn't do that if I were behind her kidnapping, would I?"

Embry and Hal glanced at each other. They didn't have an answer for Baldridge's question.

Neither did Frank, but he still thought there was more going on here than was apparent. Unfortunately, the only way to find out what it was might be to go along with Baldridge's plan.

"We're wasting time here," Trask snapped. "Baldridge, how long will it take to get to that line shack you're talking about?"

"It's been several years since I've been there, but I think we can make it in a couple of hours," Baldridge replied. He looked at the sky. "We should get there before dark, but you're right, Marshal, we don't have any time to waste." He swung around to look at Embry. "What's it going to be, Jubal? Do we go and rescue your daughter, or do we kill each other and leave her in the hands of those desperadoes?"

Embry snatched off his hat and pawed at his mostly bald head in obvious frustration. Then he clapped the hat back on and said, "All right, blast it! I still don't trust you a lick, Baldridge, but I'll go along with you . . . for now! But if this is a trick, you'll be mighty sorry."

Baldridge nodded and said, "I'll fetch Brady, and he can get his men. We'll be ready to ride in ten minutes."

"Better not be any longer than that, or we'll know you're up to something," Embry warned.

That didn't make a lot of sense, Frank thought, but Embry was so used to being angry and hostile where Baldridge was concerned that he had to spout something.

After Baldridge had gone inside, Laura said quietly from the doorway, "Frank."

He turned toward her. She stepped out onto the porch. Salty and Kitson had gone down into the ranch yard to untie their horses, and Trask was talking to Jubal and Hal Embry. That meant Frank and Laura were alone on the porch for the moment.

"I just wanted to tell you to be careful," she said. "I don't know what will happen up there where you're going, but I'm sure it'll be dangerous."

"Life is dangerous," Frank said. "Even when you do everything you're supposed to, sometimes things don't work out."

She smiled. "You're talking about the two of us, aren't you?"

"The two of us . . . Brady . . . everything we've gone through over the past twenty odd years, I suppose."

She reached out and touched his hand. "If you had known then what you know now, would you have done anything differently?" she asked.

"That question has been plaguing everybody since the dawn of time, I reckon." Frank shook his head. "And I don't have an answer for it any more than most folks do."

"I know what my answer would be," Laura said with a smile.

Before she could elaborate, Brady stalked out to the porch and glared at the two of them.

"Let's go," he said curtly to Frank. "We've got things to do."

"I reckon that's true," Frank said. He put his hat on and nodded to Laura. "I'll see you when we get back."

"I'll be watching for you," she promised.

CHAPTER 27

Brady Morgan and six other men from the B Star joined the group of Boxed E riders headed for the mountains on the trail of the kidnappers. The other members of Baldridge's crew were out tending to their ranch duties, too far from headquarters to summon, Brady explained.

Baldridge and Embry both urged their horses to the front of the group. They were flanked by Brady and Hal, and just behind came Frank, Trask, and Salty. Bill Kitson had fallen back with the other Boxed E hands.

"My men used to use this line shack we're looking for when I had herds grazing in the highest pastures during the summer," Baldridge explained. "I stopped doing that several years ago because it was simply too much trouble to fetch the animals down every fall, and too many of them got lost up there in that rugged country. I have plenty of range just as good lower down." He shot a glance over at Embry. "Of course, when I was able to graze my stock anywhere I wanted, even west of Loco Creek, it was much easier."

"There's still room enough for both of us," Embry said. "The valley's plenty big."

"Don't try to pretend to be the voice of reason, Jubal. It doesn't suit you."

Embry was about to make an angry retort when Hal spoke up instead, saying, "How about this, Baldridge? Your herd is bigger than ours. What say we lease you some range during the winter when you need it more?"

Embry and Baldridge both looked at him in surprise. Embry said, "What . . . what are you doin', son? I don't want to do business with this polecat!"

"Why not?" Hal asked stubbornly. "The two of you used to get along all right. I've been thinking about it, and I don't see any reason why you can't work together again."

"But we're suing each other!" Baldridge protested.

"You wouldn't have to, if you'd just come to an agreement," Hal insisted. "Mr. Baldridge, you could admit that my pa's claim to the western half of the valley is legal, and Pa, you could admit that we've got a little more range than we really need. Seems like it would work out better all around if you'd just cooperate."

Brady said, "He means if you'd just slink away with your tail between your legs like a whipped dog, Gaius. Is that what you want to do?"

Baldridge had been looking confused and seemed to be considering Hal's suggestion, but at Brady's sharp question, his expression firmed up and he shook his head.

"No, of course not. I won't let any man run roughshod over me."

Hal began, "That's not what I was saying —"

"Forget it, boy," his father growled. "Thinkin' ain't never been your strong suit. You'd best leave that to me."

Actually, Frank thought, what Hal had proposed made a lot of sense. If Embry and Baldridge had been willing to go along with the idea, it would have solved a lot of the problems in the valley. Sure, the hard feelings between the two spreads would have taken some time to fade away, but eventually they would have.

Brady had jabbed a sharp stick into Baldridge's pride before Baldridge could even give it any serious consideration, though. Brady didn't want peace in the valley. That would mean he was out of a job. The only way he would make a profit was if Baldridge and Embry stayed at each other's throats . . .

A frown creased Frank's forehead as several bothersome thoughts stirred in his brain. He asked himself who else might have something to gain if the Boxed E and the B Star were at war with each other.

The answer was obvious, and while he didn't like it a bit, it didn't particularly surprise him, either.

A couple of other questions were nagging at him, and he had a feeling that if he could answer those as well, the whole picture would be visible to him.

"Blast it!" he exclaimed as he hauled back on Goldy's reins. "My horse has gone lame for some reason."

Salty frowned and said, "Are you sure, Frank? I didn't see nothin' —"

"Yeah, I felt him pull up just now," Frank went on quickly. He started to dismount. "I'd better check him over. Maybe he just picked up a stone in one of his shoes."

The whole group had come to a stop now.

"We don't have time for this, old man," Brady complained.

Frank swung down from the saddle and waved them on toward the mountains. "The rest of you go on. Salty, why don't you and Bill stay here with me and give me a hand? We'll catch up to the rest of you in a little while."

"I don't like splittin' up like this," Embry said.

"There are only three of those kidnappers," Frank pointed out. "You've got about thirty men. If ten-to-one odds don't make them surrender, having the three of us along isn't going to make any difference."

Brady sneered and said, "It sounds to me like the great Frank Morgan is tryin' to duck out of a fight. Maybe that reputation of his was just a mess of hot air all along!"

"Sonny, you don't know what you're talkin' about!" Salty said. "Why, I've seen this man take on a whole passel of varmints single-handed!"

"Let it go, Salty," Frank said. "I don't care what Brady thinks."

"You will one of these days," Brady said, "when it comes time for a showdown between you and me."

Frank ignored him. Bill Kitson edged his horse up and said, "I don't know, Mr. Morgan . . . I think I ought to stay with the boss . . ."

"I just thought if you hung back with us for a little while, you could ride after the others and let them know if Salty and I have to turn back," Frank explained.

"That makes sense," Embry said. "Stay here with Morgan and Stevens, Bill, until he sees how bad off his horse is."

Kitson nodded but still looked uneasy as he said, "Sure, boss. Whatever you say."

He dismounted and stood there holding the reins of his horse and fidgeting a little as Frank started examining each of Goldy's hooves in turn. The rest of the men rode off, with Brady directing a disdainful glare toward Frank as they left.

Salty leaned over and put his hands on his knees as he studied the sorrel's hooves as well. "I don't see nothin' wrong so far, Frank," he said. "Goldy's pretty dependable, though, so if he tried to pull up, there must be somethin' botherin' him."

"I'll find it," Frank said, "no matter how long it takes."

He noticed that Kitson looked even more impatient at that comment.

"Mighty pretty country around here," he went on, apparently making idle conversation while he checked over the horse. "I don't reckon I've ever seen anything prettier, though, than Miss Faye standing under that waterfall with that water running all over her." He grinned, even as Salty frowned in puzzlement. "How about you, Bill? You ever seen anything like that?"

Kitson ducked his head, but he couldn't completely hide the surprised frown that appeared on his face.

Frank laughed as he set down the hoof he'd been examining.

"You've seen her like that, haven't you, Bill?" he prodded. "I can tell by the look on your face."

Bill turned away. "I don't reckon I want to talk about that."

"Come on, Bill, you're among friends. You and Faye were sweet on each other for a while. You went out there to that waterfall with her a few times, didn't you?"

"That's none of your business, Mr. Morgan," Kitson said. He was starting to sound annoyed now.

"Hell, son, it's nothing to be ashamed of," Frank persisted. Salty was staring at him now in utter confusion, knowing that Frank wasn't the sort of man to talk about a woman like that, but Kitson had his back turned and couldn't see the old-timer's expression.

Frank gestured to Salty, trying to tell him to play along, and continued, "A couple of healthy young people like you two, there's nothing wrong with stripping down buck-naked and romping a little in a pool like that —"

Kitson swung around sharply, and now his face was flushed with anger.

"That's not the way it was!" he said. "I knew about that waterfall and wanted to go out there with her, but she wouldn't let me! I had to sneak out there to get a look at her, and she —"

He stopped short and stepped back with a look of apprehension on his face.

Frank took a quick step toward the young cowboy. "She caught you," he said, "and told you that everything was over and done with between you. She probably called you a few choice names and threatened to tell her pa about what you'd done, too, didn't she?"

"You . . . you don't know what you're talkin' about, Mr. Morgan," Kitson forced out.

"I think I do," Frank said. "She was furious at you, probably said all kinds of things that made you mad, but in the end she promised not to say anything to Embry. But you couldn't forget how humiliating it was to have her treat you like that, could you, Bill? You were still in love with her, but she didn't feel the same way anymore. And you couldn't stand that."

Kitson shook his head and took another step back. "You don't know what it was like," he said. "Having to see her around the ranch all the time, knowin' that she hated me now, knowing what we might've had together if I hadn't been so blasted stupid . . ."

"So to get even with her you decided to sell out the Boxed E." Frank's voice was hard as flint now. "You went over to Baldridge's side and started feeding information to Brady Morgan. Maybe you didn't mean to let it slip about Faye going out there to the waterfall, but you said something to plant the idea in Brady's brain. If Faye Embry was raped and murdered by a couple of Baldridge's gun-wolves, it would get a war started in this valley for sure."

Kitson gasped and exclaimed, "No! No, I never meant for Faye to be hurt. He promised me —"

"You believed a snake like Brady Morgan?"

"He's *your* son!" Kitson accused.

"That doesn't make him any less of a snake. Or you, for that matter. You slipped out of the bunkhouse last night and rode over to the B Star, or wherever you met Brady to pass along your information, and told him that Faye was going to Pine Knob today. As soon as he knew that, he hatched a plan to have her kidnapped. That gunman called Cotter and the other two, they never quit Baldridge. That was a lie. They're still working for him. And everything Brady and Baldridge said when we rode up was just an act."

"I . . . I don't know anything about that," Kitson insisted.

"Sure you do." Frank's words lashed out like a whip. "You know Jubal and Hal Embry and the rest of the Boxed E crew are riding into a trap right now! It's all a double-cross. The rest of Baldridge's gunnies are waiting up there in the mountains to ambush them and wipe them out!"

Frank hadn't seen all of the plan laid out in detail at first, but it had come together in his mind as he was talking. Now that he had put his hunches and half-formed theories into words, he knew it was all true.

He knew as well that Brady hadn't come up with such an elaborate scheme on his own, not on such short notice. And neither had Baldridge.

He saw Laura's hand in this. She was cunning, and she was ruthless, and she knew how to get what she wanted. She had probably been pulling Baldridge's strings from the start, with Brady's help. Frank wasn't sure exactly what she hoped to gain from pitting Baldridge and Embry against each other. But if Baldridge wiped out his only rival and then married Laura, and something was to happen to him after that . . .

Laura could easily wind up owning the entire valley.

There was more to it than that, Frank thought, and it probably had to do with the railroad since Laura's late husband Frederick Wilcoxon had been involved with building spur lines all across the frontier. Laura might want to run such a line through the valley, and she stood to make a fortune if she controlled all the rights-of-way. Or rather, a bigger fortune, Frank thought, since she was already a wealthy woman.

But would too much ever be enough, where Laura was concerned?

Those thoughts were racing through Frank's head, and they almost distracted him to the point that he didn't see Kitson suddenly grabbing for the gun on his hip.

"I won't let you tell anybody!" the young cowboy yelled.

Frank didn't reach for his gun. His right fist shot forward instead, crashing into Kitson's face just as the man's Colt cleared leather. The force of the blow sent Kitson reeling backward. Frank went after him, grabbing the gun and twisting it out of Kitson's grip. Then he swung a powerful backhand that cracked across Kitson's jaw and sent the cowboy sprawling senseless on the ground.

"Good Lord, Frank!" Salty burst out as he scrambled forward with his old hogleg clutched in his hand. He covered Kitson and asked, "How in tarnation did you figure out all that? It's as tangled up as a skillet full o' snakes!"

"Just put together a few things I saw and heard along the way," Frank said. "Keep him covered, Salty, while I tie him up. We don't want him getting away and trying to warn Brady and Baldridge."

"Wait a minute," Salty said with a frown. "Did Goldy really go lame or not?"

"We'd better hope not," Frank said, "because we'll really have to light a shuck if we want to catch up to Embry and his men in time to stop them from riding into that ambush!"

CHAPTER 28

It didn't take long for Frank to lash Kitson's wrists and ankles together so securely that the young cowboy wouldn't be going anywhere until somebody came along and cut his bonds.

Since they were out in the wilds of the B Star range, Frank decided it would be all right to leave Kitson without gagging him. There was no one around to hear his shouts.

"We'll come back to get you later," Frank told Kitson as he swung up into the saddle.

"Either that or you'll lay out here until you starve to death, you double-crossin' polecat," Salty added with a malicious cackle.

Kitson said dully, "It'd be better if you'd just go ahead and shoot me. It's all I deserve after what I've done." He groaned in despair. "A bunch of my friends are gonna wind up dead because of me!"

"More than likely," Frank said. "You

should've thought about that before you let your head get all twisted up by a woman."

He heeled Goldy into motion and rode away without looking back at the forlorn Kitson. Salty rode alongside on the pinto.

"How are we gonna find that line shack, Frank?" the old-timer asked. "Baldridge is the one who knows where it is."

"They left enough sign we can follow their trail," Frank said. "I've got a hunch that when we get closer, we'll be able to tell where they are."

"We'll hear the shootin', eh?" Salty asked grimly. "There's a good chance you're right about that."

They pushed their horses hard in hopes of catching up to the men from the Boxed E before they reached the ambush. But Goldy and Salty's paint had already traveled quite a distance today, and there was only so much the horses could do. Frank knew that running their mounts into the ground wouldn't accomplish anything.

The mountains rose sharply along the northern edge of the valley, with only a narrow band of foothills before the tree-covered slopes. A larger range with snow-capped peaks bulked to the northwest. The mountains bordering the valley were smaller but still rugged. The high pastures had good grass, but it was too much work getting stock up to them and back down again when summer was over.

Thirty horsemen couldn't travel through those pastures without the grass getting beaten down. Not all of it had sprung back up again just yet, so Frank and Salty had no trouble following the trail. The terrain climbed in front of them and fell away behind them, so when Frank glanced back over his shoulder, he had a good view of the entire valley.

It was a beautiful place, just as he had said to Bill Kitson. Worth fighting for, no doubt about that, but at the same time plenty big enough for two ranches. Hal Embry had been on the right track with his suggestion.

Unfortunately, it was probably too late for a peaceful solution. With everything he knew now, Frank was sure that Gaius Baldridge was in on the plan hatched by Laura and Brady. He had to be. That meant he had gone along with the idea of kidnapping Faye, and he was aware that Brady planned to bushwhack the rescue party and murder all the men from the Boxed E.

There was no turning back from that. Even though Frank figured Baldridge had been manipulated by Laura and Brady, he had been a willing victim. He had crossed a line and couldn't come back.

"What do you reckon's gonna happen when they get to that line shack?" Salty asked.

"Embry will charge it like the loco old buffalo bull he is," Frank said, "and the rest of his bunch will be right behind them. Brady and Baldridge and the men with them will open fire from behind, and I figure the rest of Baldridge's crew is hidden somewhere close by where they can start shooting, too. Probably won't take long to butcher everybody from the Boxed E."

"Frank . . . I don't want to say it, but I'm thinkin' maybe Miz Wilcoxon has got somethin' to do with this."

"You're not telling me anything I don't already know, Salty," Frank replied.

"If we can put a stop to this, what's gonna happen to her?"

"I don't know," Frank said honestly. "Right now I just want to keep Embry and Hal and the rest of them from getting slaughtered."

The horses were tiring even more. Goldy was strong and valiant, and Salty's pinto was a real scrapper. But they were only flesh and blood and had their limits. The fact that the trail had gotten even steeper didn't help matters.

Frank grimaced as the sound of shots suddenly reached his ears, drifting down from higher in the mountains.

Salty heard the gunfire, too. "We're too late, damn it!"

"Maybe not," Frank said. He pulled his Winchester from its sheath. "We've got to try to help them."

They called on their mounts for one last burst of speed. The animals thundered up a long slope. The ground leveled out into a pasture about two hundred yards wide that stretched for twice that distance to a sheer cliff jutting up a hundred feet or more. Rocky ridges flanked the pasture on both sides. At the far end of the pasture, near the granite cliff, stood the old line shack. It was built of logs with a stone chimney and appeared to still be pretty sturdy.

A number of riderless horses milled around the shack. Frank recognized some of the Boxed E mounts. He didn't see Brady or any of the B Star gunnies. Sensing that the situation wasn't exactly what he had expected to find, he reined in and motioned for Salty to do likewise. They stopped in the shelter of some trees at the entrance to the pasture.

"What in blazes is goin' on here?" Salty asked as gray puffs of powdersmoke spurted from behind boulders and trees on the ridges. "I figured we'd find Embry and the rest of the Boxed E bunch shot to pieces."

"So did I," Frank said. Shots came from the windows of the line shack as well. Frank pointed to half a dozen dark shapes sprawled on the ground between them and the shack and said, "It looks to me like Embry or somebody else in the bunch must have figured out they were riding into an ambush. That line shack was the closest cover, so they lit out for it just before the shooting started. A few of them didn't make it, but most of the bunch did."

"What about the kidnappers and those two gals?"

Frank shook his head. "They were probably never in the line shack to start with. That was just a ruse to get Embry and his men up here."

"Where are the gals, then?"

"Being held prisoner in Baldridge's house, maybe," Frank guessed. "We'll figure that out later. Right now we've got the survivors from the Boxed E holed up in that shack, and Baldridge's hired killers up on the ridges trying to smoke them out."

"What about us?"

Despite the desperateness of the situation, a grin flashed across Frank's face, the reaction of a natural-born fighting man.

"We're the wild cards, Salty," he said. "Neither side knows we're here. It's up to us to even the odds a little."

"Now you're talkin'," the old-timer said. "Where do you reckon Baldridge and Brady got off to?"

"We didn't meet them coming up here, so they must still be around. Chances are when the trap didn't close all the way, they headed up on one of those ridges to throw lead at the line shack, too."

"If we could get our hands on Baldridge . . ." Salty mused.

"I was thinking the same thing," Frank agreed with a nod. "Then we'd have a bargaining chip of our own." He lifted Goldy's reins. "Come on. Let's see if we can work our way around to that ridge on the right."

Staying in the cover of the trees where they weren't as likely to be noticed, the two men rode east. After a few minutes of making their way toward the ridge, Frank suddenly stiffened in his saddle as the smell of tobacco smoke drifted to his nostrils. Someone nearby was smoking a quirly.

He motioned for Salty to stop and dismounted. After handing his reins to the old-timer, Frank started through the trees on foot with the Winchester held slanted across his chest. He followed the smell of smoke until he came to a clearing where a dozen saddle horses were tied to bushes and saplings. Those mounts had to belong to Brady's men. The gun-wolves had left them here to climb to the ridge and take their positions for the ambush.

One man stood next to a tree, sucking on a quirly as he kept an eye on the horses. His back was half-turned toward Frank. With the stealth that his long, perilous life had taught him, Frank moved closer to the guard in almost complete silence.

Frank wasn't the only one with sharp senses and instincts, though. The gunman, who wore a buckskin shirt and a brown hat with a rounded crown and turquoise-studded band, must have picked up some sort of warning. He threw the cigarette down and spun around, clawing at the holstered revolver on his hip.

Frank didn't want the man to get a shot off, because that might warn the bush-whackers on the ridge that something was wrong down here. He sprang forward and lifted the rifle, lashing out with the stock. He drove the Winchester's butt into the middle of the guard's face and felt bone crunch under the blow's impact. The man fell back against the tree and dropped the gun that he had just yanked from leather. Frank pulled back the rifle and hit him again.

The guard slid down the tree trunk until he was sitting against it. Then he slowly toppled onto his side and lay there motionless. Frank kicked the man's gun out of reach and knelt to see if he was dead.

The guard had breathed his last. Frank figured that bone shards from the crushing blows had penetrated his brain. Even though the rifle butt had battered the man's face out of shape, Frank recognized him.

This was Vince Cotter, one of Brady's men. And the last time Frank had seen him, Cotter had been struggling with Katie Storm in the kitchen of the Feed Barn.

Finding Cotter here, watching over the horses, was more evidence supporting Frank's theory of what had happened. Cotter and the other two gunmen must have taken Faye and Katie back to the B Star. Probably they had never even come close to the line shack with the prisoners. And chances were, Faye and Katie were locked up in the ranch house right now . . . and had been when Frank and the others were there earlier.

If Frank had had any doubts about Laura's

involvement with this murderous scheme, they were gone now.

And Cotter was dead, which was good riddance as far as Frank was concerned. He left the gunman where he had fallen and hurried back to Salty.

"What did you find?" the old-timer asked anxiously.

Frank told him, then added with a grim smile, "That's one down. More than a dozen to go, though."

"Shoot, we've got 'em outnumbered," Salty said. "The dang varmints just don't know it yet!"

CHAPTER 29

They left Goldy and the pinto with the killers' horses and started climbing the slope to the crest of the ridge. Dog went with them, staying close to Frank now instead of ranging ahead, as the big cur often did.

Gunshots continued to echo in the late afternoon air, which was a good sign as far as Frank was concerned. Silence now would mean that all the men from the Boxed E had been wiped out.

The gunshots also served to guide Frank and Salty once they reached the top. By following the nearest reports, they located one of Brady's men stretched out on top of a slab of rock as he fired down at the line shack. Frank and Salty were about fifty feet above him.

Frank knelt and lined his sights on the man's back, but his finger didn't press the Winchester's trigger. Salty leaned close and whispered, "You don't want to drill the son of a buck in the back, do you, even though he's got it comin'?"

"I never have cared for back-shooting," Frank said.

"We can fix that."

Before Frank could say anything else, Salty reached down, plucked a fist-sized rock from the ground, and chucked it at the gunman. The rock thudded hard into the man's back and made him jump and yelp. He rolled over, bringing his rifle around with him, and as he spotted Frank and Salty, his eyes widened in surprise and he tried to swing the repeater's barrel into line.

Frank's Winchester cracked. The hired killer jerked as the slug hit the tab of his tobacco sack hanging from his shirt pocket and bored on into his heart. The man arched his back in a death spasm, then slumped flat on the rock slab again with his arms outstretched at his sides.

"There you go," Salty said. "You didn't have to shoot him in the back. I call that a fair fight."

Frank didn't . . . but it was close enough considering the sort of men they were dealing with.

With the battle going on around the line shack, Frank didn't think one extra shot would be noticed, and it would be a while

312

before Brady and his men realized that no more bullets were coming from this position. That's what Frank was counting on, anyway.

"Let's go," he told Salty quietly, and they moved on to locate the next gunman.

Again the sound of gunshots guided them. They weren't going to be able to get to this man as easily, though. Instead of lying out in the open, he was concealed in a thicket of trees and brush. Frank couldn't get a clear shot at him from above.

"I'm going to have to go down there," he told Salty.

"With all them pine needles on the ground, you're gonna have a hard time gettin' close to him without makin' some racket," the old-timer warned.

Frank nodded and said, "I know, but I don't see any other way to do it."

"Well, be careful. I'm a tough old bird, but I ain't gonna be any match for this whole gang o' killers all by my lonesome."

"Don't worry," Frank said with a smile. He handed Salty his Winchester. "Here, hang on to this for me."

"What're you gonna —" Salty began, then stopped as Frank drew the knife from the sheath on his belt. "Oh."

Frank had never been particularly fond of

313

knife-fighting, but for a quiet, close-range weapon, it was hard to beat a blade.

He moved into the trees and began his stealthy approach, relying on the continued banging of gunshots to cover up any small sounds he made. He could hear the carpet of pine needles rustling under his feet, but he hoped the gunman couldn't.

So far he hadn't gotten a good look at the man. All he had seen was a rifle barrel thrusting out from the brush. What if this was Brady he was sneaking up on, Frank asked himself? Could he drive eight inches of cold steel into his own son's back, or cut his throat if it came down to that?

Frank had no doubt that if the tables were turned, Brady would kill him without hesitation. Brady would probably even enjoy it.

The boy had chosen his own trail, Frank told himself. And innocent lives were at risk. If that was Brady hidden in the trees . . . well, father and son would each have to take his own risk, that was all there was to it.

Frank pressed his back to a tree trunk and slid around the pine. He caught a glimpse of a denim-clad leg through the undergrowth about ten feet ahead of him. The whipcrack of a rifle shot nearby confirmed it. He was almost on top of the bush-whacker.

Branches and creepers clawed at him as he forced his way through the thicket. One of the branches caught on his shirt and suddenly snapped with a sharp crack. The unnatural sound caused the hidden gunman to exclaim in surprise.

Lowering his head, Frank bulled his way through the brush and came out in the little open space where the killer had taken cover. The man had twisted around with the rifle in his hands, and he got a shot off as Frank charged him. The slug whined past Frank's ear. He thrust the knife out, aiming to bury it in the man's chest.

But the gunman was fast, too, and he blocked the thrust with his Winchester. Metal rang against metal as the rifle barrel clashed with the knife and knocked the blade aside. The knife flew out of Frank's hand.

He was too close to stop, but also too close for the gunman to use his rifle again. Frank rammed his shoulder against the man's torso and drove him backward against a tree trunk. The man's head hit the tree hard and bounced off, but even though he seemed stunned, he didn't stop fighting. He tried to ram the Winchester's muzzle under Frank's chin. Frank jerked his head out of the way just in time, but the sight still scraped his jaw.

He got his hand on the barrel and wrenched it aside. It was hot from firing, but he hung on anyway. At the same time he drove his other fist into the gunman's midsection. The man's breath puffed out in Frank's face, bringing with it the smell of rotting teeth.

The man lowered his head and tried to butt Frank in the face. They wrestled back and forth in the brush for a moment, until Frank's ankle tangled in a tree root. His balance deserted him and he fell, pulling the gunman down with him.

The struggle continued on the ground. The undergrowth was so thick they couldn't roll back and forth very much, but they wound up with Frank on the bottom and the hired killer on top, trying to get his hands around Frank's throat with the obvious intention of choking the life out of him.

From the corner of Frank's eye, he saw the late afternoon sun glint redly on something lying in the pine needles to his right. He slapped his hand down over there and felt the handle of the knife he had dropped. His fingers closed around the grip. Just as the gunman got his hands on Frank's throat and started trying to dig in his thumbs, Frank shoved the blade in under the man's ribs, angling it up so the point pierced the heart.

The man's eyes widened in pain and shock. He still tried to crush Frank's windpipe with his thumbs, but his strength was leaving him too fast. Frank ripped the knife out and drove it in again, this time opening a wound that gushed blood hotly over his hand. He grabbed the man's shirt with his other hand and heaved him away to the side.

The gunman landed on his back and gasped out the last few breaths of his life. Blood trickled from his mouth. A violent shudder went through him, and he lay still after that as his wide-open eyes began to glaze over.

Frank rolled onto his side and pushed himself up. He cleaned the blade on the dead man's shirt and slid it back into its sheath. Then he climbed to his feet, picked up his hat, which had fallen off during the fight, and made his way out of the thicket to rejoin Salty.

A grin wreathed the old-timer's whiskery face when he saw Frank coming.

"I was startin' to worry a mite," he said. "You'd been gone a while, and I could see that brush wavin' around down there like there was a grizzle bear in it goin' after the honey in a beehive!"

"I'm fine," Frank said. He wiped away a small trickle of blood from the scratch on his jaw that the rifle sight had opened up. "Let's see if we can whittle down those odds a little more."

From where they were now, they could see the puffs of powdersmoke marking the locations of the other bushwhackers on this side of the pasture. Six more men were pouring lead down at the line shack.

Frank wished he could see into the shack. He wanted to know how many of the Boxed E men were left alive. He was especially worried about Embry, Hal, and Gage Carlin because he had grown closer to those three than any of the others during his time in the valley. But he didn't want to see any of them wounded or dying, and when he looked down into the pasture at the sprawled bodies of the men who had fallen in the first volley, anger burned inside him.

Brady Morgan and Gaius Baldridge had a lot to answer for. And as far as Brady was concerned . . . Frank wasn't even going to think of the killer as his son anymore. Brady was just an accident of blood, a vicious murderer who had to be dealt with.

The next ambusher knelt in a cluster of small boulders just below the ridge crest, with open, rocky ground around him. Frank and Salty couldn't approach him without being seen. Like it or not, there was no way to dispose of this man without shooting him down with no warning. Frank stole a little closer, crouched behind a tree, and lifted the Winchester to his shoulder to draw a bead. He squinted over the rifle barrel and settled his sights on the side of the man's neck.

The Winchester bucked against his shoulder as it cracked.

Frank had aimed for a killing shot that would sever the man's spine and drop him straight down like a sack of rocks. Instead, the gunman shifted slightly just as Frank squeezed the trigger, and the slug ripped through the front part of his throat, missing the backbone. Pain sent the man lurching to his feet. He let out a strangled cry as a stream of crimson fountained from his torn neck a good ten feet in front of him. He pawed at his throat, trying futilely to stem the flood, but only for a second before he collapsed.

"Lord have mercy," Salty breathed.

"Come on," Frank said. There was no mercy on B Star range today.

There was more proof of that only an instant later, as Salty cried out and stumbled. Frank caught the old-timer's arm and kept him from falling, but as he steadied Salty he saw the red stain spreading on the side of the checkered shirt.

"Dagnab it!" Salty gasped. "I'm hit!"

Before Frank could check and see how bad it was, more bullets began to whine around his head like angry bees.

CHAPTER 30

With bullets whipping around them, Frank had no choice but to tackle Salty and knock the old man off his feet, even though Salty was wounded.

There was a deadfall not far away where a large pine tree had toppled over, possibly after being struck by lightning in a storm.

Frank didn't care why the tree had fallen; he just wanted to get behind it.

More bullets smacked into the ground around him and kicked up rock chips as he started dragging Salty toward the deadfall. A few yards away, Dog whined as if he wanted to help.

"Hunt, Dog!" Frank ordered the big cur. Like a streak, Dog bounded away, which got him out of the immediate line of fire. That was Frank's intention, but at the same time he had unleashed a dangerous force up here on the ridge. Dog would assume that anyone he encountered other than

Frank or Salty was an enemy, and he would react accordingly.

And because of that, some of Brady's gunmen were in for a heap of trouble.

Somehow Frank managed to get Salty behind the fallen tree without either of them getting hit again. Frank lay there catching his breath for a few seconds while more bullets thudded into the thick trunk that shielded them. When his heart wasn't pounding quite so hard in his chest, he turned to Salty to see just how badly the old-timer was hurt.

Salty seemed to have passed out, but his chest was rising and falling rapidly and Frank could hear the breath rasping in the old-timer's throat. After pulling up the bloody shirt, Frank saw that a bullet had plowed a shallow furrow across Salty's side. The wound was messy but not life-threatening, especially if Salty got some medical attention in the reasonably near future. Blood still welled from the crease, so Frank took out his bandana, folded it into a thick pad, and used Salty's belt to bind it into place over the wound.

With that done, Frank turned his attention to the problem of who had ventilated the old-timer and tried their best to kill him, too. He supposed the defenders in the line shack could have spotted the two of them, mistaken them for some of Brady's men, and opened fire. Frank didn't think that was likely, however. The angle of the shots that had buzzed around his head seemed wrong, and so did the trajectory of the bullet that had struck Salty.

No, he decided, those shots had come from the bushwhackers on the other ridge, the one on the far side of the pasture. Somebody over there must have seen that gunman lurch to his feet with blood spouting from his neck and figured out that there were enemies on this ridge. After that it would have been just a matter of waiting for Frank and Salty to show themselves . . .

Frank had hoped to get rid of more of the hired killers before his and Salty's presence was discovered. That hope was dashed now. Not only that, he was going to have to carry on alone from here, since Salty was wounded too badly to fight.

More bullets continued to smack into the log from time to time, but the bushwhackers on the other ridge weren't concentrating their fire on it anymore. They must have figured out that Frank and Salty were pinned down here and had returned to trying to smoke out the defenders in the line shack. Those occasional shots were just to keep Frank and Salty honest and force them to keep their heads down.

Salty let out a groan as his eyes flickered open. "What . . . what in blazes happened?" he managed to ask as he looked over at Frank through watery eyes.

"One of the varmints winged you," Frank explained. "You've got a crease in your side. It's bled some, but you'll be all right."

"I didn't think . . . they even knew we was over here!"

"They didn't at first," Frank said. "I figure they must have spotted that fella who died so spectacularly, and that made them look for us."

Salty licked his lips and looked around. "Where's . . . Dog? The mangy son . . . didn't get hit . . . did he?"

"I sent him hunting," Frank said grimly.

"Good!" Salty croaked. "I hope he chews up . . . a whole passel o' them skunks. Just hope he don't . . . catch hydrophobia from 'em!"

Frank chuckled. Salty had lost some blood, but none of his spirit.

"I've got my bandana tied over the crease to slow down the bleeding," he said. "This deadfall is good cover, so I reckon you'll be all right here."

"Now wait . . . just a dang minute! You

sound like . . . you're plannin' on leavin' me here."

"Not much else I can do," Frank said. "You've lost enough blood that you're too weak to keep going."

"Dang it! I reckon that's . . . my decision to make . . . not yours." Salty tried to push himself up on an elbow, but with a groan, he slumped down again. "Son of a gun! Maybe . . . you're right."

"Sorry. I know how you hate to miss out on a good scrap."

"That's the . . . dadgummed truth." Salty reached out and clutched at Frank's sleeve. "You're gonna . . . keep tryin' to rescue those fellas . . . who're holed up down there?"

"Yeah. I reckon I'm the only chance they've got."

"You listen to me . . . Frank." Salty paused, and Frank leaned closer. The old-timer rasped, "If you come up against . . . Brady . . . don't you hesitate . . . don't you think about nothin' else . . . except gunnin' the buzzard. 'Cause he's got it comin', Frank . . . you know he does . . . and his life ain't worth a thing . . . compared to yours."

"You just take it easy, Salty," Frank said. "Don't worry yourself."

"You mind . . . what I done told you!" Salty looked around again. "Where's my . . . rifle?"

"You dropped it when you got hit," Frank explained. "I had my hands full getting you behind cover. I didn't have a chance to grab your rifle, too."

"Oh, well. Still got . . . my old hogleg . . . and a couple dozen rounds for it. Anybody who ain't on our side . . . tries to bother me . . . I'll blow a hole in 'em."

"I don't doubt it." Frank squeezed the old-timer's shoulder. "I'll see you around."

"Yeah . . . if we don't get back together here . . . we'll meet up in Mexico."

"In Mexico," Frank repeated, knowing what Salty meant. "I'll be looking for you."

No bullets had struck the deadfall in the past couple of minutes. Frank reared up suddenly and brought the Winchester to his shoulder. He cranked off five rounds as fast as he could work the rifle's lever, raking the opposite ridge with lead. He didn't know if he came close to any of the gunmen over there, but he hoped that he made them duck their heads, anyway.

He surged to his feet and broke into a run.

There were more trees about fifteen yards away. Frank wasn't as nimble as he had once been; years of riding and cold nights spent on the ground had taken their toll on his muscles. Boots weren't made for running, either.

But he could still move pretty fast when he had to, and this was one of those times.

Bullets sizzled through the air close enough for him to hear them, but he didn't feel the heat of their passage. A few slugs kicked up dirt and rocks behind him. Then he plunged into the trees, moving so fast that he lost his balance and went down into a rolling tumble. He came to a stop on his belly, still holding the Winchester. The men on the other ridge continued to fire blindly for a minute or two, but the bullets only smacked into tree trunks and clipped small branches from the pines — none of them came close to Frank.

He caught his breath again, reached out to retrieve his hat, and clapped it on his head. Using the rifle to brace himself, he climbed to his feet. There were still gunmen on this ridge. The more of them he could render useless, the better the chance the Boxed E men would have to escape from this trap with their lives. It was still possible that Gaius Baldridge was over here, too, and it might change things if Frank could get his hands on the rancher.

Frank started to make his way through

the trees, wondering briefly what had happened to Marshal Roy Trask. He had been unable to get a good look at any of the men who had been killed in the ambush. Trask might be lying out there in the pasture, dead.

Or could the lawman have been in on the plan with Baldridge and Brady? That didn't seem likely, but Frank couldn't rule out the possibility. Plenty of star packers had turned crooked in the past. Maybe Trask had finally chosen a side and decided that Baldridge was going to come out on top. Frank had seen some things that made him curious about Trask, but he didn't have any answers, even though his gut told him Trask wouldn't have gone along with wholesale murder.

He could figure out the truth about Roy Trask later, he told himself . . . assuming he survived this dust-up and Trask did, too. If they didn't . . . well, it wouldn't matter then, would it?

During a lull in the shooting, he heard the distant rataplan of hoofbeats. He turned to look and saw four riders galloping across the far end of the pasture, where the slope leading up to it ended. Those had to be some of Brady's men, Frank thought. Brady — or at least somebody over on that opposite ridge — must be sending them over here as reinforcements.

They would be hunting him and Salty, Frank thought bleakly. He and the old-timer were caught between two forces now. If the killers who had come over from the other ridge found Salty, he wouldn't stand much of a chance against them.

Frank had no choice but to turn back; otherwise, he was condemning Salty to certain death.

He'd be killing Brady's men either way, whether he went forward or turned back, he thought as a grim smile tugged at his mouth, so he might as well try to save Salty's life.

When Frank reached the edge of the trees, he paused. He could see behind the deadfall from here. Salty had pushed himself up into a half-sitting position and had the old revolver in his hand.

"Salty!" Frank called. He waved a hand to catch the old man's attention.

Salty's eyes were big as he turned his head to look at Frank. "What're you doin' back here?" he demanded. His voice sounded stronger. "We just had that touchin' farewell a few minutes ago. See you in Mexico and all that."

Frank grinned and pointed back along the ridge. "More hostiles coming from that direction," he explained. "I thought I'd come back and help you deal with them."

"You ran across that open ground once without gettin' hit. I ain't so sure you can do it again."

"Neither am I," Frank admitted. "That's why I thought I'd get you to cover me."

Salty hefted the revolver. "This smokepole won't reach that other ridge."

"No, but my Winchester will. I'll toss it over to you. You can get it and cover me while I make a run for it."

Salty nodded and shoved his iron back into leather.

"Let fly with it!"

Frank threw the Winchester with all his strength. The rifle was heavy, and it wasn't meant for throwing. But it made it most of the way to the log, falling short by only a couple of feet.

Salty crawled to the end of the deadfall and stretched out his arm as he groped for the Winchester's barrel. More shots suddenly peppered the ground around the weapon. Salty jerked his arm back and let out a stream of colorful profanity.

When he finished turning the air blue, he made another try and this time latched on to the barrel.

"Dadblast it!" he yelped as he dragged the

Winchester behind the deadfall. "Those ringtailed rannihans like to blowed my fingers off!" He shook his hand, as if to make sure that all the fingers actually were still attached, then called to Frank, "Come on anytime you're ready!"

"Make that rifle sing and dance, Salty!" Frank yelled. He burst out of the trees as Salty thrust the Winchester's barrel over the log and opened fire.

CHAPTER 31

Salty fired the Winchester so fast the sound of the shots blended into one long continuous roar as he swung the barrel from left to right. Frank lunged ahead, running at top speed. He felt a tug on his shirt and knew a bullet had just come within a shaved fraction of an inch of hitting him.

But that was the closest any of the hired killers came. Frank left his feet in a dive that carried him behind the log next to Salty. The old-timer ducked down again.

"Pretty spry for somebody your age," he commented.

"Yeah, well, I'll feel it in the morning," Frank said.

"Better hope so, anyway."

Frank understood. If they were dead, they wouldn't feel anything.

The exchange of shots had drawn the bushwhackers' attention to the deadfall again. A hail of lead chewed into the log for a moment, sending splinters and chunks of bark spraying high into the air. The gunmen stopped firing fairly quickly, though, as they must have realized that their bullets weren't doing any good.

"Now what?" Salty asked.

"Hand me that Winchester," Frank said. "I've got more cartridges for it in my pocket."

He didn't have an endless supply, though, and there was still a lot of fighting to do. There was more ammunition in the saddlebags on Goldy's back, but under the circumstances, the sorrel might as well have been a million miles away.

Frank thumbed more shells through the Winchester's loading gate until the magazine was full again.

"We'd better make all our shots count from here on out," he told Salty.

"Yeah, we wouldn't want to run out of bullets before we run out of varmints that need killin'. Speakin' of which, you said there were some comin' up behind us?"

"That's right. And we shouldn't have to wait very long for —"

As if they had been listening to the conversation and waiting for their cue, four horsemen burst out of the trees, charging toward Frank and Salty with guns blazing.

Frank hadn't expected them to be able to get their horses up the slope onto the ridge. They must have found another trail, he thought as he rolled from his side onto his belly and brought the rifle to his shoulder. The Winchester cracked and one of the gunmen went flying out of the saddle. The dull boom of Salty's revolver filled the air as well. One of the horses went down, sending its rider flying wildly through the air. The man crashed to the ground, rolled over a couple of times, and came up on a knee just in time for a slug from Frank's rifle to smash into his chest and send him over backwards.

The other two gunmen yanked their horses around, threw a couple of last shots at Frank and Salty, and galloped back toward the trees.

"Dadgum it!" Salty exclaimed. "I was hopin' they'd keep comin'. That was our best chance of killin' 'em."

Frank thought the same thing. Now the men could take potshots at them from the safety of the trees, and from that angle, the deadfall didn't offer any cover for them.

"We can't stay here, Salty," he said. "They'll pick us off if we do."

"If we get up and make a run for it, the varmints on the other ridge will get us,"

Salty objected. "It'll be dark in another hour or so. If we could hold out until then —"

"We can't," Frank said. "We've got a minute, maybe less, before those two open fire on us again. Come on."

"What're you — Whoa!"

Salty let out the exclamation as Frank grabbed him around the middle with one arm and surged to his feet. Salty wound up draped over Frank's shoulder. Frank broke into a run toward the trees where he had gone a few minutes earlier, only to have to turn back to rescue the old-timer.

Salty howled curses with every jolting step, and Frank knew the wound in his side had to be hurting him. But it would be a lot worse if they stayed where they were.

He stumbled as a bullet burned across the back of one thigh. The muscles in that leg still worked, though, so he knew the slug hadn't penetrated. Another bullet kicked up dirt in front of them. The bushwhackers on the other ridge would have the range soon. Frank wasn't a fast runner to start with, and with Salty's extra weight slowing him down, he was reduced to plodding.

"They're comin' up behind us again!" Salty yelled. He started firing, and the revolver's boom was deafening at this close range.

That fifteen yards was the longest of Frank's life. It seemed to take an hour to cross it. But finally he staggered into the trees. Dropping to his knees, he lowered Salty to the ground behind one of the pines.

"Lord, Frank!" Salty gasped. "I didn't know you was so strong!"

"Neither . . . did I," Frank panted. He had called on the reserves of strength that came to a man when it was either do what had to be done . . . or die.

They weren't out of danger yet, though, because bullets were still zipping through the trees around them. Frank helped Salty to his feet, and together they made their way deeper into the growth. Salty groaned from the pain of his wound.

"Feels like I'm bleedin' again," he said.

"I'd be surprised if you weren't," Frank told him.

They came to a little hollow, about half the height of a man, and slid down into it. Salty propped his back against the slope while Frank checked the bullet crease. The bandana he had tied on there earlier was soaked with blood. He replaced it with a pad he made from a strip cut off Salty's shirt.

"Sure wish we had a jug of whiskey right now," Salty said.

"Yeah, it would help to clean that wound."

Salty snorted. "I was thinkin' more of drinkin' it!" he said.

Frank set the rifle next to him. "This is a good spot. You've got cover all around. I'm going to leave the Winchester with you and see if I can get a few more of them."

"You're liable to need that rifle," Salty protested.

Frank shook his head and said, "No, I've got a hunch it'll be close work from here on out, but it might come in handy for you if those varmints try to sneak up on you."

"If they do, I'll give 'em a hot lead welcome, that's for dang sure!"

"I never doubted it," Frank said with a grin. "So long."

"Vaya con Dios."

That was all they said this time in the way of farewells, but it was enough.

Frank made sure he had a full wheel in his Colt, even the chamber where the hammer rested, which normally was empty. He moved through the trees, limping slightly from the bullet burn on the back of his left leg. He paused and felt back there. The slug had torn his trousers, but there was no blood.

He made his way to a point of rock where he could see down into the pasture but was shielded by a pair of boulders. Shots coming from the line shack still peppered the ridges, so he knew at least some of the defenders were still alive.

One of the gunmen was off to his right, firing down at the shack. Frank started in that direction and came up behind the man, who hadn't noticed him.

"Hey!" Frank called.

The hired killer whirled, but Frank's Colt was already out. The revolver roared, and the gunman doubled over as the slug punched into his belly. The rifle in his hands cracked as his finger jerked involuntarily on the trigger, but the barrel had sagged and the bullet went harmlessly into the ground.

Since it usually took a while for a gutshot man to die, Frank strode over to him, picked up the fallen rifle, and slammed the butt down on the gunman's head, crushing his skull and putting him out of his misery . . . and eliminating even the slightest possibility of the man threatening anyone again.

Frank glanced at the sky as he moved along the ridge. The sun had dipped close to the western horizon. Another half-hour and the shadows would be thick . . . too thick for accurate shooting. If the defenders could hold on for that long, they might be able to slip out under the cover of darkness.

The sound of rifle fire behind him made Frank look over his shoulder. Salty was swapping lead with those two gunmen, he thought. From the sound of the shots, the fight was hot and heavy. Frank said a brief, silent prayer for the old-timer and continued working his way toward the cliff, which not only backed up to the cabin but cut off both ridges at the far end.

From time to time a bullet sliced through the branches nearby. He didn't know if the shots were coming from the line shack or the bushwhackers on the other ridge, who might be firing blindly, hoping to hit him since they couldn't see him.

The sight of a pair of legs and booted feet sticking out from behind a rock made him freeze momentarily, but then he realized those limbs were motionless. When they didn't move for a good two minutes as he watched, he approached cautiously, his gun held ready, and looked behind the rock.

One of the bushwhackers lay there with his head in a pool of blood that was soaking slowly into the ground. The blood came from his throat, which had been torn open by savage fangs.

Dog had been here, Frank thought with a

grim smile. He resumed his own deadly hunt.

He came to a pair of gunmen crouched behind some rocks as they sniped at the line shack. So far he hadn't seen any sign of Brady or Gaius Baldridge, so it was looking like they were probably on the other ridge. They would have to be dealt with eventually, but right now Frank was doing all he could on this ridge.

He crept up to within fifteen feet of the two bushwhackers. Leveling his Colt at them, he called, "Hold it! Drop those rifles!"

Neither man followed that order. Frank didn't really expect them to. Instead they wheeled around and opened fire. He dropped to a knee as slugs racketed over his head and triggered three swift shots. Both gunmen crumpled under the deadly accurate fire.

Frank was checking them to make sure they were dead when he heard a man yell somewhere close by, followed by some fearsome snarling and growling. Breaking into a run, Frank came up to the battle just in time to see Dog break the wrist of the man's gun hand with a crunch of powerful jaws. The man screamed and dropped the revolver he had been trying to line up on the big cur.

In a flash, Dog knocked the man down

and ripped his throat out. None of his wolf cousins could have done it any better, or with more brutal efficiency.

"Dog!" Frank called softly. The big cur turned and loped happily back to him, blood dripping from his muzzle.

That was the last of the bushwhackers on this ridge, Frank realized. Against seemingly overwhelming odds, he and Salty and Dog had succeeded in opening one side of the trap. There were still the two men behind them, but from the sound of the sporadic shots coming from back there, Salty was keeping them pinned down.

As soon as it was dark, he could make his way down the slope to the line shack and let the men inside know that there was a way out over this ridge. The sun was down now, and gloom had started to descend on the rugged landscape. It wouldn't be long until the darkness was thick enough for Frank to make his move.

Then something happened that changed all that.

CHAPTER 32

The sound of hoofbeats drew Frank's attention to the far end of the pasture. A large wagon being drawn by six horses was headed toward the line shack. The back of it was piled high with hay. Several men rode behind the driverless wagon, yelling and shooting into the air to keep the team moving.

Frank knew instantly what the purpose of this maneuver was. Brady's men were going to drive the wagon up close to the line shack and set the hay on fire. The light from the blaze would reveal anyone who tried to escape from the building. The bushwhackers would be waiting to gun them down if they made the attempt.

That ruined his plans before they ever got under way. He couldn't reach the line shack now, and the men holed up in there couldn't get out.

The only thing he could do now was try

to get up the cliff, which was only about forty feet high at the end of the ridge, cross over to the other ridge, and pick off as many of the hired killers as he could, just like he had done on this side.

Unless . . .

The idea that sprang into his brain held some promise, but he didn't know if it was possible. That depended on something that was largely out of his control and would require a great deal of luck. But he couldn't rule it out just yet.

As the dusk thickened around him, he holstered his gun and started back along the ridge. Since he knew there were no bushwhackers between him and the hollow where Salty was dug in — no live ones, anyway — he didn't have to be as careful and could move faster. Within minutes he was close enough to call softly, "Salty!"

"Frank?" the old-timer's voice came back. "Is that you?"

"Me and Dog," Frank replied as both of them slipped down in the hollow. "Are you all right?"

"Yeah, they ain't hit me again. I'm thirsty as hell, though, prob'ly because of that blood I lost. I'm so thirsty I'd even settle for a drink o' water instead of whiskey."

"Maybe it won't be too much longer."

"Yeah, because I figure those two buzzards'll try to sneak up on me once it's good and dark. They'll have a surprise waitin' for 'em when they realize you're here, too."

"I won't be," Frank said. "I've got something else to do. But I'll leave Dog with you. He's worth any two fighting men."

"I can't argue with that," Salty said. "But what have you got in mind?"

"Before it started getting dark, did you see where that extra horse went?"

"The one where you shot the hombre ridin' it out of the saddle?" Salty sounded confused. "The last I seen of that hoss, it had wandered off over yonder to the left and was grazin'. Don't know where it is now."

"Thanks, Salty. That gives me a place to start looking for it, anyway."

"What do you want with that horse? You gonna cut and run and leave me up here, Frank?"

"You know better than that," Frank said. "If you weren't wounded I'd kick you in the butt for even asking such a thing. I'm hoping I can find what I need to get those men out of that line shack."

"Unless that nag can sprout wings and fly down there, I don't see how it's gonna help." Salty sighed. "But I reckon you know what you're doin'. You always do."

Frank chuckled. "Thanks for the vote of confidence." He added, "Dog, stay here with Salty. If those varmints charge him, you know what to do."

He patted Dog on the head, squeezed Salty's shoulder, and moved off into the twilight, which was not far from being full-fledged night now. The sky was fading from dark blue to black overhead, and some of the millions of stars had already popped into view.

An orange glow climbed into the sky above the pasture. Frank knew Baldridge's men had fired the hay in the wagon. It would burn fairly quickly, but they might have more wagons ready to move in if they needed to.

Frank heard something moving in the brush not far away. He drew his gun in case it was some of the hired killers, but a moment later he spotted a dark shape larger than a man.

"Hey," he called softly. "Take it easy. I'm a friend."

The words didn't mean anything, but the tone of voice did. He continued to speak in calm, steady, soothing tones as he approached the bulky shape. As he came closer, he could see that it was a riderless horse, the mount that had belonged to the man he'd killed earlier. The horse acted a little spooked, but it stayed put until Frank was close enough to catch hold of the reins.

Feeling a human touch on the reins, the horse settled down instantly. Frank patted the animal's shoulder and then ran his hand over the saddle. His fingers tightened on the coiled rope he found hanging there from a strap.

That was what he needed. Luck was with him, at least this far.

But there was still a long way to go.

He took the rope loose from the saddle and draped the coil over his left shoulder.

"You can go back to grazing, old hoss," he told the bushwhacker's horse. "And I hope your next owner is an improvement on the last one."

With the rope on his shoulder, Frank practically ran back to the cliff at the end of the ridge. He had to move carefully since now it was getting too dark to see very well, but he hurried as much as he could.

The haystack was still burning down below in the pasture, he saw. Baldridge's men, or Brady's men, or whatever they ought to be called, had turned the vehicle so that its back was toward the line shack.

That had allowed them to use the wagon itself for cover as they cut the team loose and led the horses away. The glare from the burning hay lit up the front of the shack almost as bright as day, and it spilled out to the sides, too.

But it didn't reach the very back of the building, Frank noted, and right now, that was all he cared about.

Working mostly by feel, he began to climb the cliff. He had gotten a good look at it earlier, before the sun went down, and he had seen that its face was pitted and scored, offering quite a few footholds and handholds. He pulled himself up carefully, testing each grip before he trusted his weight to it. If he fell it could prove fatal not only to him but also to all the men in the line shack who were still alive.

The climb seemed to take forever, but really it was only ten minutes or so. When Frank reached the top he pulled himself over the edge and sprawled out for a moment to catch his breath. Then he rolled over, came to his feet, and started along the cliff.

He suspected that the view from up here would be spectacular during the day, offering a panoramic vista of the entire valley. Right now, though, all he could really see was the pasture below, lit up by the light from the burning hay wagon. That allowed him to find the spot he wanted, directly behind the line shack. He tied one end of the rope around the sturdy trunk of a pine and dropped the rest of it over the brink.

The rope fell in the stygian darkness between the line shack and the cliff. Frank couldn't tell whether it reached the ground or not, but it was as long as it was and would have to do. He leaned against it, testing the strength of the tree and the knots he had tied.

Satisfied with both, he let himself over the edge and started walking down the cliff, thankful that its face was rough enough to give his boots purchase and that his hands, wrists, arms, and shoulders were strong enough to support most of his weight.

The climb down seemed even longer than the one up. If it had been daylight, he would have been an easy target for the hired killers on the ridge. The glow from the blaze didn't reach quite far enough to reveal him . . . or at least so he hoped. It helped that none of the bushwhackers would be expecting someone to climb down the cliff like this.

His arms and shoulders ached and throbbed by the time he reached the end of the rope. Frank knew he was almost to the ground, so he let go and dropped the rest of the way. The fall was no more than six feet. He landed heavily and dropped to a knee but came up quickly.

The shooting had stopped now except for an occasional blast as the standoff continued. Frank went to the rear wall of the shack and drew his gun. Reversing it, he used the butt to rap sharply on one of the logs. He hit it three times, paused, then struck three times again in an unmistakable signal.

After a moment, a voice he recognized as Jubal Embry's called, "Who the hell's out there?" Embry sounded utterly shocked.

Frank put his mouth close to a small chink in the mud between the logs and said, "It's Frank Morgan, Embry. I've come to get you out of there!"

"Morgan!" Embry exclaimed. "How the hell —"

"There's no time for that," Frank said. He drew his knife and started working at the mud to enlarge the chink. "We need to get some of these logs out."

He heard scraping from inside the shack as some of the men in there went to work on the same task. He didn't know yet how many survivors there were, but they labored industriously to remove the earthen mortar that held the logs together.

"Some of you keep shooting now and then," Frank advised through the gap he had created. "That way they're less likely to think that something else is going on."

A few shots rang out. Frank got his hands through the opening and took a firm grip on the log. He heaved on it and felt it shift a little.

Embry said, "I'll push on it from inside while you pull, Morgan. Ready?"

"Ready," Frank said.

It took several minutes of grunting effort, but the log came free and dropped to the ground outside the shack, making Frank hop back nimbly to keep it from crushing his toes. By then some of the other men had loosened another section of log, and with Frank pulling outside and the men inside pushing, it came out as well. That weakened the wall even more. Minutes later, they had another log out and an opening big enough for men to crawl through.

"How many men in there who aren't wounded?" Frank asked.

"About a dozen," Embry replied. "We got six or seven more who got plugged when the treacherous sons o' bitches opened fire on us." His voice choked for a second. "And we lost half a dozen or so in the pasture."

"I saw them out there," Frank said. "I'm

sorry. But I need the men who are able to fight."

"You heard the man," Embry said. "Get on out there, and do what Morgan tells you. He's in charge."

"Pa, I'm not leaving you here."

Frank recognized that new voice in the darkness. It belonged to Hal Embry.

"That bullet busted my ankle," Jubal Embry said. "Whatever Morgan's got in mind, I ain't gonna be spry enough for it. You go, Hal. Settle the score for the Boxed E."

If Embry had a broken ankle, he was probably in a lot of pain, Frank thought. And yet he hadn't been able to tell it from the rancher's voice, which sounded as strong as ever. Jubal Embry was a tough old bird, true pioneer stock.

Hal didn't argue with his father. He crawled through the opening they had made in the wall and was followed by eleven other men, among them Gage Carlin. Frank was glad to see that the middle-aged cowboy was all right.

The feeling was likewise, because Carlin gripped Frank's hand and wrung it.

"I didn't expect to ever see you again, Frank, not this side of the hereafter, anyway. Where are Salty and Bill?"

"Salty's up on the eastern ridge, holding

down the fort there. Kitson's not here."

"Damn! You mean he's dead?"

"No, but he's not in this fight," Frank said. Time enough to go into the details of Kitson's treachery later. Right now it was more important to take the fight to the enemy. "Everybody still have ammunition?"

He got a chorus of affirmatives from the men, although some of them said they were starting to run low, then he showed them the rope dangling from the cliff top.

"Climbing that cliff won't be easy, but you can do it. When you get to the top, wait for me. We're going to make our way to the western ridge and give Baldridge and his men a surprise."

The Boxed E punchers seemed to like the sound of that. Hal said, "I'll go first," and jumped up to grab the rope. He got his feet braced against the cliff and started climbing.

While they were doing that, Frank ducked down and crawled through the opening into the line shack. It was dark as pitch inside, so he said, "Embry?"

"Here," the rancher said.

"Who else is in here?"

Embry named five of the hands from the Boxed E, then added, "And the marshal."

"Trask?"

"Yeah," the lawman said in a hoarse, strained voice. "I'm here, Morgan."

"How bad are you hit?"

"Bad enough," Trask replied. The note of fatalism in his words was obvious. "But it doesn't really matter. I didn't have much time left anyway."

"Consumption?" Frank asked.

Trask sounded surprised as he said, "How did you know?"

"I saw the way you were coughing back in town a couple of times, and I spotted some blood on your handkerchief. It was pretty easy to figure out from that."

Trask sighed and said, "Yeah. You wanted to know where I was right after the inquest, when the fight broke out. I was in my office coughing up what looked like half of my lungs, that's where I was. But I didn't want anybody to know about it. I never wanted anybody's damned pity."

"You should've spoke up, Marshal," Embry said. "Maybe somebody could've helped you."

"There was no help for me," Trask said, "and now with a bullet through me, there sure as hell isn't. But the rest of you can get out of here and settle things with Baldridge and that blasted Brady Morgan."

"How did you know it was a trap?" Frank asked.

"Brady tried to spring it too quick," Embry said. "That boy's kill-crazy. He opened the ball before his men expected him to, I guess. Anyway, we were able to hotfoot it over here to this line shack while we were tradin' shots with the varmints up on the ridges. I never trusted him or Baldridge, neither one."

"And you were right not to," Frank said. "I didn't want to think Baldridge would sink to that level, but I reckon he did."

"It was the woman," Trask husked out. "I hate to say it, Morgan . . . I know she's the mother of your son . . . but both of them are no good."

"You're not telling me anything I don't already know, Marshal," Frank assured him. "And I'll deal with Brady if I get the chance."

"What can we do to help?" Embry asked.

"Those of you who are able to pull triggers, keep shooting. Make them think nothing has changed down here. We'll be working our way around behind them. Give us about twenty minutes to get in position, and then burn powder for all you're worth so they all start shooting back. We'll need their muzzle flashes to locate all of them."

"It's gonna be a helluva scrap," Embry said. "Wish I could be in the big middle of it with you. But we'll keep 'em busy until then, Morgan. Don't worry about that."

Frank reached out in the darkness, found the rancher's shoulder, and clapped his hand on it.

"I never had any doubts, Embry."

From outside the shack, Gage Carlin called, "Everybody's up that rope but you and me, Frank."

"I'm coming," Frank said. He crawled back out and joined the cowboy at the base of the cliff.

"Who's goin' first?" Carlin asked.

"Go ahead," Frank told him. "I can use a few more minutes to rest."

"I'm gettin' too old for dust-ups like this," Carlin said ruefully.

"I keep saying the same thing . . . but somehow folks just keep shooting at me."

CHAPTER 33

Frank held the end of the rope as Gage Carlin climbed up. When Carlin reached the top, he tugged the rope three times to signal Frank. After drawing in a deep breath, Frank gripped the rope and started the ascent. His shoulders still burned from the previous exertion, but he ignored the discomfort and kept climbing.

When he made it to the top, Hal and Carlin were there to grasp his arms and help him over the edge. Frank stood up, rolled his shoulders to ease their ache, and then in a low voice explained his plan to the men gathered around.

"In a few minutes, the men in the shack will be stepping up the pace. Move as quiet as you can and spread out along the ridge. When the shooting picks up, you ought to be able to see the muzzle flashes from the bushwhackers. Hit 'em hard then. We'll be taking them by surprise, and the odds are pretty even."

"We'll get them, Mr. Morgan," Hal promised. "We'll settle the score for the Boxed E."

"Let's go, then," Frank said. "Somebody bring that rope. We'll need it to get down to the western ridge, but that'll be a lot easier than climbing that cliff."

That prediction proved to be accurate. After Frank found a good place to tie the rope around a rock, the men scrambled down without any trouble. They assembled where the cliff met the ridge.

Frank had been trying to count off the seconds in his head. He knew the men in the shack would start firing fast and furiously any moment now.

"Spread out," he ordered the men in an urgent whisper. "Find those bushwhackers!"

He spotted a muzzle flash and headed for it as the group scattered. It would have been good if they could have attacked together, but that wasn't the nature of this battle. This skirmish was more a man-to-man fight. Unfortunately, that meant the Boxed E punchers would be going up against professional killers, but Frank was counting on the element of surprise to make the odds more even.

The hay was still burning, but the flames

had died down some and their light wasn't as bright. Bright enough, though, to reveal the man who threw open the line shack door and stumbled out into the glare. He yelled, "You sons of bitches!" Then he flung up his arm, and started firing the revolver in his hand.

Trask!

Frank barely had time to wonder what in the world the marshal was doing before he realized the answer. Baldridge's men all along the ridge opened up on the defiant lawman, riddling Trask. But even though he jerked and staggered under the impact of the bullets, he stayed on his feet and kept pulling the trigger of his Colt until it was empty.

And every bushwhacker on the ridge had revealed his location by firing again and again, accomplishing exactly what Trask must have hoped he would accomplish by this fatal distraction.

Frank charged forward, bounding from rock to rock as he closed in on his quarry. The gunman kneeling behind a boulder must have heard him coming, because he tried to turn.

Frank shot him in the head, blowing the man's brains out through a fist-sized hole in the back of his skull.

Frank raced along the ridge. Rifles cracked and pistols boomed, filling the night with a cacophony of death. Muzzle flashes split the darkness. One of them lit up the face of a hired killer right in front of Frank, and a split-second later his slug smashed through the bridge of the man's nose and into his brain. For thirty seconds that seemed much longer, chaos reigned along the ridge.

Then Hal Embry shouted, "Boxed E, hold your fire! Hold your fire!"

Frank raised his voice, calling, "Hal! Gage! Boxed E! Gather up! Hold your fire!"

They had to regroup. If they didn't, they ran the risk of shooting each other. Frank hoped they had done enough damage to Baldridge's forces that they weren't cutting their own throats by halting the attack.

When the Boxed E men held their fire, though, the shooting stopped entirely. Hal ordered, "Sing out!" and the men did. As they gathered in the darkness, Frank realized they were all there except for a couple of the men.

"We did it!" Hal said exultantly. "I think we got them all!"

"Except for a couple who lit a shuck out of here," Carlin growled. "I think it was Baldridge and Brady Morgan, but I didn't get a good enough look at them to be sure."

"We need some light," Frank said. "Somebody gather up some pine needles and make a fire."

Soon they had several branches burning as makeshift torches. When they spread out again over the ridge, several armed men going with each man who carried a torch, they found that all of Baldridge's hired killers were either dead or badly wounded.

Two of the Boxed E cowboys had been killed in the fighting as well. They would be buried as heroes, Hal Embry declared.

But they didn't find Brady Morgan or Gaius Baldridge. It came as no surprise to Frank that the two ringleaders had fled.

Frank knelt next to one of the wounded gun-wolves and gripped the man's chin, jerking his head around so the gunman had no choice but to look up at him. Blood trailed from a corner of the man's mouth.

"Where did Baldridge and Brady go?" Frank asked.

"Why don't you . . . go to hell?" the man rasped defiantly.

Frank dug the muzzle of his Colt under the man's jaw.

"You'll be there first," he promised. "There are still three more of you left alive. I'll go ask one of them if you want me to pull this trigger right now."

The gunman's eyes widened in fear, but he said, "You're . . . bluffin'!"

Frank leaned closer and asked in a flat voice, "Do I *look* like I'm bluffing, mister?"

"The ranch!" the wounded gunman yelped. "I saw Brady grab Baldridge . . . he said they were goin' . . . back to the B Star. Said they had to get those girls . . . to make sure they got away safe."

That confirmed Frank's hunch that Faye and Katie were being held at Baldridge's headquarters. He pulled the gun away from the man's throat and let his head fall back.

"Come on," he said to Hal. "We need horses. We're heading for the B Star. Gage, you and the rest of the men can mop up here and tend to the wounded in the line shack. Salty's up there on that other ridge, too." Frank was relieved when he saw Dog come loping up. "Dog, go to Salty. Somebody needs to go with Dog and help Salty."

Carlin nodded. "I'll take care of it, Frank," he said. "Count on it."

Frank and Hal ran along the ridge until they came to a place where they could descend fairly easily. They reloaded their guns by feel as they hurried toward the line shack to reclaim a couple of the Boxed E horses milling around nearby. Some of the animals had been killed in the fighting, but several were still unharmed. By the dwindling light of the burning hay, Frank and Hal grabbed two mounts and swung up into the saddles.

"Can you find your way back to the B Star in the dark?" Frank asked as they rode out of the pasture where so much killing had taken place.

"Yeah," Hal replied. "When I was a kid, before there was any trouble between my pa and Baldridge, I roamed all over this valley. I know my way around, even on Baldridge's range."

Brady and Baldridge had a lead on them, so Frank didn't expect to beat the two men back to the ranch. He just hoped they could get there in time to prevent them from taking the two young women and leaving.

Would Baldridge really abandon the B Star, Frank wondered, or was he being forced to do so by Brady? With the crew of gun-wolves all either killed or captured, Baldridge couldn't hope to seize the valley by force anymore, and trying to wipe out Embry and his men the way he had done was bound to weigh against him in court. Baldridge had no reasonable way to salvage the situation now. Maybe he *would* cut and run. What other choice did he have?

Hal Embry proved as good as his word.

He led Frank straight to Baldridge's headquarters. As they approached the big house, Frank saw lights blazing in most of its windows. Before they got there, he motioned for Hal to stop and reined his own mount to a halt.

"We'll go ahead on foot so they don't hear us coming," he said.

"How do we know they're still there?" Hal whispered.

"There are a couple of horses standing by the porch," Frank pointed out. "The way their heads are drooping, they've been ridden pretty hard getting here. But the saddles are still on them, and I don't think all those windows would be lit up if the place was abandoned."

"I hope you're right. If they've already taken Faye and Katie, we've got to get on their trail as fast as we can."

"We will," Frank promised. "Let's just check out the house first."

With guns drawn and staying in the shadows as much as possible, they stole toward the house. Frank stepped onto the porch and pressed his back to the wall to the right of the front door, gesturing with his Colt for Hal to take the other side. He edged toward the door.

A couple of the windows were open to let

fresh air into the house. Through them came the sound of loud, angry voices. Frank couldn't make out the words, but he recognized Brady Morgan's voice, along with Baldridge's.

Then Laura's voice cut through the hubbub, clear and penetrating but no less angry.

"Both of you, just shut up!" she said. "Gaius, go fetch those girls." She paused. "Brady, you had them all trapped! How could you let them get away?"

"We didn't have them all," Brady said, and he had to be closer to the window now because Frank understood him. "We didn't have Frank, and somehow he turned it all around. Damn him! Father or no father, if I had him in my sights right now —"

"You idiot!" Laura cried. "Frank Morgan's not your father!"

On the porch, Frank stiffened in surprise. Inside, Brady sounded just as shocked as he said, "What? But all those years, you said —"

"I told you a fairy tale," Laura snarled. "A convenient fairy tale about how your father was the big bad gunman who abandoned us and never loved you!" She laughed, and a hysterical edge crept into the sound. "And it worked, didn't it? You grew up to be just the man I wanted you to be! A man who would do anything I wanted, kill anybody I told you to kill!"

Frank's heart slugged heavily in his chest. Laura had no reason to lie now, and what she was saying to Brady had the ring of truth.

It was also as sick and twisted as anything he had ever heard, but that no longer surprised him.

"Gaius!" Laura's voice lashed out. "All of you stop right there. Brady and I are going to Great Falls. We'll catch the train to Helena. Once we're there safely, my lawyers will take over."

"Take over?" Baldridge repeated. "I don't understand. After everything that's happened, what can your lawyers say?"

Frank moved so he could look through the window as Laura replied, "Exactly what I tell them to say."

She was standing at the top of the stairs, on the second-floor balcony that ran around the large main room of the ranch house. She had a small pistol clutched in her hand. Brady stood a few yards away on the balcony, also holding a gun.

Between them were Gaius Baldridge and the two prisoners he had just herded out of their confinement. Faye Embry and Katie Storm had their hands tied in front of them, and both young women were gagged. Their faces were pale with terror.

Baldridge looked scared, too, but more confused than anything else. He shook his head and said again, "I don't understand."

"You went mad and tried to wipe out Jubal Embry and his men," Laura said. "When that didn't work, you came back here and tried to kill everyone in the house. You murdered Miss Embry and Miss Storm here, but then Brady saved my life by killing you."

Brady appeared to still be shaken by the revelation that Frank Morgan wasn't his father, but he didn't let that stop him from raising his Colt and aiming it at Baldridge and the two young women.

"And no one will ever be able to prove differently," Laura said as Baldridge's mouth sagged open in comprehension and horror.

That was when Frank kicked the front door open and thundered, "Brady!"

CHAPTER 34

Brady whirled toward the balcony railing as Frank charged into the room, followed by Hal. Frank started to fire up at him, but he held off as he saw that Brady had been seized by a violent trembling. Brady lowered his gun. He controlled the trembling with a visible effort and said, "You may not be my father, but you're still fast on the draw. I'm faster, though. Holster it, old man. Let's give a try, just you and me."

"Brady, no!" Laura screamed. "Kill him!"

Brady ignored her and sneered at Frank. "How about it?" he asked softly. "Scared?"

Laura jerked around and fired the little pistol in her hand. Frank felt the bullet spear into his shoulder. He took a step back.

Brady's gun flashed up and spouted flame.

Frank fired at the same instant. He felt the wind-rip of Brady's bullet past his ear and saw Brady rock back as Frank's slug plowed through his body at an upward angle. Eyes widening in shock, Brady dropped his gun and swayed forward. The railing caught him at the waist, and he tipped over it, plummeting to the floor of the main room with a crash.

Laura started pulling the trigger of her gun as fast as she could.

Another bullet whipped past Frank. He swung his Colt toward her, but Laura had already swept her gun hand toward the prisoners and Baldridge. The rancher thrust Faye and Katie behind him and charged Laura with an incoherent cry of rage. Bullets thudded into his chest, but the pistol wasn't a heavy enough caliber to slow his momentum.

He crashed into Laura and she went over backwards with a scream.

Both of them tumbled down the stairs, wildly out of control. They didn't stop until they reached the bottom.

By the time they did, Frank was there, ready to kick the gun out of Laura's hand.

There was no need. When she and Baldridge came to a stop, she lay on the bottom with her head twisted at a grotesque angle on her neck. The life was already fading from her eyes.

Frank reached down, grasped Baldridge's shoulder, and rolled the man onto his back.

While Frank was doing that, Hal rushed past him and charged up the stairs to see to Faye and Katie.

Laura's bullets might not have stopped Baldridge, but they had penetrated far enough to be fatal. Blood soaked the front of his shirt. He was still clinging to life as he looked up at Frank and said, "Morgan . . . I'm sorry . . . she . . . she deceived me . . ."

"You're not the only one," Frank said. Baldridge didn't hear him, though. The man was already dead.

Frank dragged Baldridge's body aside to make more room as Hal brought Faye and Katie downstairs. Katie looked at Frank and exclaimed, "Mr. Morgan, you're hurt!"

Frank glanced down at the blood on his shirt that had leaked from the wound in his shoulder.

"I'll be all right," he assured them. "Lord knows this isn't the first time I've been ventilated like this."

"You saved our lives," Faye said. "Those lunatics would have killed us."

Frank looked at Brady and Laura. Brady had been loco, all right, no doubt about that. His mother had made him that way. Laura, on the other hand . . .

Frank had learned long ago that some

people were just pure evil. But sometimes the reminders were still mighty damned painful.

The rocking chair squeaked a little as Salty rocked back and forth on the front porch of the Boxed E ranch house. Frank sat beside him in another rocker. Both men had bandages bulked under their shirts where they had been wounded. Several days had passed since the kidnapping of the two young women and the epic battles that had followed, and while Frank and Salty were healing well, according to Dr. Hutchison, it would still be a while before they were able to travel for any great distance.

That was fine with Frank. He was enjoying the tranquility of life on the Boxed E now that peace had returned to the valley.

With the thumping of crutches, Jubal Embry stumped onto the porch, the leg with the broken ankle held up so that no weight was on it.

"You're supposed to be inside resting with that leg propped up," Frank reminded him.

"The hell with that," Embry said with a snort. "I ain't the sort to lay around doin' nothin'. I'm used to bein' outside. There's work to be done."

"I think between them, Hal and Gage

have everything under control."

Embry snorted again.

"Gage, maybe. Hal's head is too full of sparkin' that Katie gal to think about work. She's a bad influence on him, mighty bad. Why, with her stayin' out here, the boy speaks up for hisself and talks back to me too much. I'll be glad when that crotchety ol' uncle of hers is recuperated enough for 'em to open up the café again."

Salty chuckled and said, "Café or no café, I reckon you best get used to that gal bein' around, Jubal. I don't think Hal's gonna let her go anywhere, 'cept maybe down the aisle of the church."

Embry propped himself up on his crutches and leaned against the porch railing.

"Well, I got to admit, I'd rather go back to the church for somethin' like that than why we were there yesterday."

A solemn silence gripped all three men for a moment. A day earlier, they had journeyed into Pine Knob for Marshal Roy Trask's funeral. Trask had died a hero, charging out of the line shack to draw the fire of Baldridge's hired killers before Embry or anyone else could stop him.

There had been no services for Baldridge, Laura, or Brady. They had been laid to rest in the local cemetery with no mourners on hand except Frank. He instructed Omar Finnegan to put "Brady Morgan" on Brady's tombstone. He had no idea what other name to use, and that was as good as any, Frank supposed.

Faye came out of the barn and walked toward the house, trailed by Dog. The big cur had taken a liking to her, maybe because they both had their savage streaks, Frank mused. Faye had wanted to have Bill Kitson hanged for betraying the Boxed E . . . after he'd been horsewhipped, of course.

But Jubal Embry had overruled his headstrong daughter for once, telling Kitson instead to light out of the valley and never come back. He would be shot on sight if he ever set foot on Boxed E range again.

"I've got the buggy hitched up," Faye said now as she came up to the porch. "I'm sending a letter to that lawyer in Helena instructing him to find out who Baldridge's heirs are. I think we should buy the B Star from them."

"Buy the B Star?" Embry repeated. "What in blazes would we do with it? We don't need that much range for our herd!"

"Well, we'll buy Baldridge's stock, too, of course," Faye replied. "Once we do that, we'll have the biggest spread in this part of Montana."

"I never had no interest in being the biggest, just the best," Embry said.

"All right, then," Faye said without hesitation. "Give the B Star to me. I'll run it . . . and I'll make it the best."

Embry cocked an eyebrow and let out a hoot of laughter.

"A gal runnin' a ranch? And makin' it a better spread than mine? That'll be the day!"

"You think so, do you?" Faye's eyes narrowed. "We'll just see about that!"

She turned and headed for the barn, ready to take the buggy to town. Embry snorted and went back inside, muttering something about daughters who were vexations and needing a drink.

"Frank," Salty said when they were alone on the porch again, "I was thinkin' maybe we ought to stay around here for a while, but with those two goin' at it, I ain't so sure anymore!"

"I reckon you're right, Salty," Frank replied with a grin. "We'd better head for Mexico as soon as we're able; otherwise, we're liable to find ourselves smack-dab in the middle of another range war!"

ABOUT THE AUTHOR

William W. Johnstone is the *USA Today* and *New York Times* bestselling author of over 220 books, including the popular *Ashes, Mountain Man,* and *Last Gunfighter* series. Visit his website at www.william johnstone.net or email him at dogcia@aol .com.

Being the all around assistant, typist, researcher, and fact checker to one of the most popular western authors of all time, **J.A. Johnstone** learned from the master, Uncle William W. Johnstone. Bill, as he preferred to be called, began tutoring J.A. at an early age. After-school hours were often spent retyping manuscripts or researching his massive American Western History library as well as the more modern wars and conflicts. J.A. worked hard — and learned. "Every day with Bill was an adventure story in itself. Bill taught me all he could about the art of storytelling and creating believable characters. *'Keep the historical facts accurate,'* he would say. *'Remember the readers, and as your grandfather once told me, I am telling you now: be the best J.A. Johnstone you can be.'* "

The employees of Thorndike Press hope you have enjoyed this Large Print book. All our Thorndike, Wheeler, and Kennebec Large Print titles are designed for easy reading, and all our books are made to last. Other Thorndike Press Large Print books are available at your library, through selected bookstores, or directly from us.

For information about titles, please call:
(800) 223-1244

or visit our Web site at:
http://gale.cengage.com/thorndike

To share your comments, please write:
Publisher
Thorndike Press
10 Water St., Suite 310
Waterville, ME 04901

CPSIA information can be obtained
at www.ICGtesting.com
Printed in the USA
FFOW05n0349030214